Death in Dark Waters

Tony Read

Death in Dark Waters
By Tony Read

ISBN - 978-1-906755-88-1

Spinetinglers Publishing
22 Vestry Road
Co. Down
BT23 6HJ
UK
www.spinetinglerspublishing.com

Chapter One

Dusk lies skulking near at hand; the departing sun casts long shadows in the fast fading light. At a far corner of a distant pasture, where the land climbs steeply, mongrel bitches run off leash, ignored for the moment by the men who saunter arrogantly behind them. Here they are kings. The laws of trespass mean nothing. Like their fathers and grandfathers before them, they stalk the wild and mysterious hare wherever it roams free, and they acknowledge no man's right to prevent them. Savagery courses through their veins. The predatory need to chase and then to kill is inbred; it permeates every fibre of their being and is untameable.

Silently they stride through the long grass, now wet with dew. Lights from the stone cottages in the nearby town begin to sparkle like fire flies in the advancing gloom; a lone star soon becomes a galaxy. Darkness holds no fear for these two men of blood, but many inhabitants of the town will not walk the meadows at night and even in the dying embers of the 20th Century local folklore frightens children with tales of ghosts and demons.

With confidence they approach a place of infinite sadness. Three hundred or more years ago a gibbet was erected on top of the hill they climb, within clear sight of the town, by the side of a deeply rutted track used by weary travellers as a short cut to the coach road lower down the valley. For more than two centuries thereafter there were times when the bodies of the condemned hung and rotted there while birds pecked their carcasses clean. Magpies were the worst, those feared foretellers of doom or joy, and carrion crows too had their fill; but little songbirds also gorged on human flesh. The eyes were always gauged out first, perhaps because these were succulent and tasty, or maybe just because they were soft targets for sharp beaks to pierce.

Relatives of the executed were sometimes driven mad by grief. Local legend tells of the torment of a pregnant girl who was carrying the unborn child of a young man hanged for stealing a goose. His offence had been born of hunger and of a desire to feed his starving family, but that had mattered not, the crime of theft had been prevalent, others before him had been lucky and had escaped without punishment; an example had to be made so he had to pay the price. Imagine the torment of the love he left behind, powerless to prevent his death and unable ever to reclaim his body for Christian burial. It is said that night after night, she sat beneath the rusted cage with its gruesome contents and lamented her "Pretty Joe". She barely ate, and when the time came that her child was due, weak and undernourished, and in a raging storm, she struggled one last time to reach this place of lost souls. She died there alone in the agonies of child birth. The baby, a boy, was still-born; feral dogs had already found the pathetic corpses by the time they were discovered by the local priest. Long after all trace of the ghastly structure that had topped the grassy mound had disappeared, when the wind moaned and wailed in the dark trees, simple folk still swore they heard the cries of tortured souls calling to them across time in eternal despair.

But now a new noise silences ancient myths. It is a distant clamour coming from the town, faint at first, but getting louder every minute, growing like thunder in a fast approaching storm. It is the sound of shouting and jeering and the beating of makeshift drums, struck with a power and a passion that seems to transcend the constraints of civilization. The poachers feel no alarm, but like the hunters that they are, they know when to stay and when to fade into the ever deepening darkness, wrapping the night around themselves like a blanket: this temporary interruption will soon pass and they will set loose their dogs again, on many nights, to good effect; but tonight it is better for them to slip away unseen.

A rowdy procession makes its way through the cobbled streets, the light from their flaming torches much brighter than the orange glow of the street lamps that each evening fight a losing battle against the blackness of night. Two hundred people, maybe more, old and young, rich and poor, male and female, many carrying placards or banners, and others seemingly intent on waking the dead with their banging and screaming, all crammed together into the confined spaces of the old town. Outside locked wrought iron gates that stand taller than a man they halt. Chants of "Bitch" and "Slag" and "Cheat" rent the night air. Stones are thrown, but not in great numbers, and to no good effect, landing as they do harmlessly on the winding driveway that stretches into the distance. The heavy oak doors of the impressive mansion that lies at the end of the immaculately cobbled roadway remain tight shut; nobody from within ventures outside, no face appears at a window, no sign is given that any occupant of that building has the slightest interest in, or concern about the events unfolding just outside the high stone walls which surround this very private property

At the vanguard of the procession two men hold aloft an effigy, a thing of straw and paper but wearing surprisingly good clothes. To those who know it is clearly a representation of the lady of the house, the broad- brimmed hat and Burberry raincoat are unmistakable; there is a howl like hounds baying at a kill when the mob see the loathed facsimile hoisted up towards the stars. For several minutes the people linger, and continue to fill the night air with shouts of protest and abuse, but, finally, the men carrying the reviled object of detestation set off on the last stage of their journey to take it to the place of ultimate retribution.

The blazing torches cast dancing shadows on the narrow path as the procession now snakes its way across the empty meadow to the gibbet hill and there the unholy pilgrimage ends. Four large men emerge from the shadows carrying heavy, rough-hewn lengths of wood, just as some two thousand years earlier, in a faraway land; Jesus Christ carried his own cross to a place of crucifixion.

There is utter silence now, except for the grunts of the hard-handed men who struggle to erect a tall scaffold on the grassy knoll. Poles are lashed together with stout ropes and, when the structure is complete, one man, his face hidden behind a black scarf, holds up a noose to the assembled congregation, like a priest holding aloft a chalice of communion wine for benediction, he then places this over the head of the hated representation. The crowd roars its approval and the effigy is pulled high into the night sky; at that instant the twentieth century becomes a distant memory and time seems to embrace an earlier age.

For a moment silence reasserts itself; then a chant of "Burn, Burn, Burn!" destroys the unnerving calm. A young woman dressed in white steps into the limelight, she takes a flaming torch from the masked man, and this she holds out to the crowd as if in veneration. Like a High Priestess, she approaches the scaffold, the only sound that can now be heard is the hooting of distant owls and they too fall quiet as she caresses the extremities of the grotesque doll with her naked flame.

The fire takes hold, at first just timidly scorching the extremities of this thing of sacrifice, then greedily devouring the whole entity, and as it consumes the symbol of the crowd's disgust the drums beat out an ever more frenzied rhythm, until not one shred of garment or tiny scrap of stuffing survives.

Chapter Two.

It was warm, it was very warm indeed; even at midnight the air was hot and sticky and with little or no prospect of a change in the weather occurring any time soon, Helena and Mark Hobson foresaw that many more nights of disturbed sleep lay ahead of them. They thought about the people living in the system built brick houses on the new estates at the edge of town and considered how much worse their plight would be; to some degree at least the thick stone walls of their 18th century cottage did keep them cooler than their ultra-modern neighbours, but not much. The heat wave had already lasted for a fortnight and looked set to carry on for many weeks to come; people were beginning to complain and a general air of irritable inertia now affected many of the inhabitants of the small Peak District town of Burrdale.

Other parts of the United Kingdom were suffering even more; in Kent, and in much of the south east temperatures had topped 31degrees for the tenth consecutive day and old and vulnerable people were collapsing through de-hydration and with heat exhaustion. Across the country as a whole there had been at least twenty deaths attributable to the extreme weather. Helena worried constantly about her father, who was awaiting a heart bypass operation, and telephoned home daily to ensure that he was drinking enough water and that he was not undertaking any ill-advised physical exercise in the heat of the day.

She was a beautiful, gentle, graceful woman, who at 33 years of age was some ten years younger than her husband Mark. He was a big man, with great physical strength, but as Helena knew so well, he had great tenderness too: he was also clever and brave and he adored her, and his faults of occasional bouts of impatience and odd moments of impetuousness hardly seemed to weigh anything in the balance. She had first met him when she was in hospital beginning the slow process of recovery from injuries she had received when a car she had just got out of had been destroyed by a bomb planted inside it which had killed outright her wealthy employer. Mark had helped her through her ordeal and had then protected her from the vicious campaign of harassment that had subsequently been waged against her, and quite literally, he had saved her life; twice himself being shot in the process of doing so.

Helena looked at her husband, who, just for a moment had dozed off in his armchair, and reflected upon how completely her life had been changed by him She had some friends who could only see how much she had lost: the London flat, the London salary, the clothes, the cash, the excitement of working for the country's leading entrepreneur, but they totally missed the point. Mark was honest, Mark was decent and his passion for her was overwhelming; even two years after their marriage true friends still noticed how sometimes, without realising it, he would glance at his wife and his face would soften as he gazed upon her.

Their wedding day had been a joy; Helena had looked radiant and Mark in turns had looked awkward, apprehensive, nervous, relieved, relaxed and then blissfully happy, and the feeling each had for the other had been obvious for all to see. Those feelings were as strong today as they had ever been, and if possible, even enhanced by the experience of sharing their daily lives. Of course it hadn't all been plain sailing. Shortly after they were married Mark's mother had suffered a stroke and, although she had now made a reasonable recovery, she was no longer the confident, energetic, forthright personality that she had been before it occurred. Mark's mum's state of health was one of the reasons why Mark had sought a transfer from the South Yorkshire police to the smaller County police force in Derbyshire.

Another reason for the move concerned Helena's father, who had started to experience chest pains within weeks of Mark's mother's illness; a heart specialist confirmed that there were serious problems and that her dad would need surgery, but although she and Mark had offered to pay privately for his treatment, her father had refused to allow them to do so and was now awaiting a heart-bypass operation on the N.H.S. The town of

Burrdale was only 18 miles away from Helena's parents' Cheshire home and 15 miles at most from the hospital where the operation would be carried out so relocating there also meant that Helena was now readily available in the case of an emergency, which to a degree had helped to put her mind at ease.

When Helena became pregnant both she and Mark had been overjoyed and when she miscarried eleven weeks later they were both desolate. Helena had wept for the loss of the baby and she had felt an overwhelming sense of failure, but most of all she felt that somehow she had let Mark down. Mark had felt great sadness, as he had been so proud and excited when he learnt of the pregnancy, but his real distress was at Helena's unhappiness; it seemed so unfair that she who had been through so much, needlessly, and without fault had yet again to suffer hurt.

Largely through the support and encouragement of Detective Superintendent Tim Gratton (as he now was) Mark had been persuaded to try for promotion and had been successful and Tim had done everything he could to facilitate Mark's transfer to the Derbyshire force.

The last six months had been hectic, moving house is always a stressful experience, and the fact that to begin with they just missed out on two properties they had liked had done nothing to reduce that stress. Eventually, when they were beginning to feel that they never would, they had found a cottage that seemed to be perfect and the sale had gone through without any major hitch; but as the house had stood empty for a long while a lot of work needed doing to the property before they could move in. In the midst of all this upheaval Helena had discovered that she was pregnant again and Mark had started his new job and had had to contend with resentment from certain officers now under his command who were distrustful of an outsider brought in over their heads from a city force. By a combination of knowledge and long perfected people skills and simply by demonstrating that he was very good at his job, in a comparatively short period of time Mark had managed to win most of the doubters round.

Helena's unexpected pregnancy, although a joy for them both, was not without its problems. Some women blossom when they carry a child, but things hadn't been easy for her; she was still being sick every day, even after twenty two weeks, and had twice been admitted to hospital because she was unable to keep down fluids. Mark marvelled at the fact that she never complained, and on the plus side the baby seemed to be developing quite normally. The physical tasks of decorating, renovating and moving in had often been arduous, and Mark and Helena were still far from being settled. Mark had been insistent that she shouldn't do too much and it was only when he was at work that Helena felt free to organise rooms in the way she wanted them to be. Many, many items still remained packed up in crates and some of these had been placed in the loft for the time being in the full knowledge that it might be a long while before they could be properly sorted out. It was whilst Mark was putting a couple of tea chests out of harm's way that he had discovered a battered box file hidden under the glass fibre loft insulation.

The contents of this file had intrigued both of them. Initially they had seemed to be harmlessly nostalgic. The box contained diaries, scrap books, newspaper cuttings and photographs dating from a period nearly a quarter of a century before and the only mystery appeared to be why something so innocent had been cast to one side and left untouched and unlooked at for over two decades. On a quiet August evening, when they were both too tired and too drained by the heat to do anything more demanding, Helena and Mark had sat outside on the rear patio and together they had examined the secret records of one person's memories of a bygone age.

The earliest histories were happy portraits of life in a small town in the last quarter of the 20th Century. There were photographs of carnivals, school trips, fund-raising scouts, street parties to celebrate Queen Elizabeth's silver jubilee, as well as many publicity shots for the local amateur dramatic society, and there was a simplicity about all of them which left Helena in particular thinking how nice it must have been to have lived in Burrdale during those years. Mark, whose daily work brought him into contact with drug addicted crime, drunken violence, mindless vandalism and petty incidents of anti-social behaviour doubted if things had ever really been that idyllic, but even he could see how much nicer life seemed to have been then.

The period dealt with in this private chronicle covered the years from 1975-1979, and then the record came to a sudden and abrupt halt. The winter of 1978-1979 was the "Winter of Discontent" and one of the coldest winters of the century. Mark had seen photographs in a local pub showing men digging out a country road, dwarfed by drifts of compacted snow that must have been at least 15 feet high. At the time he'd been with Alan Nadin, a long serving detective sergeant, who was now coming towards the end of his police career, and he'd commented on the photographs to him. Alan had said that the pictures didn't lie and that he'd been told by the locals of many nights of hard frost, and weeks of heavy snowfall; the snow sometimes driven horizontally by bitterly cold north easterly winds. Roads had been blocked and traffic chaos had ensued. The situation had not been helped by the fact that council employees were on strike and, because they had refused to work, roads hadn't been cleared or even gritted. Domestic rubbish had been piled high in the streets and as the bin men wouldn't shift it, the heaps of garbage had frozen solid in the sub-zero temperatures which had persisted both day and night for weeks at a time. On the few occasions when the thermometer had struggled to reach three or four degrees centigrade there had been cold rain or heavy sleet, but never enough to strip the hill tops of the white cloak of snow that they had permanently worn for three months, and always thereafter winter had come back with a vengeance. The licensee of the pub, who was himself a native of Burrdale, confirmed without hesitation Alan's account and told stories, which he swore were true, of wood pigeons dropping from the sky, exhausted and weighing next to nothing at all, because the deep snow and thick ice had denied them access to all food and water.

It was as the account of that awful winter unfolded that the joyous shades of colour which had so far illuminated this portrait of a time long past began to darken and the events now recounted became uncomfortable and sombre. The dramatic change started with a press cutting about an 8 year old boy who had disappeared from home and the article in the local newspaper described, in graphic detail, the large scale manhunt that had been organised by the police, who had been aided by a vast number of volunteers. The hillsides and valleys had been searched, but to no avail and the child had remained missing. His name was Lucas Norton and his father was the local butcher Richard Norton: Helena had seen Norton's Butcher's shop in the town's market square and she wondered if it was still owned by the child's father.

One week later the story remained front page news; the little boy was still unaccounted for and the temperatures had by then reached record breaking lows; all hope for the child had been lost but his body still hadn't been found. It was not until the following week that the tiny remains of Lucas were discovered trapped under a tombstone of thick, thick ice, which covered a pool in a peat bog that had been formed when a glacier retreated from the wide Burrdale valley 10.000 years before, at the end of the last ice age. Nobody knew what the boy had been doing there, or how it was that he had come to drown. When he was found the ice was so solid it couldn't be broken by pick axes, and somehow, with great difficulty a compressor and pneumatic drills had been manually dragged to this inaccessible place, and the boy's father had watched in tears, as the men battled against the elements to release his adored son from his frozen tomb. The sorrowful task had taken all day and it had been evening before the ice had finally released its prisoner. An ambulance couldn't be brought to the scene and the local mountain rescue team had had to carry Lucas off the hillside, followed by his father, whose cries of anguish drowned out even the barking of the foxes and the screeching of the owls.

In an unhappy postscript to this sad story, later editions of the local newspaper reported the inquest into Lucas's death. A nine year old boy had admitted to his mother that he and Lucas had been playing in the snow, watched by an older teenage girl who he didn't know and who he had never seen before. For some reason the two boys had squabbled and the girl had encouraged them both to fight. The boy had pushed Lucas and he'd fallen onto the ice which had given way under his weight. The boy couldn't swim; he told the inquest that he'd wanted to run for help but the girl told him it was too late. She said that he'd killed Lucas and that that was murder, and that if anybody found out he would be locked up in prison until the day he died. The boy was not a bright child and had believed everything the girl had said to him. For two weeks he told nobody but he couldn't sleep; he started to have horrible nightmares and he began wetting his bed; his mother had become frantic with worry and finally she had extracted the whole story from him, and it was she who had told the police what had occurred and where the body of Lucas could be found.

There was a final chapter to this very unhappy tale; it was contained in the report of a court case at Derby Crown Court. Richard Norton there pleaded guilty to charges of using threatening behaviour and to causing many hundreds of pounds worth of damage to the property of Mr. and Mrs. Chadwick, the parents of the nine year old boy. He had forced his way into their home, armed with a crowbar and a butcher's knife. He had made the most extreme and appalling threats of violence and he had slashed every piece of upholstered furniture in the building. By the time the police arrived, and they had responded quickly, every piece of electrical equipment in the house had been damaged, every pane of glass, every mirror, every framed photograph and every ornament that would break had been destroyed and the Chadwick family had been found huddled together in a corner of the room, seemingly in abject terror, so violent and uncontrolled had been Richard Norton's rage. With verbal ferocity he had cursed Shane Chadwick who was the boy who had killed his son, and the child had been so traumatised that forever after he believed that curse.

The effect of Norton's behaviour was dramatic. The Chadwick family had gathered together what remained of their possessions and left Burrdale the very next day; never to return again. The local magistrates had declined to deal with the case, feeling that their powers of sentence were inadequate, and it had been committed to Derby Crown Court for sentence. The judge was sympathetic towards Richard Norton and to his overwhelming grief; he might easily have been persuaded that at the time of this outburst the balance of his mind had been disturbed but Norton refused point blank to let his counsel put forward such a plea. He expressed no regret or remorse at what he had done; nor for one second did he deny intent. The judge had had no option. Norton received a custodial sentence of 12 months imprisonment, although half of that sentence had been suspended in view of the wholly exceptional circumstances of the case.

Chapter Three

The smell inside the council chamber of Burrdale Town Hall was made up from an unappetising cocktail of cheap deodorant, lavender furniture polish and plain unapologetic human sweat. The room was airless and clammy and far too small to hold the large number of people who were tightly crammed into it. Once it had had grandeur or, if not grandeur, the solid oak panels had at least expressed a sense of Victorian self-confidence, but much of the impact had been destroyed by an unsympathetic refurbishment of the building carried out in the late 1960's. White P.V.C. double-glazed windows had replaced the old sash windows and chrome framed chairs, upholstered in red synthetic leather, had banished most of the simple wooden benches (which had reigned supreme for over 80 years and which had served both councillors and members of the public well), on the grounds that these venerable old retainers were now too hard for sensitive bottoms to rest upon. Progress it seemed demanded that nobody should be obliged to endure even the tiniest degree of discomfort in their daily lives in the last years of the 20th Century.

The mood in the chamber was angry; tempers were short and people were at boiling point. The Bank Holiday break, although only a couple of days before, now seemed to most to be a distant memory and, however much the people present might have benefited from having a few days to relax, all that good was now being undone because of the level of tension in the room. Every person who was packed into that odour filled sauna was struggling to control feelings of outrage, resentment or disbelief; and these feelings threatened to overwhelm the collective ability of the large crowd to remain calm.

The Council Chamber had of course seen anger on many occasions in the past, and the night when the then lady Chairman had thrown water into the face of a local magistrate and then slapped him so hard that it had left a stinging red handprint on his cheek, had slipped into folklore. Stories were still told about that night, even though twenty five years had elapsed, but although feelings were running high, tonight wasn't going to see a repeat of any such clan warfare. For once, and maybe just for once, there was a unity of purpose and the room was not split upon party political lines, as so often in the past had been the case. The only rivalry that existed between normally bitterly opposed political enemies was the extent to which each group tried to outdo the other when expressing their condemnation of what had occurred. Loudest and angriest of all the people present was Tony Patterson, a Labour councillor from Burrdale West Ward and always something of a firebrand with out-spoken, although often ill-thought out, views on a wide range of issues.

He was a small man, but with a disproportionately large beer belly. His hair was long and curly and always in need of combing and, although it had once been defiantly ginger, it was now generously flecked with grey. On principal he never wore a tie and tonight his ill-fitting short sleeved shirt, unbuttoned to the navel exposed to public view the tattoos that adorned both of his arms and also substantially revealed the golden eagle that soared across his disconcertingly hairy chest. He had been a merchant seaman for many years until an injury to his back had prevented him from doing manual work, and thereafter he had claimed Disability Living Allowance. With time to kill he had developed an interest in local politics, firstly in Liverpool and then in Derbyshire, and now he spent most of his waking hours stirring up as much trouble, as any man with a left wing political agenda, could decently hope to achieve. The pleasure he got from this was immense; to get one over on some stuck up Tory toff was orgasmic, much better than normal sex; it even surpassed the satisfaction he got from rubbishing the attempts of members of his local camera club to produce a decent still life photograph. He preferred to photograph movement, and animal life in all its shapes and sizes. He was very good at doing this, although he seldom entered any of his work in competition."

"It's a swindle," he roared; his deep rough sounding voice betraying his Merseyside roots, "The greedy cow can't be allowed to get away with it. It was a solemn promise, everybody understood that. She knows exactly what her husband intended to do, and she knows what she should do, but the hard faced bitch can only think of herself. She's got to be bloody well stopped. She should be tarred and feathered and driven out of town on the back of a muck wagon, the penny pinching, money-grubbing avaricious tart!"

Many of the people present shouted out their support. In vain the Chairman of the Council tried to keep order, but she found it quite impossible to make herself heard over the murmurs of assent that had come from all parts of the room, and from some totally unexpected quarters. "Ladies and gentlemen," she squealed in a plaintive high-pitched wail, "Calm down and please, please moderate your language; intemperate and sexist remarks are completely unacceptable in this council chamber."

"Is what she's done acceptable?" responded a very well-spoken, well-dressed older woman. "I never thought I'd hear myself agreeing with Tony Patterson, but I applaud his sentiments, even if I myself might have chosen to use somewhat less colourful language to express them."

"Of course it isn't: it's a bloody disgrace," shouted out another man; "and its cost this town and this council a great deal of money."

"I told you we should have purchased Ludgate's field when we had the chance to do so," said a pale-faced, skinny fellow in a suit and tie, visibly wilting in the steam room that this overheated gathering had become. "We had the money to spend and we chose not to do so; it's not much good to us now though is it?" he added rhetorically.

"At the time we all thowt that it were the reet decision; everybody knew and liked Jack, everybody trusted 'im, he were a good man who'd done a hell of a lot fer all of us. He were straight as a dye, 'ad been so all his life and the three acre site at Plunkett's Stand was bigger, and far, far better situated than Ludgate's bloody field," cried out an old man with large hands, and a face that had been sculpted and defined by the weather and the seasons for more than three quarters of a century.

"But nobody reckoned on her did they?" bellowed Tony Patterson, "Whatever did he see in her, the stone-hearted harpy? It isn't that she ever seemed to make him happy; they weren't natural bedfellows, in fact, I can't imagine that they were bedfellows at all! She was far more interested in Henry fucking Osbourne than she was in Jack. I'll bet a pound to a penny that that bastard's dipped his quill in her inkwell more times in the last few months than I've had hot dinners."

"Please, please, please," twittered the chairman, "this isn't helpful; we need to work out what is to be done."

A man with horn-rimmed spectacles and a shiny bald head turned to her, "The only thing you can do," he said, "is to try to persuade

Mrs. Brocklehurst to change her mind and to honour her late husband's wishes. You have no legal redress. Jack may have promised that he would give the land to the town and that he would make a very significant contribution towards the building costs of the new Amenity Centre; and knowing Jack as I did I've no doubt that he would have kept his word if he hadn't been so tragically killed in that appalling road traffic accident at Chesterfield: but the simple fact is he's no longer here with us and his widow is not bound by anything he said. It would be different of course had there been any sort of contract, but Jack wanted nothing for the land, and without consideration the law won't intervene."

"But we've spent thousands on a geological survey, feasibility studies and preliminary architect's designs, in anticipation of this gift being made, does that count for bloody nothing?" exploded Tony Patterson. "Surely the courts can't ignore that fact; we wouldn't have spent a penny if we hadn't been led to believe that a deal had been struck."

"You may have believed that," said the solicitor, "but you were wrong to do so. At the time when everyone was getting very excited I advised caution, but nobody seemed at all interested in my advice. You all acted as though you had won the Lottery, but no prize is secure until it's claimed. I regret to tell you that this was a case of counting chickens well before they were hatched and being left with nothing but a pile of broken eggshells."

"So if we want it, we have to beg for it," screamed Patterson, his face crimson and flushed with fury, the purple veins in his forehead standing proud from his overheated skin and seemingly in danger of bursting under the immense pressure they were being subjected to.

"I'm afraid that's just about it," replied the solicitor coolly.

"I'd sooner spit in the face of my dying mother than give that evil witch the time of day," snarled Patterson, his words exploding like cluster bombs destroying the last vestiges of serious discussion and causing the meeting to collapse into near anarchy. For several minutes there was uproar and the accusations and recriminations became so strident that it seemed that any second the room would erupt into chaotic and violent disorder. Eventually somebody blew a whistle, nobody ever knew who, and its shrill tones rose like a lark ascending into the white hot stratosphere that overhung the clamour and tumult. Gradually an element of proportion began to reassert itself and finally a degree of calm was restored. When at last he could be heard the solicitor spoke once more to the crowd.

"I cannot recommend this to you," he said, "but you as a community could decide to have no dealings whatsoever with Mrs. Brocklehurst. You'd need to be sure that nobody did anything silly, and that no illegal threats were made, and that all decisions are taken individually so that there could be no grounds to allege conspiracy to cause harassment, alarm or distress; but, provided no pressure was put on any person to take part in this action against his or her own will, and all who took part chose of their own volition to do so, you could all decide to have absolutely nothing to do with Mrs. Brocklehurst. You could leave her without services and you could refuse to do any paid or unpaid work she wanted doing. It's just possible that if she found herself totally shunned and at the same time relentlessly exposed to the full glare of public disapproval she might decide that it was in her best long term interest to think again about her stated position."

"That's about as likely as Hell freezing over," snorted Patterson. "If Plunkett's Stand ever gets planning permission for housing development, and that decision won't be taken by this council and may well be influenced by the Government's policy of increasing affordable housing in rural areas, the land will be worth millions. Anyone can put up with a bit of rejection and condemnation if they stand to pick up a seven figure sum; she'll simply wave two fingers in our faces and laugh at our fucking impotence as she staggers to the bank weighed down by a shed load of cash."

"What would happen if she died now?" somebody shouted out from the back of the room. "Wouldn't the estate pass back to

Jack's children under the rules of intestacy? They're both very unhappy at the moment; they feel that they've been cheated out of their inheritance! It's rumoured that they're considering making a legal challenge to the will; I'm certain that if they had the estate they'd be only too willing to honour their Dad's wishes."

"The only way that the estate could pass to them would be if it could be clearly established that there had been some sort of fraud, and past experience tells me that that would be extremely difficult to prove." said the solicitor. "If the will is valid, and I am virtually certain it will turn out to be so, then if Mrs. Brocklehurst were to die tomorrow, and there is little or no prospect of that happening, the house and land and all the other property would pass to her heirs. No doubt they would wish to maximise their interests by raising as much money from the sale of the assets as they could possibly do. I'm afraid I don't think the situation would be in any way improved by Mrs Brocklehurst's death."

"Except that there's no doubt that we would all feel the world was a better place without her," shouted out the same voice, "and we could all become just a little bit fitter than we are now by dancing on her bloody grave!"

Chapter Four

John Winston looked around the classroom with a feeling of disappointment. Numbers were down on the Easter term, but then again the Easter term had been phenomenally successful, and it was still possible that more people could yet join the group: Winston normally reckoned that it was only by week three that the size and vibrancy of any particular class became clearly established.

The students sitting in front of him were also markedly less diverse than last term's assembly had been. They were predominantly the *usual suspects*, retired middle class pensioners of adequate means who had time on their hands, but he was pleased to note that one or two of the younger couples who had joined in the spring had maintained their interest. There was also a very pretty pregnant young woman, who was a complete newcomer; she had come along with Kathy Latimer, one of the practice nurses at the local health centre. Winston smiled, he liked attractive women and frequently bemoaned the fact that most of the females who attended his classes had *passed their sell by dates*, but despite that fact he always flattered them excessively and often flirted with them in a quite outrageous manner. The more mature ladies were universally charmed by him; his impact on the younger ones was less certain and that fact profoundly irritated him.

Winston's first love had been English. He had trained as an English teacher after having been an outstanding student, but some ten years ago, whilst still in his early twenties and soon after starting his second year as a fully qualified school master he had suffered a mental breakdown. The cause of his brain imploding had been the collapse of a mercifully brief marriage, and the particularly unruly behaviour of a year 9 group, who he had found impossible to control. It had taken him a lot of time, and the ingestion of an incalculable number of anti-depressant tablets to recover, but in the end he had finally done so. His passion for English, however, had completely evaporated, as had his desire to bring enlightenment to *Neanderthal youth*.

Luck had then smiled on him and by good fortune he had been left a very large legacy by a distant relative which then enabled him to invest a considerable sum of money and to live off the interest and, while looking for something to occupy his mind he had developed an interest in local history. He had read widely and attended a great many courses and in the course of time had become an acknowledged expert in that field. He had needed to demonstrate his newly acquired wisdom and to do that he had needed to have an audience. He had decided once again to teach, but this time to teach older, more receptive souls and for the past four years he had run well received evening classes at the local high school. He was an eloquent speaker, with a rich, refined voice and an enthusiasm for his subject which was infectious, and his generally shambolic appearance had fortunately done nothing to detract from the power of his presentation. He was now a man at the top of his game and brimming with the self-confidence that a spectacularly successful last course had given him.

He couldn't quite explain why a series of lectures which he had entitled "Myths, Mobs and Mayhem: three thousand years of Anarchy" had touched a nerve in the manner that it had, but people who never went to night school classes had come to that one. As well as the normal core constituency, which was so well represented here tonight, there had been farmers and lorry drivers, postmen, policemen, plumbers and even a smattering of unemployed youth: Winston had been gratified that the course had actually attracted two heavily built skinheads and, unbelievably, that they had maintained their interest in it throughout the entire series of twelve lessons.

It had been exciting stuff, of course. There had been tales of blood and gore, of ritual sacrifice and Celtic burials, and he had touched upon witchcraft and superstition as well as giving examples of revenge killings, arson, looting and violence that had from time to time taken place over the last three millennia. In different periods of history different groups had been made scapegoats for the ills of the world. Gypsies and Jews had suffered many times at the hands of the mob; and during the reign of Elizabeth 1st Catholics had been the target of much discrimination and abuse.

In addition to all that Winston had found time to consider sexual immorality and the consequences of it if you were found out; it was an area of research he was particularly interested in. He was especially pleased to have unearthed a specific episode which had occurred in the late 18th century. The local incumbent, who was married with seven children, had entered into a forbidden relationship with two sisters at the same time, causing both of them to become pregnant. When their conditions could no longer be concealed there had been an outcry and the vicar had been terrified that he would be exposed. Despite being placed under almost intolerable pressure neither sister had been prepared to name the father of her unborn child because they both wanted to protect him from disgrace and ruin. When it was clear to him that he would not be denounced the vicar rewarded their silence by preaching against fornication and both girls, one only fifteen, had been driven out of town by a jeering rabble, never to return to live in Burrdale again. The vicar's hypocrisy was never revealed and eventually he rose through the church hierarchy to attain the exalted position of Bishop.

There had been comical interludes too. Willie Carter, a slow witted cobbler had formed an attachment to the spouse of Thomas

Pardew, a wheelwright with a fearful reputation for drinking, and a bare knuckle fighter of some repute. When he discovered his wife's infidelity, in a drunken rage Pardew went looking for Willie and his wife, swearing that he would kill them both, but on the way to find them he slipped on wet limestone and fallen awkwardly. His head struck a large boulder which shattered his skull and thus by God's intervention Willie and Pardew's errant wife were both saved. Many of the townsfolk felt that justice demanded that they shouldn't escape without retribution and a "Stang" ride was hastily organised. Willie came across the raucous crowd and was excited by the commotion; he enthusiastically joined in the procession: it was only when the mob stopped outside the door to his love nest that he realised who the intended victims of this public shaming were actually going to be.

Winston smiled as he remembered the reaction there had been to this historical oddity, particularly from one of the persons present in the class, who it transpired claimed direct descent from the unfortunate Pardew; but now was not the time to re-live past triumphs, he had a new class to teach and a new theme to develop for the next 13 weeks. He warmly welcomed all the students and compiled the class register, asking members who were old hands to introduce themselves for the benefit of new members. After this had been done, in his most reassuring tones he asked the young woman who he had noticed immediately he had entered the room to introduce herself to the class.

She spoke in a clear, soft, easy to listen to voice, without the trace of any apparent accent. She had the bluest of blue eyes and a healthy, natural looking skin and the teacher had to resist an urge to engineer bodily contact between him and her. It was too soon, he was unsure of his ground, he had to wait; in due course, he told himself, there would be other opportunities.

She said her name was Helena, and that she was married to Mark Hobson, who was the new Detective Inspector stationed at Burrdale. She told the class that they had recently moved into a stone cottage on Bear Post Lane (so called because once there had been a wooden pole set firmly in the cobbles to which bears had been tethered and then baited by terrier dogs, urged on by unruly crowds of half-drunken layabouts and wastrels). In the past such cruelty hadn't been unusual, and Burrdale was by no means unique in staging them, but Helena had been surprised to learn that these barbaric practices had continued well into the 19th century, although by then no longer officially tolerated by the authorities. She expressed a hope that she would be able to attend most of the classes that term, but she added that events could determine otherwise and she glanced down at her bump as she spoke.

Winston listened attentively, and wondered why her face seemed familiar to him, but he couldn't think where he had seen it before. He would have liked to have spent more time breathing in her perfume and hearing her soft words, but there was a job to be done and he couldn't concentrate on just this one individual, although he wished that that could be the case. He explained to all the students that this year's course, which he had entitled "Looking forward to the Past: how History shapes our Future" would examine recent events and place them in a historical context, to seek to discover if, as he believed to be the case, the modern world was really only a new coat of varnish on an old canvass and that, beneath a wafer thin veneer of modernity, timeless and constant pre-ordained rules still governed the way we live.

He apologised in advance to his audience that the contents of the course would probably be less dramatic than the previous term's extravaganza, but ultimately he felt that they might be more relevant to everyday experience. He promised that there would be some very interesting new material on the scandals of the 19th century workhouses and he offered a striking insight into the abuses that had occurred in the local mental hospital, even as late as 1968, shortly before it finally closed. In addition, if the weather permitted, he said that there would be a field trip to the site of a newly excavated Bronze Age settlement which would reveal some absolutely fascinating facts about the lifestyles of our long dead ancestors. He did his selling job well, everybody showed keen interest in his words and by 9pm, when the lesson ended, he was sure in his own mind that few, if any, of the persons gathered there that night would fail to return in one week's time.

As the class was breaking up Winston took the opportunity to speak to Helena Hobson again. It was only then that he noticed the faint scar over her left eye, and that slight mark suddenly unlocked his memory and he recalled a story that had been in all the newspapers only a few years before.

The deranged wife of a multi-millionaire had murdered her husband and one of his unsavoury employees. She had then kidnapped and planned to disfigure and kill his beautiful personal assistant, who she suspected had had an affair with him and only the last minute intervention of the police had saved her life. Helena Hobson was that intended victim. Winston couldn't explain why that knowledge suddenly excited him, but excite him it did; perhaps it was when he started to fantasise about her terror, but something caused his face to flush and his hand to shake. He explained the tremor as a muscular spasm; he knew that he hadn't been believed.

From inside a briefcase he produced a full set of course notes for the last term's series of lessons and offered them to Helena, asking her if she would like to have them as he thought she might find them interesting. Helena thanked him for his kindness and her voice sent tingles down his spine. She was genuinely pleased to be given the folder of documents and told Winston that a friend of her husband was visiting next week and that she was sure he would be intrigued by this chronicle of crime and retribution.

Winston basked in her approval; he asked Helena if her friend was coming up for the Scarecrow Festival, which was now one of the biggest in the north of England, and he showed off his learning to her by explaining the mystic properties that had historically been attributed to these sometimes scary creations. Helena said that it was just a short holiday, and that the Scarecrow Festival was a lucky bonus, although she was sure the he would enjoy the atmosphere of the oddly surreal event.

Chapter Five

The second week of the Burrdale Scarecrow Fortnight was drawing to a close and, apart from one area of controversy, and one bizarre happening, it had been a highly successful event. The numbers of visitors was well up on previous years and the early September sunshine which had so far smiled on the festival on every day bar one, had made sure that when the tourists came they had been tempted to linger and to spend money in the town's restaurants and bars. Even today, although the high cloud was just beginning to turn the sky a pastel shade of blue, it was still plenty warm enough to wander the paved streets of the old town without a jumper and to drink beer in the open air, and dozens of families and many young couples were taking the opportunity to enjoy what could well be the swan song of this long, hot summer Cold winds and heavy rain were waiting in the wings and the final few days of the festival looked like being far less benign than the first 10 days had been.

Mark and Helena strolled down the narrow streets in the company of Tim Gratton and his new girlfriend Amanda. Red, white and blue bunting fluttered in the breeze and Burrdale was a picture of colour and tranquillity. On every street corner and at virtually every lamp post stood a scarecrow, and it was obvious that a lot of people had spent a great deal of time making costumes and painting face masks. The only criticism of the pageant that had been voiced in some quarters was that some of the scarecrows on display were too perfect and too well dressed ever to be thought to have been made for the humble task of putting hungry birds to flight.

In the Market Place they halted: it was still too early to eat, and, in any event their table at the Burrdale Bistro was not booked until 7-30 pm. To find a pleasant way of killing time they stopped at a small cafe/bar overlooking the ancient market cross and the Tudor stocks which had given the little restaurant its unimaginative, but utterly appropriate name. The two men drank beer from the wood; Helena drank sparkling mineral water, although she had promised herself one glass of wine when they dined, Tim's girlfriend sipped a gin and slim line tonic.

At both ends of the cobbled square decking had been laid to create two display areas of equal size and prominence. Upright poles had been inserted into the wooden platforms at evenly spaced intervals and to each of these posts a scarecrow had been attached. The theme for the festival was "Fame and Infamy" and many heroes and villains occupied their respective plinths. On the stage set aside for wickedness and depravity Adolf Hitler stood next to Vlad the Impaler, Cruella-de-Ville propositioned Jack the Ripper, Lady Macbeth succeeded in tempting her husband to commit regicide and Myra Hindley and Ian Brady plotted acts of unspeakable repugnance.

On the platform reserved for heroes and heroines Marilyn Monroe touched the heart of Superman, James Bond exerted all his charms on Florence Nightingale, Mother Theresa of Calcutta discussed the meaning of life with Albert Einstein and Mohammed Ali shared a joke with Dr Martin Luther King; and there were many other recognisable figures from the fields of sport and television and the arts.

Some use had been made of the stocks themselves. Sitting alone on the bench reserved for miscreants, with its feet firmly locked in place, was a figure which, as the printed card alongside it explained, was a representation of the current Member of Parliament. Mark told his friends that the man was generally well liked and that he could take a joke at his own expense: next to him there was an empty space and, as Mark would explain later, thereby hung a curious tale.

As they sipped their drinks and relaxed Tim looked at his friend's wife and could not help putting into words how fortunate he thought he was. "You are looking absolutely gorgeous Helena my dear, pregnancy obviously suits you," he said "Mark's a very, very lucky man."

"I look like a beached whale," laughed Helena, "and for 26 weeks I've been sick every day and I'm a total embarrassment to Mark and to everybody else but somehow today I do feel a great deal better, I think that must be down to you and to Amanda;" and she smiled and leant across the table to give Tim a gentle peck upon the cheek.

Amanda Faversham was Tim's new girlfriend; at 23 years old she was quite a bit younger than her boyfriend. She was a bright, seemingly self-confident girl, although Mark suspected that there was a certain brittleness and insecurity behind the outgoing, extrovert facade. She was an up and coming actress, who had already co-starred in a television adaptation of Jane Austen's "Pride and Prejudice" and she was currently appearing in a new version of "The Taming of the Shrew" at a Manchester theatre, and in which she had received rave reviews.

"I could stay here forever," she said in slightly languid manner, "It's so quaint I really do envy you living here."

"It isn't always like this," replied Mark. "There are a lot of things simmering away quietly just beneath the surface and it is seldom as calm and peaceful as it is tonight. I'll tell you about something very odd that happened only a couple of days ago and which, seemed to involve just about everybody in town to demonstrate to you just how wild things can sometimes be."

Mark's words grabbed Tim and Amanda's attention. He pointed to the vacant seat at the stocks alongside the town's Member of Parliament. "If you'd been here on Saturday or Sunday you'd have seen a figure sitting there," he said. "You might not have known who she was, but there is a piece about her in the local paper, and before we eat I'll show you a picture of her scarecrow as it was at the weekend; her inclusion in this year's festival caused heated debate in some quarters."

Mark then told his friends how a lady called Virginia Brocklehurst had attracted universal condemnation for failing to honour her late husband's wishes by not giving to the town a piece of land for a new Amenity Centre to be built upon, even though his intentions couldn't have been clearer. Mark also explained that she had refused point blank to make any financial contribution whatsoever towards the costs of the project despite her late husband's promise that he would make a generous donation to the scheme.

"There was uproar in the Council Chamber," he said. "We received a call to attend because things had become so heated, but fortunately they had calmed down a touch by the time the police arrived so there were no arrests. Because everyone believes that she's a selfish cow, Mrs Brocklehurst is now shunned by the whole town and none of the local shops or tradesmen will have any dealings with her. Then on Monday night it happened."

"What happened?" asked Amanda.

"Well, people say it was a spontaneous uprising," answered Mark, "but I'm sure it wasn't. Everybody seemed to know exactly what to do. It was as if there had been some sort of historical flashback. There was shouting and chanting and banging and clanging and the figure of Mrs Brocklehurst was stolen from the stocks and paraded through the streets and then finally it was burnt in a field just outside the town, at a spot where an old gibbet used to stand. The uniform officers hadn't got a clue how to deal with the situation, there was no Inspector on duty that night to advise them, so they just kept well away, which was probably the wisest thing they could have done in the circumstances."

Tim's eyes opened wide with excitement. "You know what that was, don't you Helena?" he asked.

She nodded. "I read my Thomas Hardy," she said. Mark and Amanda didn't get the allusion.

"In Hardy's novel *The Mayor of Casterbridge* explained Tim, "he describes a "Skimmity ride" in which the effigies of a man and a woman are placed upon a donkey and then paraded through the town accompanied by a makeshift band of musicians playing ram's horns, trombones, serpents and an assortment of tuneless instruments which beat out a noisy overture. Historically speaking the practice allegedly owes its origins to a certain Mrs Skimmington, who completely dominated her pathetic husband to such an extent that he became a figure of mockery. The town's people reacted to her abuse of him by making an image of her and carrying it through the town. I think the figure was jeered and booed and that it was then destroyed in one way or another. Other places then copied this crude pantomime and the term "Skimmity ride" was born. "Skimmity" is a corruption of "Skimmington." So far as I know its first recorded use was in the early 17th century. It was, and here it apparently still is, an expression of social disapproval. Sometimes, as in this instance, the effigies were set on fire, in Hardy's book they were thrown into the river. Even as late as the 1880's local newspapers in Dorset describe an event at which male and female figures were burnt on a gallows, erected right outside a local pub. The reason for that happening was sexual immorality; indeed that was generally, although not exclusively, the case. The most frequent occurrences seem to have been in the counties of Somerset, Dorset and Wiltshire, but the practice was known in Nottinghamshire and also in Scotland where it was called "Riding the Stang."

"That's what John Winston called it in his night school classes," interjected Helena. "I wonder if in some way his lessons inspired this incident to take place."

"This is so very exciting," cried Amanda, "just like the *Wicker Man*; you know what happened to the police inspector in that story don't you Mark?"

"That's not going to happen to me," laughed Mark "Shall we go and eat before we all start frightening ourselves into serious bouts of indigestion?"

En route to the restaurant they passed the window of the local newspaper office and stopped to gaze at the photographs on display there.

"That's Mrs Brocklehurst," said Mark, pointing to a photograph of two scarecrows seated in the stocks, "and that's her in real life," he added, pointing to a picture from page four of the same edition of the newspaper.

"It is a remarkable likeness," commented Tim. "You'd almost think that it had been lovingly created; there's so much attention to detail."

"I don't think that lovingly is entirely the right word," laughed Mark, "but I can see exactly what you mean."

As they made their choices from the Bistro's superb a la carte menu, the conversation still revolved around the strange events.

"This town is very set in its ways," said Mark, "and sometimes I think we just police the surface. People have very long memories and forgiveness isn't an over-used commodity round here. There's so much I still haven't got to grips with. There's a bright young detective sergeant, stationed at New Mills, who has only been here a couple of months longer than me, but he seems to understand the mentality of the people who live here a great deal better than I do. I thought I was a quick learner, and I've done my very best, but he's streets ahead of me: instinctively he seems to know what's going on, perhaps it's having a local girlfriend that gives him an unfair advantage."

"There are a lot of very nice people here," countered Helena. "The doctors have been wonderful and Kathy Latimer, the practice nurse is lovely; the children at the school all seem to be happy and all the shopkeepers are so friendly. It's so different from London. It feels so very safe; I've got no regrets at all about moving here."

"Neither have I my love," said Mark, "neither have I", and he kissed his wife gently on the forehead.

The rest of the evening was spent talking about music and art and drama and politics. Amanda explained how she had first met Tim and talked about the play she was in and about the Manchester audiences; Tim talked about his new job and his new car and reminisced about old times with Mark; Mark talked about Helena and the house and pending fatherhood at his time of life and Tim thought how much he had changed since the occasion of their first inauspicious meeting. Those changes were surely down to Helena, she had overwhelmed Mark and in the end she had even touched him with her courage and tenderness. One day he hoped he might emulate Mark's happiness; he hoped there was a chance that it might be with Amanda. Helena listened to everyone; she had the gift of making other people feel relaxed and want to talk and was the best of company in any social occasion.

The two men and Amanda finished their meal with coffee and liqueurs. Helena just had coffee; one glass of wine was all she permitted herself to drink whilst she was pregnant. Later, as they strolled back to Mark and Helena's cottage a tawny owl screeched in the church yard: Mark teased everyone by suggesting that it might have seen a ghost; Helena stopped his mischief by lightly touching his lips with her finger and they continued on in silence under a demurely veiled moon.

Chapter Six

Virginia Brocklehurst ate her breakfast alone; she was used to doing that and it didn't upset her. There had been a time when she had shared a table with Jack and she had listened to his plans and been a sounding board for his ideas. She wondered if she had ever really understood the man she had married; she was totally convinced that he had never really understood her. They had been so very different, he was charming, easy going, generous, even profligate with his money, well liked and well respected in the community and, in her opinion, a soft touch for every hard luck story that was fed to him. He had been born and bred in Burrdale and he loved the town and its people. Virginia had seen him as a sort of enlightened feudal overlord who had an over developed sense of duty, and it was that sense of duty that really frustrated her, particularly if this concern for the general good led to Jack's financial detriment, which was what she thought very frequently occurred. Jack had been a dreamer; she was always the arch realist: his life, although not without its problems had been privileged; her life had been difficult and whatever she had achieved had been earned by hard work and a ruthless determination to succeed.

When talking about Jack behind his back, some people had asked the question "Why the Hell did he marry her?" She had been aware of the snide comments and they hadn't bothered her. She had frequently asked herself the same question and had concluded that it was her intelligence that had attracted him. She also felt sure that there must have been a void in his life following the death of his first wife through cancer, and that she had been chosen to fill that void. His children were away at university, for a sociable man it must have been very lonely. She was sure that other women must have tried to attract him, but perhaps they had tried too hard, and maybe he had seen through their too obvious attempts to entice him. She had not tried to do that, she hadn't pretended to be anything other than what she was, and Jack had admired her honesty.

She had always been wise beyond her years, she understood people, and her mental toughness was clear for all to see. Once in the course of an argument with a property developer, he had called her "a cold, calculating cow" because she had refused to be railroaded into agreeing to advise the company she was working for that a series of interim payments should be made. This was not a comment on her appearance; an attractive, well-groomed woman deserved no such description, but it reflected the impotence of the man when he couldn't overcome her cast iron will. She was good at making people feel impotent, she revelled in that power. The image she presented to the world was of a person without an Achilles heel, indestructible, unbeatable and unflappable. It was just an image, of course; inside her breast feelings of anger and hurt burnt as fiercely as they had ever done, and for a while these had been supplemented by an overwhelming sense of dread, but now miraculously that dread had disappeared as quickly as it had arrived.

Knowledge is always the key. For many weeks now she had been sure that she was unmasked and that thought had terrified her; but life is a card game, and sometimes fate deals a player a winning hand. For the first time in months she was confident that her knowledge now trumped every other card in the pack.

People had asked her how she had felt when she learnt that Jack had been killed, and her feelings had been mixed. There had been genuine sorrow. Jack had been kind and loving, and she had recognised his goodness and his decency, and she was not surprised to discover how much of a hole his passing had made in her life, but this feeling of loss hadn't been the dominant emotion. The overwhelming sensation she had experienced was one of liberation. At last she had a chance to be totally herself and to do things entirely her own way, without reference to any other individual and, although she hadn't been without means before she met Jack, she now had money to enable her to do virtually anything that she wanted to do. One of her first actions deeply astonished her. Whilst Jack had been alive, there had been many times when he had been absent from home. Like a queen bee she needed the attention of drones, and Henry Osbourne had fulfilled a useful role. Now she reigned supreme she had an unfettered right to choose. She no longer had need of little Henry. He was so very shocked when she told him that his services were being dispensed with; the sounds of bursting ego and feeble protest were immensely pleasurable sounds, and potentially very addictive ones.

She rang a bell and Jack's Spanish housekeeper appeared. She was no friend to Virginia, but she had lived in England for a number of years and she had no desire to return to Madrid; a job was a job, and at present mistress and maid had a shared interest. She needed work and Virginia needed a servant; she could not do without the wage and Virginia had not the slightest chance of recruiting a replacement locally if she left. For the time being therefore a fragile truce existed between the two women.

The housekeeper cleared away the breakfast dishes in an unnecessarily noisy manner and Virginia curtly told her to take more care. Virginia then said she was probably going out soon, but that she expected to be back for lunch, although she was awaiting a phone call and it was possible her plans might change at short notice. Whilst the housekeeper finished removing the last of the pots, Virginia drank a second cup of coffee and re-read the local newspaper. The ridiculous episode of the effigy made her smile; if the intention had been to drive her from town they had seriously misjudged their victim. It was a ludicrous, laughable stunt, probably dreamed up by John Winston, who no doubt enjoyed playing the part of agent provocateur. His whole life had been one long performance; if ever a man did better not to truly know himself then that man was John Winston. The only thing that really irritated her about the whole pantomime was the scarecrow itself; it was far too big. Virginia looked at herself in the mirror, she was a trim size 10, and the coat the absurd creation wore must have been at least a size 18. She was proud of her slim body; to represent her as overweight was petty but then again it was typical of the man who she suspected was the chief architect of the malign charade.

A very long time ago she had come to understand that life owed her no favours; that she could depend on nobody and trust no-one. Memories of her childhood flooded back, and these were not pleasant: being the only daughter of a single mother who had lived with a succession of unsuitable partners had left its mark and the many times that she had been farmed out to distant, uncaring relatives, sometimes for days at a time, without knowing whether the banishment would ever end had planted within her a deep rooted sense of insecurity. As a little girl she had yearned for love, but all too frequently had met with rejection, although there had been times when she was older when rejection was the kindest thing that could have been wished for. As the years had passed, she had learned to become invisible and that had protected her until the curves of her body finally burst through the flimsy fabric of her dresses.

She had become a woman too soon, with appetites and passions no child should ever have known, and there were pages from her past that she now wished could be torn out. Her assets had been her looks and her brains and she had made good use of these. Natural cleverness, combined with beauty and ambition had taken her a long way and by the time she met Jack she was already a qualified accountant, working in Manchester, with her own apartment at Salford Quays.

She had started wearing Burberry long before it was hijacked by *Chavs* and football hooligans because the brand had had a dependable quality. When she began to make good money, more than one friend had suggested that she move with the times, clear out her wardrobe, send dated garments to the charity shop and indulge herself by buying a whole new range of designer clothes. She had been appalled at the very idea. The thought that people who had never saved and who had led feckless lives, squandering their cash on booze, bingo, and many worse things, could profit from her hard work deeply offended her. She had resolved there and then, and she had always stuck rigidly to this afterwards, that when she no longer wanted or could no longer wear a coat, jacket, suit or dress it would go directly to the wheelie bin or to the incinerator; and over the course of the years some very exclusive labels had been summarily disposed of.

She was interrupted in her thoughts by the jarring tones of the telephone bell. Like a general on the field of battle preparing to negotiate terms of surrender with a defeated enemy, she strode purposely to the point of confrontation. There must be no hint of weakness in her voice; total victory was the only outcome that could be agreed: *Surrender or Die* that could be the only message.

"Yes," she said, "they should meet face to face." A disembodied voice on the end of a telephone line she knew could lose its potency with the passage of time but the look in the eye of the person who can destroy your world at an instant can never be forgotten; it permeates every fibre of your being and is the stuff of endless nightmares and every time the vanquished wakes from sleep in a cold sweat, the safer the victor sleeps at night.

"No," she agreed, "a public meeting would not be a good idea." Nosey people can overhear things they should not hear, prying eyes can see things they shouldn't see and this matter needed to be kept secret. She would name the venue, she would set the time and there could be no argument; there was a firmness in her voice that demanded total obedience.

When she finally put down the receiver it was with a feeling of triumph; she was euphoric. The last remnants of self-doubt had gone, all moments of indecision were behind her; she was in complete control and the feeling was a heady one. Power was an aphrodisiac, she could build or she could destroy: she felt invincible!

She looked out of the big bay window and down the long swirling drive towards the town. It was a grey day, with more than a hint of moisture in the atmosphere; she turned, left the room and walked towards the hall stand. For just a fraction of a second she hesitated. She wondered, for a brief instance, if she should wear the trench coat, or seek anonymity by putting on a little used Berghaus, which would also be more in keeping with the wild countryside and the journey that she had got planned for that morning. The spot was remote, why she had suddenly thought of it, she didn't know, but she always trusted her instincts and saw no reason not to do so now, and certainly there would be the privacy she needed. She realised immediately that whatever practical advantages the red anorak might have, in reality there was only one choice. If she wore the Berghaus and people saw her in it, they might infer that she had been intimidated by their campaign of harassment and, if they thought that, she laid herself open to public expressions of derision and contempt.

With an air of defiance she put on the Burberry and the fedora hat and, closing the solid oak door behind her, with her head held high, she walked confidently into town, The damp streets were not busy, the joyous air of yesterday had disappeared, and the few people who were out and about seemed to bolt for cover when they saw her. What weaklings they all were; even now, if somebody had had the guts to approach her and to challenge her, she might have been won over by their courage; but nobody did. She felt eyes stabbing her in the back, but nobody was brave enough to confront her face to face. There was not a man amongst them. As she left the market square to head out into the open countryside she glorified in being an outcast. Jack and his decency had almost made her see Burrdale in a different light, but he was gone and he had been the only good thing about this place. It deserved to fail and she was glad that it would do so. When she left it would be on her own terms and through the front door, and that would be a joyous day, but that day was not today.

She needed time to plan the legacy of disappointment that she would bequeath to this backward looking, claustrophobic little town.

Chapter Seven

It took Emelina Delgado, the Spanish housekeeper two and a half days to report her mistress missing. She attended the drab Burrdale police station in the late evening when she knew the streets would be largely deserted: as the servant of the despised Mrs Brocklehurst she had frequently been subjected to verbal abuse and insults and, although she never stuck up for her mistress, her command of English was too poor to allow her to make it clear to her tormentors that she was really on their side.

At the enquiry desk she spoke to a civilian clerk. The clerk gained the distinct impression that the housekeeper had no concern for Virginia's safety and that she was merely trying to cover her back should she, at some time in the future, be accused of failing to act with due diligence by an obviously unloved employer. This assessment of the situation was, in truth, entirely accurate.

To begin with Virginia's absence had been a rare treat for Emelina, mainly because, most unusually, the maid hadn't been left a lengthy list of tasks sufficient to occupy a whole battalion of cleaners for a fortnight, to be completed during the short time the mistress was usually away. Emelina had made good use of her unexpected freedom by drinking countless cups of coffee and watching mind rotting day time television, but always with one eye on the long driveway so that, if Mrs Brocklehurst should return without warning, she could switch from self-indulgent inertia to frantic activity to create an entirely false impression that she had been hard at work throughout the period of her employer's absence

By the end of the second day an unwanted thought had wormed its way into her brain. Suppose Virginia had been out walking and had somehow slipped and injured herself; Emelina knew that the Burrdale valley was notorious for mobile phone black spots; if she was lying helpless somewhere and if nothing had been done to look for her then there would be Hell to pay when she was eventually found. If that proved to be the case there was only one possible outcome and that was that Emelina would be sent in shame back to the poor suburb of Madrid from whence she came to live with her large family in their cramped and airless down market apartment on the sixth floor of a crumbling multi-storey block of flats. Despite the fact that her life had become much harder since the premature death of her master, it was still better than anything she had known at home and she didn't want to be driven back to her former life in disgrace by an enraged and vindictive mistress.

The girl on the enquiry desk took down the particulars with the minimum of fuss, although at times she had struggled to understand Emelina's faltering English, and on occasions she had needed to ask the Spanish maid to talk more slowly to be sure that she recorded every detail correctly. She had had the sense to realise that potentially the disappearance of the hated Mrs Brocklehurst could become a media event, although there remained a good chance that it might fizzle out into nothing, if in due course Virginia returned home unharmed having simply gone off on a whim on some spur of the moment self-indulgent jaunt. However, no chances could be taken and given the degree of public ill feeling the missing woman had generated; she decided that it was safer to pass the matter straight away to a uniformed police officer who could determine what steps, if any, needed to be taken.

Constable Ollerenshaw was that officer. He was a good old fashioned bobby, not known for his super intellect, nor had he ever topped any Arrests Made league table compiled by Derbyshire Constabulary, but everyone in Burrdale knew him, and he was the policeman most likely to be stopped on the street and to whom snippets of information were most frequently passed. He listened intently to everything the housekeeper had to say, and recorded on paper all the details she related. When she had finished, he took time to consider what to do for the best. He concluded that it was not yet appropriate to launch a full scale missing person inquiry. There were no compelling reasons to suppose that Mrs Brocklehurst had come to harm and, if she had arranged to meet somebody, particularly in circumstances as outlined by the housekeeper, when she had appeared very eager for that meeting to take place, it was quite possible that after the meeting she and the person she had met could have both decided to go somewhere together on a whim. Lack of luggage wouldn't be a problem for a wealthy woman like Virginia; so after some deliberation Ollerenshaw formed the opinion that at this stage it was better to wait and see what developed before taking any precipitous action.

A few hours later however, the situation altered dramatically when a rambler arrived at the enquiry desk. The leather purse he brought with him was very wet, but not completely sodden. It was large and fat and, when opened, it contained £35 in coins and £780 in bank notes: in addition to the money there were credit cards and a photo card driving licence all in the name of Virginia Brocklehurst. The man, who came from Salford, was keen to know if there was likely to be a reward and, on being told that there was nothing on the table so far, began to question to himself the wisdom of honesty and to regret that he hadn't succumbed to the initial temptations that had afflicted him. He became even more despondent when Detective Sergeant Alan Nadin asked him to show him exactly where the purse had been found and to complete a form detailing all his personal particulars and the full circumstances that had led to the discovery of the wallet. Two hours later, and not in the best of humour, the reluctant good citizen finally left the police station to continue his walk; rain was now falling steadily, it was cold and dismal: he wasn't in any way warmed by the knowledge that he had done the right thing.

Alan Nadin went straight to Mark after he had finished dealing with the man. "I don't like it Gov," he said, "Virginia Brocklehurst isn't the sort of woman to suddenly take off into the hills alone, nor is she the type of woman to accept the loss of her purse without doing anything about it. I've got a feeling in the pit of me stomach about this one."

"I've got the same feeling Alan. If the purse has simply been lost I'm certain she'd have missed it by now. I think it's possible that Mrs Brocklehurst currently has no cash and moreover, she no longer has the means of getting any without returning home or going to a bank to get emergency funding. In normal circumstances, you'd expect her to report the loss to us, wouldn't you? I think the fact that she hasn't done so could potentially be significant, it could mean that she's lying injured out on the hills unable to use her mobile, or it could mean something far worse. A great many people would be chuffed to little mint balls if the lovely Virginia were found with her toes pointing skywards."

It was thus shortly after 4pm, Mark called in the Mountain Rescue Service and a full scale search of the area was begun.

The weather was by now appalling. Heavy persistent rain was

being driven across the wide Burrdale valley by a stiff north easterly gale and after months of drought, during which they had all but disappeared, hillside streams were finally awakening from their slumbers, rock hard clay was becoming saturated and limestone paths were becoming slippery and difficult and dangerous to walk upon. Visibility was non-existent, particularly on the hill tops which were covered by a waterlogged cloak of low cloud and everywhere black faced and Herdwick sheep were pictures of dejection. Nature was not treating the searchers kindly, only blizzard conditions could have been worse; it was therefore no surprise to Mark that at the end of Day One when the search was called off for the night, no trace of the missing woman had yet been found.

The next morning, soon after first light, the search began again. The number of police involved had increased considerably and, to the credit of the inhabitants of Burrdale, a good number of its townsfolk had turned out to assist in the task.

"I wouldn't leave a dog out in these conditions," said one man, "I can hardly treat a fellow human being less well, even if she is a greedy tart." Other people expressed broadly similar views, although, not all of them, were so delicately understated!

The sea of humanity that now braved the elements slowly fanned out across the misty hillsides, the dark colours of police uniforms mixing with the reds, greens and yellows of the civilian searchers, mimicking the diverse shades of autumn which were beginning to tint the broad leaved trees that grew in the more sheltered spots at the foot of the valley alongside the meandering Burrdale Brook. Rescue dogs ran hither and thither, wagging their tails excitedly as they criss-crossed the moorland slopes, and from time to time, a police helicopter flew overhead, although the low cloud severely hampered its effectiveness.

Gradually the area of search grew wider and wider and further away from the spot where Virginia's purse had been discovered. Higher and higher up the hillsides the people went following the rocky paths that lead to the grit stone ridge that separates Burrdale Valley from the more dramatic Hope Valley. The views from the top on a clear day are breath taking and on good days the two great industrial cities of Manchester and Sheffield are both visible even at distances of over 20 miles; today visibility was often little more than 20 metres and all anybody could think of was getting the job done and then getting indoors out of the wind and rain as quickly as they could.

It was as tired legs were beginning to ache and cold teeth were beginning to chatter that the cry went up. By now the main body of the search party was carefully edging its way back down a steep gully towards the distant town. The area had been searched before, but at a time when the downpour had been at its hardest, and it was therefore understandable that things might have been overlooked. Beneath a slimy outcrop, not far from the brown waters of a peaty pool, a shapeless and sodden felt hat was discovered. It had suffered a disastrous transformation, but there was no doubt that it had once been identical to the one habitually worn by Virginia Brocklehurst. Much later, when it had been dried out and hair samples had been lifted from its crown it was conclusively established that it was without doubt one and the same.

The next step was obvious. There was no alternative. The stagnant tarn would have to be dragged and police frogmen would need to brave the algae and the pond weed in order to uncover what if anything these muddy waters might be concealing.

As dismal afternoon finally gave way to dire evening the secret hidden at the bottom of the pool was finally revealed. The body of a woman was raised to the surface of the lake and steered by the police divers to the water's edge where other hands helped to haul the corpse out onto the slippery bank. Even her closest friends would have had difficulty recognising her, and Virginia Brocklehurst had precious few of those left now. Her dark hair was caked with dirt and slime, as if some giant slug had crawled over her head, leaving a noxious trail of puss in its wake, and the rotting leaves that clung to her face looked for all the world like black leeches that had grown fat sucking out her life's blood, but there was no doubt: this grotesque parody of the woman she once had been was the missing business woman. The long search for Jack Brocklehurst's widow was at an end. Once heads had turned to look at her when she passed, now heads turned away to avoid looking at her. To the few who continued to stare, the most terrible sight of all was the ligature of thick cord that cut deeply into the dead woman's neck.

Mark Hobson was already at the scene, he had been alerted when the hat had been found and the police frogmen had been called in, and the discovery of the body confirmed his worst fears. This was now a crime scene, all unnecessary personnel had to be withdrawn. The body could not be moved until the pathologist for the High Peak had examined it in situ, but it would only be much later, when it had been stripped of the last vestiges of dignity in the operating theatre and sharp blades had sliced open its chest and vital organs had been hacked out and microscopically examined, that the cause of death would be fully known, but even at this stage the necklace of hemp argued eloquently for a finding that the murder had been committed. How had she ended up in the water? Was she alive or dead when she was thrown into the pool? Had she been beaten before she was strangled? These and a hundred more questions besides needed to be answered, but Mark Hobson was fearful that many of them never would be. Big booted Bobbies and small booted civvies had all skidded and slithered across the muddy terrain: tracks and trails may once have existed, footprints could have provided important clues, but all these now lay submerged under layers of squelchy glop that covered the entire land area around the pool.

Chapter Eight

Dr Gerald Grimshawe universally referred to as "The Grim Reaper" by disrespectful police officers, was the pathologist for the High Peak. He was at a seminar in Huddersfield when the summons to attend Burrdale Tops was received. The call didn't thrill him for, although the topic being discussed was one that barely interested him, he had been looking forward to meeting the few of his colleagues who did not profoundly irritate him after the event, and sharing with them a pint or three of real ale before making a leisurely journey back home. He was not a hypocrite. Doc Grimshawe didn't preach to others the virtues of a healthy lifestyle while ignoring that advice himself and he had never been a zealot in the cause of moderation. He liked a pint and a good cigar, and he had not attained his barrel-like figure by turning up his nose at roast beef dinners and steak and ale pies. There were some in his profession who despaired at his political incorrectness, who saw a country hick in ill-fitting tweed suits whose shameless self-indulgence they believed damaged the standing of doctors in the eyes of the general public, but these were people who didn't know him well. To those people who did the reality was very different: behind the persona of a grumpy, curmudgeonly old man was hidden a world renowned expert in a highly specialised field who was blessed with a brain the size of a small planet.

"I'll be with you in about an hour," he told the timid young police woman who had ruined his cherished plans.

"Can you be a bit more precise please?" she had asked.

"No," he had replied curtly, before slamming down the receiver to rule out the possibility of any further conversation.

Having to wait for the pathologist wasn't all bad news for D.I. Hobson. It gave him the chance to return to his vehicle which he had left parked in a field gateway three quarters of a mile down the valley and from the relative warmth of the driver's seat telephone Detective Chief Superintendent Stan Hardy, who was the Senior Investigating Officer for the whole of North Derbyshire; it also gave him a chance to make a quick call to his wife Helena.

When D.C.S. Hardy was told the facts, he instantly realised how much media interest there would be in this suspicious death.

"I know you'd like to head this one up Mark," he said, "but the press will expect a higher ranking officer to lead the inquiry. I'm going to ask Detective Superintendent John Lomas to be in charge, but the killing happened on your patch so I'm pretty certain he'll choose you to be his Deputy S.I.O. He's an easy bloke to work with; I think you'll make a good team. I'll get on to him straight away; meanwhile you'd better get yourself back up the hill to wait for Doc Grimshawe. If you're not there when he arrives, he'll be grumpy as hell, and I wouldn't wish a crotchety Grim Reaper on my worst enemy."

"As you wish Sir," said Mark, disappointed but not surprised by this turn of events.

It was nearly another hour and a quarter before the pathologist finally turned up, red faced and breathless from his difficult trudge up the steep hillside, looking like an ungainly, lumbering snowman in his white boiler suit, but one whose head had been replaced by a gigantic over-ripe tomato.

"God in Heaven," he snorted, "Why couldn't the silly bitch have chosen a more accessible place than this to get herself bloody killed!"

The initial examination at the scene was mercifully quite short.

"That neck- tie that she's wearing hasn't done her any good at all. I think she was probably dead before she was lobbed into the water, but I can't say that for definite until I've taken a look at her lungs. There look to be some facial abrasions, but until she's been properly hosed down I can't tell the extent and, by the way don't send your divers home yet, there's still some work for them to do."

"Why's that?" asked Mark, "What do you expect them to find?"

"I'm not a bloody clairvoyant, but your slutched up water baby appears to have had both her wrists slashed, and there's also a puncture wound to her chest. You can advise them to search for Captain Flint's treasure if you've a mind to, but if you're wise I'd limit their ambition to finding a broad bladed knife, or something very much of that ilk."

"Any idea as to the time of death?" Mark asked.

"Oh sometime in the last three days, but given that she's been hugging the bottom of the pond I can't be any more precise than that at this time."

It was very late when Mark finally arrived back home. No knife had been found, but the search would resume the following morning. The area around the pool had been cordoned off for the night, and the volunteer searchers had long since been sent on their way. Mark had had a long telephone chat with Detective Superintendent Lomas, and found himself encouraged by the senior officer's relaxed attitude and a full briefing had been time tabled to take place at 10-30am the next day. Helena had been sick twice in the late afternoon and her stomach muscles and her back ached, and both of them were too tired to offer much support to the other. If he won the lottery Mark decided he would retire. He wanted to be with his wife; he resented the fact that all too often his job didn't allow him to be so. In his dreams they spent long hours together, in reality six hours of possibly disturbed sleep lay between him and the next working day.

Even that calculation was over-optimistic. With little more than four hours rest under his belt Mark found himself depressingly wide awake. It was his job to get everything ready for Mr Lomas's briefing. He would be judged by results and he couldn't afford to make any mistakes; not if he wanted to gain the respect of the Detective Superintendent.

By eight o'clock he was at the police station. The first photographs of the scene of the crime had been developed and printed to A4 size and a map showing the pool and the surrounding area had been prepared and stuck up on the wall.

As Mark waited, he looked at the photographs which he had just put up and he felt a surge of pity for the victim. Whatever she had done, she didn't deserve to die in terror. Maybe it was the fact that the rope was still in place, maybe it was the angle of her head, or perhaps it was just the black mud, but as Mark studied the pictures he remembered a documentary he had once watched on BBC 2 about ritual sacrifice in pre-Christian times. Although he hadn't lived in Burrdale very long he knew that Lindow Common, near Wilmslow, was no more than 18 miles away and that at that location the body of an Iron Age man had been recovered from a bog where it had lain undisturbed for nearly 2000 years. When that body was examined it was discovered that it still had strands of fibre knotted around its throat, which was also found to have been slit: he might have been the victim of a violent crime, he might have been a willing sacrifice, but whatever he was, something in the manner of poor reviled Virginia's death mirrored that centuries old mystery.

The press were going to go crazy. A few years before Mark had lived through the notorious William Ludlow inquiry and his evidence had been crucial in securing a successful outcome to that case. He knew from bitter experience how much pressure the tabloids could exert and how little some journalists were constrained by minor considerations such as truth, particularly if the truth got in the way of a good story. Like that case, this case too would have much to excite them; both had very wealthy victims and, if Virginia Brocklehurst didn't have as high a public profile as William Ludlow, the fact that she had been a strikingly beautiful woman tilted the balance in her favour, and this time there was a back-drop of ancient customs to contend with plus an old fashioned market town which historically had been no stranger to macabre events. It was a near certainty that before this murder investigation was concluded a great many column inches in the less responsible tabloids would be filled with sensational speculation masquerading as hard news.

By the time John Lomas arrived, Burrdale was crawling with

reporters. The presence of the scarecrows on the streets was a godsend to T.V cameramen and press photographers and the local newspaper's report of the recent destruction of the effigy was *manna from Heaven* for the journalists. One enterprising television reporter had even managed to obtain a copy of John Winston's lecture notes from the spring term and, as a consequence, Winston himself had been questioned on camera about the town and its colourful past. He had basked in the attention, his sense of self-importance had soared and he had gleefully told the interviewer of the research he had carried out. The picture he painted was of a community burdened with a blood-soaked past and he had revelled in recounting as many chilling tales as he could possibly cram into a very short prime time slot.

John Lomas's first words to Mark were not those of a happy man. "Listen to that bloody self-opinionated hypocrite!" he exploded. "Have you ever heard such crap as that in your entire life? He's making Burrdale sound like a cross between Amityville and Moss Side which it bloody isn't but that's what the press want to believe and very soon every lunatic under the sun will be sticking in his or her two penneth about curses and vengeance and supernatural forces!"

"So is Winston talking a load of cobblers Sir? Only I looked at some stuff that he gave my wife to read and it did seem to be pretty well researched to me."

"His basic facts are probably right Mark. Burrdale is a very old town and if you study the history of any old town you'll discover enough prejudice, envy, greed, violence and injustice to fill a six volume novel. The crime rate in Burrdale is actually lower now than in most comparably sized towns in England and Wales. Just because some people here have strong links with the past and occasionally old grudges rise to the surface it doesn't turn a sleepy little market town into the "Village of the Dammed", but it suits self-obsessed pillocks like John Winston and those bloody vultures out there in the square to create that impression to further their own selfish ends!"

"I can see that Sir" said Mark, "but you've got to admit that this murder is a strange one. It's almost as if the victim has been killed twice, once to end her life and then because that wasn't enough she's been butchered a second time, maybe to put to rest some inner demon, although I know we'll have to wait for the full P.M. report before we can say that for sure. You may think I'm barking up the wrong tree, but when I look at the pictures of her body lying at the side of that pool, I keep seeing the image of the 2000 year old bloke they pulled from the peat bog at Lindow a few years ago now."

"I think that that's exactly the image the killer wants you to see" said Lomas. "I'm not sure why I think this, but I believe the murderer knew, or even intended that the body would be found and that he has very coldly, and very deliberately, set out to re-create a sacrificial killing, but why he should choose to do this I've no idea, but that's what we need to find out."

"All the talk in the town is that this murder is retribution because Mrs Brocklehurst has betrayed her husband's wishes, and certainly that betrayal has caused a colossal amount of ill feeling," said Mark, "and if she'd simply been strangled, or been beaten about the head with a blunt implement, I'd subscribe to that view myself. But there's more to it than that, I'd stake my life on it. I'm convinced however that the retribution theory has got to be a significant line of inquiry."

"I think you could well be right," said Mr Lomas, "but we can talk about motives in the briefing; we've a great deal to do, and a hell of a lot of people out there are going to be watching us doing it; let's grab a cup of tea and then get the men in and make a prompt start to the job in hand."

Chapter Nine

Most murders are appallingly run of the mill. When a man in a drunken fit of rage batters his girlfriend to a pulp there is precious little to tax the imagination of the investigators: when a drug addict, out of his skull on crack cocaine, drags an old lady to her death because she clings on tight to her handbag to prevent him stealing her pension the story is depressingly easy to unravel; but there are some murders where the difficulties facing the inquiry teams from the outset seem almost insurmountable. When such a murder happens, it generates a mood of excitement, particularly among younger officers, and they are frequently amazed at the casual attitude of the more experienced men and women who, having seen it all before regard the investigation primarily as an opportunity to earn a decent amount of overtime. Detective Sergeant Alan Nadin in his time had felt all these emotions. In a police career that stretched over three decades there wasn't much that he hadn't seen or done, and in the course of his journey from wet behind the ears recruit to case hardened C.I.D. officer he had moved a long way along the road from idealism to cynicism, but he had never quite arrived there. The job still mattered, and it was still important that it was done right. He had worked with John Lomas on many occasions in the past and this was the seventeenth or eighteenth murder they had investigated together, he couldn't rightly now remember which. He understood the man; he knew what made him tick. Lomas would demand an efficient and effective investigation, he would settle for nothing less, but he would listen to his experienced officers and make good use of their abilities.

The area around Burrdale was etched into Alan Nadin's brain. He knew the ordinary people and he knew the villains and, he was sure that his knowledge would be valued by the Detective Superintendent as it had been many times before. He didn't yet know how much his Detective Inspector would seek to involve him, but he seemed to be a clued up bloke, and one who was blessed with a fair smattering of common sense.

Police Constable Jessica Wain was a computer graduate, who was just finishing her probationary period as a police constable. She believed in technology, and was convinced that science could solve any crime. D.N.A. and data bases gave magic answers and she was sure in her own mind that too many police procedures were outdated and should be scrapped, or at the very least substantially revised and re-assessed to take account of the scientific advances that there had been in the last ten years. She was certain that if she was in charge things would be done differently and she was sure that spectacular progress would already have been made under her leadership. She was not in charge, however, and her views were not required. One day it might be different; one day she might have earned the chance to put her theories to the test but, for now, and for a long time to come, her role was to listen carefully to instructions and to follow orders. If she was wise it would pay her not to stand out from the crowd. Nobody, especially a dyed in the wool Detective Superintendent, had any time for a pushy little know-it-all.

Detective Sergeant Paul Burgess was twenty six years old and the youngest detective sergeant in Derbyshire. He was much nearer in age to Jessica Wain than he was to Alan Nadin but like Nadin he believed in tried and tested methods, although at the same time he wasn't afraid of change and innovation. He was a quiet man who kept his own counsel, but was also a clear thinker and obviously highly intelligent. His arrival at New Mills police station had caused quite a flutter among the younger female officers and civilian support staff because of his athletic build and blonde haired good looks but he had disappointed all of them by quickly entering into a relationship with the daughter of a local shopkeeper. When he was off duty, he preferred to keep company with her, rather than go out on the beer with his work colleagues. Usually he appeared content with his lot, but there were times when events in his personal life seemed to pre-occupy him and he could seem distant and withdrawn. At those times it was best to leave him to his own thoughts; ill-advised attempts to lighten his mood often lead to sharp responses. It had quickly been realised that on those occasions it was far better to let him work through his own problems without any outside interference. He had just returned to duty following a bout of sickness, which he had self-medicated. He looked pale and perhaps not yet fully recovered from his illness, and there was some concern that he had returned to work too soon. He was one of three detectives from the New Mills office who had been drafted in to boost the manpower in this inquiry.

The briefing room was packed and was a hubbub of conversation, banter and laughter, but this ceased the moment Detective Superintendent Lomas and Detective Inspector Hobson entered the room. Lomas briefly addressed the assembled officers to confirm that which they all already knew, that the police were launching a full scale murder inquiry into Virginia Brocklehurst's death and he then asked Detective Inspector Hobson to present the details of the preliminary Post Mortem examination.

After Mark had finished speaking John Lomas again took the floor and set out in general terms the lines he wanted the inquiry to follow.

"We're pretty certain of the cause of death, as D.I. Hobson has already explained," he said, "but as yet we can't be certain as to the place of death. That the body was dumped in the pool is clear enough, but we don't yet know if the victim was killed at the lakeside or killed somewhere else. Her purse was found at least two miles from where the body was recovered, but we don't know how it came to be lost. It's possible that there was a struggle and that she was murdered during that struggle. I want a fingertip search of the area to see what we can find. In particular, I'm looking for a weapon that could have inflicted the post-death wounds discovered on the victim's body. Doc Grimshawe thinks that they were probably caused by a large kitchen knife or maybe a bayonet, but a knife isn't the only thing we're looking for: there's also a missing ear stud which will be identical to the stud worn in the deceased's right ear;" and he produced an enlarged photograph of that stud for the watching officers to study carefully.

"Are we considering robbery as a motive?" asked Paul Burgess, "Only the victim was carrying a considerable amount of cash; in the past men have killed for far less than £780."

"I'm ruling nothing out," said Lomas, "but, if robbery was the motive, why didn't the murderer pick up the purse? He or she seems to have found sufficient time to inflict harm upon the body. Surely it would have taken a split second to bend down and grab the wallet? And would an ordinary robber indulge in gratuitous violence?" he asked. "Unless perhaps his mind was chasing psychedelic dragons in Cloud Cuckoo Land," he added, thus providing a possible answer to his own question.

"We know from what the housekeeper says that Virginia left the house to meet somebody following the receipt of a phone call," answered Mark. "We have to check all the incoming and outgoing calls to try to establish who that caller was. He or she could turn out to be our killer, but it's equally possible that Mrs Brocklehurst was being stalked by a completely different person. Next Tuesday, unless we've already got this one sewn up, which I think will be very unlikely, I will want a volunteer to walk the route we know the victim took into town, and to do it at the same time of day and dressed in identical clothing to that worn by the deceased to see if a reconstruction of her last walk will unlock a few memories; if she was followed by her killer, then somebody or other might just have seen something that looked a bit odd."

"Virginia Brocklehurst was about as popular as a pork chop in a synagogue," commented Alan Nadin. "Just under a fortnight ago several hundred people took part in an angry protest, which culminated with her figure being burnt in effigy. The motive for killing her could simply be a violent reaction to her treachery; certainly that's the commonest view point in town."

"D.I. Hobson has a theory about that," replied Lomas, and Mark then expanded on the argument he had put before his senior officer, that such a killing would have been spontaneous and frenzied rather than planned and choreographed in the way that this act of slaughter seemed to have been meticulously thought out.

Paul Burgess intervened again at that point, "There's a video posted on YouTube showing the destruction of the scarecrow, Sir. It isn't fabulous quality, but I think it may be possible to enhance it and I believe someone like D.S. Nadin may well be able to identify most of the people shown on it. One or two of the faces look familiar to me, but I've only been living around here for a few months and I don't recognise all that many people. Alan knows everyone who lives within a ten mile radius of Burrdale, as does P.C. Ollerenshaw; I'm certain that if anyone can pick people out as potential suspects, one of those two can do it."

"That's useful information," said Lomas "Get that video downloaded straight away and get copies to Alan and to John Ollerenshaw then we'll see who can be identified from it."

"There's another thing too, Sir. I was in the Bull's Head five or six weeks ago with my girlfriend and Henry Osbourne was already in there getting drunk. He was mouthing off about Virginia Brocklehurst, what a bitch she was, how he'd supported her when her husband was away and how much he'd done for her, and he was telling anyone who was prepared to stand and listen how she'd dumped him and how much he hated her guts. I'm certain it was the beer talking, but he made everybody feel uncomfortable, although that could have been just the embarrassment of watching a normally intelligent man making a total ass of himself."

"The regulars at the Royal Albert are sure that Virginia Brocklehurst detested John Winston and that the feeling was mutual," chipped in P.C. Ollerenshaw. "It was at some big dinner, Jack Brocklehurst was the guest of honour, and Winston was making the speech of welcome. When Jack introduced his wife to Winston after the event he was all over her, just as he is with any attractive female. She said something quite unpleasant to him and by all accounts the colour drained from his face; he apparently replied with something equally unpleasant, but unfortunately nobody can tell me what was actually said: the two of 'em haven't exchanged a civil word since. It's suspected by many that Winston was the driving force behind the disturbance at Gibbet Field and maybe it isn't entirely coincidental that Mrs Brocklehurst ends up dead less than a week on from that disturbance."

"We'll speak to Winston and to Osbourne as matters of urgency" stated Lomas, "and whilst we're considering possible suspects, does anybody else have any suggestions about other people we should be thinking about speaking to?"

"Well to go back to Henry Osbourne, Sir, lots of letters were published in the "local rag," continued P.C. Ollerenshaw, "and some of them came within a hair's breadth of being illegal, particularly stuff written by Dick Norton and by that tub thumping loud mouth Tony Patterson. Both of them need to be questioned. Osbourne took a huge risk in printing those letters. I don't think that any editor, except perhaps one with a personal axe to grind, would have touched 'em with a barge pole in normal circumstances, and I'm certain that Henry Osbourne wouldn't have printed them if he'd still believed himself to be Virginia's first choice confidante. He was getting his own back; he's a man who can't stand being made a fool of in public."

"Who organised the Scarecrow Festival?" asked Lomas, "only we must find out who made the scarecrow. From looking at the photographs in the paper it's clear somebody sacrificed a very good coat to make a convincing image of Mrs Brocklehurst and that indicates to me a pretty potent dislike of her to be willing to write off such a decent garment."

Mark Hobson had done his research, "Her name is Rowena Kelper Sir," he volunteered. "She's a newcomer to Burrdale and I wouldn't have thought she'd have any great interest in the spat between the Town Council and the deceased, but she's bound to have a record of all the entrants to the competition, so if we ask her it should be easy to find out."

"We also need to discover who acted as ring leaders at Gibbet Field. I'm sure that the vast majority of the people present were just hangers on, but those who took the main roles fall into a different category and we need to know who they were, and to examine very carefully their activities over the last few weeks."

"There was uproar in the Council Chamber when the public meeting was held," interjected Alan Nadin "and more than one person who was there remembers somebody shouting out about "dancing on Virginia's grave" but nobody who I've met so far can tell me who that person was: it's a pretty spiteful comment and I think we need to try to discover the identity of the person who made it."

"I agree, we can't afford to reject any potential leads at this stage."

"There almost certainly will be people who we are currently unaware of who have privately fallen out with Virginia," said Mark, "we need to check her diaries, correspondence, mobile phones and e-mails to see if she'd been sending out or receiving any threats. She never seems to have flinched from upsetting people when the mood struck her, and it's possible that some of the people she upset could have made their feelings known in return."

"The cord wrapped round her neck had been freshly cut from a longer piece of rope. It could be part of the guy rope for a tent. It's strong and very flexible, it's just possible some Outdoors Pursuits shop or even some Scout Troop could have been the source so one of you lucky people will have to dust off your woggle and traipse round the local Scout Huts and the Camping

Shops to see if any of them can throw some light on the matter" commented Lomas, who then spent the next twenty minutes, aided by D.I. Hobson, allocating specific tasks to specific officers, before bringing the briefing session to a close and thanking everybody for their attendance as he did so.

Chapter Ten

The flat above the Burrdale shop was large and well furnished, but tonight it lay in almost total darkness lit only by the light from a single candle; it was also a cold and joyless place, but when the despair was at its blackest Richard Norton liked it better that way. He was alone in the room, alone with his memories and a bottle of whisky which was already one third empty; he was very often alone these days. Richard gazed intently into space, far beyond the confines of the four walls that imprisoned him, and back to a time when life had seemed to hold so much promise and his hopes for himself and his family had known no bounds.

He took a good mouthful of the cheap blended spirit and visibly flinched as he swallowed the straw coloured liquid. It didn't take the pain away, nothing could do that, but sometimes it dulled it a little and it wasn't always as bad as it was tonight. The local newspaper lay crumpled at his feet, he had read and re-read the story many times and the television, which now stood inert and lifeless, had earlier been the focus of his undivided attention as he had watched the regional news. Oh, how the lead story had brought back his grief. Time didn't heal; occasionally a thin scab would cover the wound, but always something would scratch off that protection and once again it would gape open, as wild, angry and infected as it had ever been.

The police would want to speak to him there was no doubt about that. His letters to the paper and his participation in the "Skimmity" guaranteed that they would do so: it was a meeting that he did not want, but it held no fear for him. He had lost so much that he had nothing left to lose, except perhaps Rebecca, and even she was growing impatient with his sadness and was spending more and more time away from home with her handsome boyfriend. Perhaps it would be he who would come to question him, he seemed a decent enough lad, but Rebecca with all her advantages could do so much better. She should wait a while. She had her whole life in front of her. She had all the time in the world; when she finally left him, he truly would have nothing else of value to cling to. If Paul Burgess arrested him on suspicion of murder, which he very well might do, that would distress Rebecca, maybe it would drive a wedge between her and him. That crumb of consolation momentarily soothed some of his distress. Twenty years ago he had sat stubborn and defiant in a police cell, soon he might do so again, but he could still recall every detail of that first occasion with such intense clarity that it might have been just hours or even minutes before. He took another large sip of whisky; the shaking of his hands was almost imperceptible and would have passed unnoticed had anyone else been present to witness his actions.

"We understand your hurt," they had said; that was so untrue it was laughable, nobody could know the depth of his anguish; a vice made of barbed wire squeezed and tore at his heart, jackboots of steel crushed every emotion except hatred; inside he was rotting away! What could they know, how dare they even assume they had the slightest insight into his tortured mind.

"We sympathise with your loss," they had added, but what good was sympathy, it wouldn't bring back Lucas and until somebody could offer him that there was nothing worth hearing.

"He's a nine year old little boy with learning difficulties, he didn't mean to harm anybody; he is already deeply traumatised: your campaign of harassment has got to stop right now."

Stop right now he had thought, *It hasn't even begun yet. You might as well try to recall a speeding bullet or forbid a mighty river in spate from flowing; as long as any trace of that family remained in Burrdale there will never be peace.*

Shane Chadwick was a murderer. What did it matter to him if he was young? Lucas had been young and vibrant and his life had been taken away. Why should Chadwick escape scot free? A precious light had been extinguished, a beautiful boy, a blessed son was no more; natural justice demanded vengeance, there could be nothing less.

"He's below the age of criminal responsibility," they had explained. "There is nothing anybody can do," but he had already proved the absurdity of that statement. He remembered the sound of breaking glass and the fury of his onslaught which had amazed him. He had felt possessed with almost superhuman strength and he had destroyed treasured possessions without a shred of compassion. The child's father had watched in helpless fear, not daring to oppose the rage of the Banshee, and the mother had collapsed in a corner, every muscle and every limb shaking in uncontrollable fear; the child had fouled the kitchen floor in his terror as he had screamed at him in his hatred and his loathing. Somehow that night he had found a voice, a terrible voice that should never have been allowed to speak. The sound had been ear shattering, strident and unnatural, a clarion call from the depths of despair and with his face flushed with anger and so close to that of the child that the spittle from his mouth splashed onto his weeping terrified face, he yelled at him with all his might. "Murdered Murderer!" he had roared and he had sworn that the boy would never forget his evil, or that night, and that he would never in his entire life find happiness or peace.

It had been then the police arrived, but their presence hadn't tamed him. It had taken seven fit young officers to subdue him. He had been strong then, he was still strong now, and as he had been dragged fighting and cursing to the police van he had awakened half the town with his violent rage.

He had paid a price for his actions and the price had been his good name, and some people thereafter had ceased to trade with him, but it had been a price worth paying. His victory over the Chadwick family had been complete and total and they had left the town in hurried flight never to come back; but conversely that victory had also been his worst defeat. The family were hiding somewhere in their cowering anonymity, he couldn't find them; he couldn't get at them and so he could never again re-enforce the impact of that unholy night, which was something he had frequently longed to be able to do.

Prison hadn't scarred him, he had too many scars already, and most of the drug infected dregs of society who he had been locked up with had recognised that he was a powder keg capable of exploding if the touch paper was lit: even in his morose sadness he was dangerous and so he had largely been immune from the unwelcome attention that so many a first time prisoners have to endure.

For a moment his field of distance narrowed, and his eye rested on a photograph of his only daughter and just for a second his mood mellowed; perhaps the burning liquor was beginning to numb his senses after all. She had been less than one year old when Lucas had died and it was her innocence and her need that had stopped going completely mad. At those times, which had come often, when he had contemplated suicide it had been her face that had prevented him from taking his own life and her needs that had empowered him to carry on.

He had done everything for her, whatever she had wanted, she had had, to the detriment of every other demand that was made on his finances. His wife hadn't been able to cope, and long ago she had left him. He blamed Shane Chadwick for her leaving. He had declined all offers of assistance from the State, or any well-meaning third parties, and he had brought up his daughter by himself. Nothing but the best had been good enough for Rebecca, he had paid for an expensive education at the St Matilda's Convent School, and there as a pupil she had shone. The teachers had told him that she should try for Oxford or Cambridge, but they were such a long way away; Manchester was so much nearer, and it was recognised as a top university. She could go there and she could live at home, and he would protect her, and reluctantly she had heeded his advice and he had given her the world as a reward for staying.

She had turned into a stunningly attractive young woman, and of course there had been a succession of young men who had wanted to date her. It had been her choice, of course, as to whom she went out with, but he had always been there to advise her and to uncover the charlatan and the fake. Nobody would ever be allowed to hurt his daughter. One day the right man would come along, and one day she would have a family of her own, a little baby boy, who would be as perfect and as lovely as Lucas had been when he was a tiny child.

The police would know that he had been one of the loudest voices that had been raised against Virginia. His letters had contained an intensity that had set them apart from the mere whining self-pity which had characterised the complaints of so many of the other contributors to the Burrdale Advertiser: Tony Patterson's diatribes had been examples of moronic abuse which had said more about the man who wrote them than they had said about the subject, and there had been many other letters written that had simply failed to ignite the senses. Richard knew that his words had been red hot and they had burnt into the page as flames had later burned into the fabric of the facsimile. The police no doubt knew by now that he had walked at the head of the procession, and that he had carried unaided the largest and heaviest piece of timber (not bad for a man who was nearing his sixty first birthday and who Rebecca said was out of condition) and it had been his strength and his expertise that had done most to build the gallows upon which the effigy of Virginia Brocklehurst had hung and swung gently in the light breeze as fire had illuminated the night sky.

The police would ask him what wrong Virginia Brocklehurst had ever done to him, and he would tell them that she had broken a solemn promise to the town. She has dishonoured Jack's name, and Jack had stood by him when others had looked away. He had been Lucas's godfather and the silver christening cup that had been his gift was kept in a locked drawer along with photographs and toys and other treasured mementoes of a perfect son. When many had condemned him and expressed outrage at his actions, Jack had instinctively understood. It was despicable of Virginia to tarnish his reputation, and it was right for him to fight to protect his good name: the police would see him as an avenger and their files would tell them that he had righted wrongs before. Their files would not tell them of the deeper suspicions that lodged within the innermost recesses of his mind, and he didn't know for sure if those suspicions were fact or fantasy.

There was a loud knock on the door. They hadn't waited long; clearly he was high up on their list of suspects and in an odd way he was flattered by their interest. The drink had done its job; he looked forward to the joust. Paul Burgess was bright, but he hadn't lived long; he had a lifetime of wisdom behind him, there was no need to be anxious. Stumbling slightly, he rose from his seat and when he reached the door, he fumbled just a little with his keys before finding the one that fitted into the lock.

He was disappointed. His visitor turned out not to be Paul Burgess, but an older man who introduced himself as Detective Inspector Mark Hobson. The officer explained, quite unnecessarily he thought, that the police were investigating the murder of Virginia Brocklehurst, and that they wanted to ask him a few questions about the matter. He had brought with him copies of the local newspaper opened up at the letters pages; he also had with him a number of video stills taken from the video recorded on the night of the "Skimmity Ride".

There was no prevarication. "Yes," he admitted the photographs were of him, couldn't be anyone else could they? "No," he agreed, nobody but him could have written the letters, but after that he chose to say nothing else. He refused point blank to account for his actions on the days leading up to the discovery of the murder victim and he didn't try to establish any sort of alibi. At that point Rebecca had returned home. She had looked at his red face, and shuddered at his slurred speech and her eyes had revealed her annoyance and distress, but she told the inspector that her father had been with her throughout most of the critical period and, for the present, at least, that assurance seemed to have been accepted at face value and Mark Hobson had departed without any talk of an arrest. Rebecca had however been left with an uneasy feeling that it wouldn't be too long before he called again.

Chapter Eleven

Mark gazed across the room at Helena who was clearing the dinner plates from the table; they had eaten late and as usual she hadn't eaten much. She looked pale and very, very tired: in the past twenty four hours he had seen so little of his wife and once again he regretted that he had not been able to share her company for any time at all. Last night had been hard: he had had to work late and then Helena had slept badly, which was by no means uncommon, and she had only properly fallen asleep when it had been time for him to get up and get ready for work. Tonight she was upset because she hadn't felt well enough to go to her night school class and she was now worried that she might have to stop going altogether, which, with the loss of social contact that it entailed, was a thoroughly depressing thought. The visit to the doctor's in the morning hadn't helped her peace of mind because he had expressed serious concerns about her blood pressure and warned her that if it could not be brought under control quickly she would almost certainly need to go into hospital until her condition stabilised. There had been tears, Mark knew that, but she had cried alone: Mark also knew how much she didn't want him to worry about her, but he couldn't help himself, he did worry about her all the time. His life had changed forever on the day he met her and he loved her so much that sometimes it hurt. He just wanted his wife back, fit and healthy and so beautiful; if anything happened to her he knew that he couldn't go on. Life is so much easier when you don't care, but it has no meaning, and if ever he lost her there would be no point to anything else that was left

Mark hadn't wanted to know the sex of their unborn child, and to begin with, both he and Helena had tried to remain in ignorance. It was silly in a way, but having lost one baby it seemed like tempting Fate to plan for the arrival of a normal little boy or girl: he had this weird conviction that somehow if you assume too much Fate always intervenes to shatter your hopes into a myriad of tiny pieces. The difficult pregnancy and the constant monitoring had put paid to that; should Helena go full term, and should she deliver a healthy child, that child would be a son. Mark tried hard not to permit himself to dream, but on a good day he couldn't help imagining how life would be if everything turned out in the way he prayed it would.

Mark moved into the kitchen to help with the dishes and then made coffee for them both. "It won't be long now, Love," he said, "A few more weeks and then it will all be over."

"It's exactly twelve weeks, and I think those twelve weeks will be the longest twelve weeks of my life; I want this baby more than anything else in the world, but I'll be so glad when I stop feeling like this. I know I'm being pathetic, I don't want to become one of those women who moan at the slightest twinge of discomfort, but I get so scared" and her eyes moistened as she fought to control her fears. Mark reached out for her and hugged her and her closeness gave him strength: he led Helena into the living room and they sat together on the soft leather settee with their cups of coffee, each of them now content with the moment and with each other.

"I met Richard Norton yesterday. God, what an intense man that man is! I don't think I've ever met anyone with so much anger pent up inside them. He was drunk when I saw him, but he knew what he was doing. He's 61 years old. Do you know he carried a piece of timber weighing just less than a hundredweight, by himself, for over three quarters of a mile and apparently he never put it down once, not even when the procession was stationary outside Virginia's house for upwards of fifteen minutes. I'm sure her murder has re-awakened in him feelings that may have been suppressed for a long time and I'm worried that one day soon he'll explode. If he ever lost control of himself I think he'd be capable of almost anything, he's certainly not a man I'd like to tackle even though I'm a good sixteen years younger than he is, and I keep myself pretty fit."

"Poor man," said Helena, "never being able to move on from a time of loss, condemned by bitterness to constantly re-live tragic events that occurred nearly half a lifetime ago."

"It's very sad, and his grief doesn't only affect him. I met his daughter when I was at the flat, she's 20 or 21 years old and she's a beautiful young woman. She's the one Paul Burgess is going out with and, now that I've seen her; it's quite easy to understand why he fancies her. She seemed very protective towards her Dad, but I could see the hurt in her eyes when she looked at him in drink, and I sensed she felt ashamed of him. She's obviously a girl who is used to being admired: if anyone pitied her she'd be distraught. She's knows the impact that she has and she knows how to exploit it. She's been given every possible advantage in life and boy doesn't it show?"

"Except she didn't have a carefree uncomplicated childhood" commented Helena.

"Nor did she have simple happiness," said Mark.

Because they had nothing else to do, and because Helena always found the story of Lucas's death to be a strangely compelling one, Mark and Helena decided yet again to examine the contents of the hidden box; Mark fetched it from the cupboard in the utility room where it was now temporarily housed and together they re-read the reports of the tragedy and of the court case that had occurred two decades before.

"It is about drowning isn't it?" said Helena, "Or, rather, it's about dead bodies being dragged from black pools. That must be why Richard Norton seems to be so badly affected by the death of Mrs

Brocklehurst; I think that every time he looks at the newspapers or watches T.V. he sees Lucas's face staring back at him."

Helena then asked a further question, "Where exactly did Lucas die?" she said, "Only I've heard old people gossiping in the local shops about this murder and some of them claim that he died in the same pool that Virginia was pulled out of: it's probably quite wrong of course, because, if it was true, officers like Alan Nadin, and John Ollerenshaw would surely have known that and they would have said something about it to you before now. And, in any case there are lots of small pools dotted about the hills in and around Burrdale, or so I am led to believe."

"I had wondered about that," said Mark, "and I should have made more enquiries into it; that could well explain why Richard Norton has reacted in the way that he has. It would make perfect sense, and Alan Nadin and John Ollerenshaw may not necessarily have known about it. Alan once told me that after he did his basic training he was stationed in Derby for over two years, and something very similar could well be true of Ollerenshaw. In any event Lucas's death was never a murder investigation; it was simply a hunt for a missing person. There was no crime and as such it wouldn't have been recorded as one on any police data base.

Inexplicably Helena shivered, "I've had another thought." she said, and she looked unsettled by the idea that had crept unbidden into her mind.

"I think I may just have had the same idea" said Mark. "Virginia Brocklehurst was thirty five years old when she died, which makes her fourteen or fifteen at the time of Lucas's death; is it possible that she could have been the mystery girl who Shane Chadwick described at the inquest? But, if she was, how could we ever prove that fact? There are no known eye witnesses. The only person who would know for sure would be Virginia herself and of course we can't get an answer out of her: I suppose that there's a remote possibility that if we could trace Shane Chadwick he might be able to recognise her from her photograph, but by all accounts he wasn't the brightest of kids so I wouldn't hold out much hope of a successful identification after all this time. Still, it would give some kind of symmetry to this puzzle if that turned out to be true."

"I suppose that would make Richard Norton your prime suspect wouldn't it?"

"Yes, it would," said Mark, "It would give him a strong motive to kill, but there are plenty of other people who may have had motives too. While I'm playing the part of Doctor Watson to your Sherlock Holmes can we talk about John Winston?" and he told Helena of the observations made by P.C. Ollerenshaw at John Lomas's briefing.

"Well, I've only been to three of his classes," said Helena, "but from what I've seen he is very, very good. When he speaks he's a lot like Anthony Hopkins but without the Welsh accent, and he's terrifically knowledgeable about his subject. The last class I went to was a real "tour de force" and when he explained about the Poor Laws, the workhouses and the lunatic asylums he painted such vivid pictures that you could almost hear the cries of the old men and women, forced to live apart from each other. When they could no longer fend for themselves and were compelled through hunger to seek the charity of the parish, and beg for shelter at the workhouse, did you know that they were segregated the moment they crossed the threshold and not allowed from then on to live as a couple? It was heart breaking, and he explains it so well. The way he conducts his classes is pure theatre; all the old ladies see him as some sort of matinee idol, and he plays to the gallery for all he's worth".

"What do you think of him, Love? Only from something in your voice, I sort of detect that you aren't quite as big a fan as they all seem to be."

"Well, he's a brilliant lecturer, but he has this habit of coming very close to me, and sometimes I feel he's mentally undressing me and that makes me feel really uncomfortable. I wouldn't like to be alone with him in a dark place, but in a group he is witty and charismatic. I don't trust him, but he's great to watch and to listen to, and I can well understand why so many of his students think that he's the best thing since sliced bread."

"Can I borrow the lecture notes he gave you? I've flipped through them before, but that was before I knew about his hostility towards Virginia Brocklehurst. Given what I've seen of him on T.V. and, from what you tell me about him now, he certainly seems to be quite capable of inflaming a mob. Either directly or indirectly I think that he's got to be the brain behind this so called "Skemmety" protest.

"Skimmity" protest," laughed Helena. "Maybe you'd better stick to calling it "a Stang ride" I think that more your type of word."

"Bitch," laughed Mark, and he gave Helena a quick cuddle and both of them were affected by a fit of giggles.

Later in the evening when Helena went for a shower Mark started to read the extensive bundle of notes. Even on the printed page the power of the lectures was apparent and Mark could only imagine how much greater the impact would have been for the students who witnessed the bravura performances first hand. He was now sure that Winston had to be questioned urgently about the reasons for his public fall out with Virginia Brocklehurst and the icy coldness that had existed between them since that date. Mark knew he couldn't yet link the protest to the murder, but he also knew he couldn't rule out a link either. Obtaining the class register had become a top priority and he hoped that from that he might be able to identify a number of potential suspects, starting of course with John Winston himself.

Chapter Twelve

The post mortem report from the *Grim Reaper* was clear and concise. Virginia Brocklehurst had not drowned; she had died of strangulation. Not one drop of water had entered her lungs and not a single spark of life had still existed when she hit the surface of the pool. There was clear damage to her face, consistent with a theory that her body might have been dragged feet first over a rough surface, and deep cuts had been made across both wrists, but only after she was well and truly dead. Her throat had been slit, and a large knife had been plunged into her chest, the blade of which had pierced her heart and the hilt of which had cracked two of her ribs, but when it did so she would have felt no pain. The lobe of her left ear was torn where an ear stud had apparently been ripped out, which added further support to Doc Grimshawe's theory that she had been pulled unceremoniously across the floor like a dead calf being hauled to a waiting knackers' wagon.

"It's official then," said Lomas to Hobson. "All the wounds are mere decoration to the done deed, but why would anyone treat her body with such violence?"

"I don't think we're talking about sadism, or some weird type of necrophilia, but I do think that the person who did this had an irresistible compulsion to defile the body. He could have pissed in her face for all we know, but three days under water would have washed away all trace. What I can't understand is why he found it necessary to take the body of the dead woman to the pool. It wasn't simply to hide it, of that I'm almost certain; otherwise he'd never have left the hat where it was. I think that was a signpost for us and not a careless oversight. I think it was important to him that the full extent of his handiwork was discovered."

"So you don't think that this was a mindless slaughter then Mark?"

"No Sir, anything but. I believe our killer gave this matter a great deal of thought."

"A thinker eh? Interesting! Of the people we've spoken to so far who would you put into that particular category?"

"Well, John Winston for one, he's a bit of an intellectual and full of his own self-importance. Shall I take Alan Nadin and pay him a visit? I've got reasons of my own to speak to him in any event."

"Might as well, Mark. Shake him up a bit, who knows what secrets might be rattling around inside his head? Being confronted by two big buggers like you and Alan might loosen things up; something might slip out that he doesn't want us to know."

Within the hour, Detective Inspector Mark Hobson and Detective Sergeant Alan Nadin were walking down the path leading to the night school tutor's well-kept detached stone cottage.

If Richard Norton had been expecting the police to knock on his door, John Winston had not the slightest inkling that the Derbyshire Constabulary would be paying him a visit. He sat before his computer, gazing intently at the monitor totally focussed on the images that appeared on the screen. He had so very often been tempted to investigate the erotic sites on Google and Yahoo but he lacked the courage to do so. He had read far too many articles in the gutter press publicly exposing stupid people who had failed to comprehend that credit cards could be traced back to their owners and that erased computer memory could always be retrieved by experts in the field of computer misuse. With no little degree of frustration, he contented himself with looking at legal soft porn. Nobody knew and nobody cared but, even so he was sure that his particular interests were best kept well hidden as he was convinced that they would not show him in a good light if subjected to the glare of public scrutiny. He had seen disgrace before, and it was not a pretty sight. As a child he had often been to stay with his Uncle Crawford, who had lived on a farm at Burrdale Tops, and he had enjoyed those visits because his uncle had been fun to be with and always very generous and often there had been other children to play with and new and exciting games to take part in. It was nearly ten years after the end of his childhood when three of these children made complaints to the police alleging sexual molestation, and he had sat, numb and appalled, in the public gallery at Derby Crown Court while his uncle was sentenced to 3 years in custody, having been convicted after trial on fourteen counts of indecent assaults on children, the youngest victim being just ten years old. The prison experience had utterly broken him and on release from custody he had been subjected to humiliating ridicule and bullying; John Winston had once witnessed the degrading spectacle of Uncle Crawford being spat at in the street by an uncouth woman with bleached blonde hair and he had wept to see his one-time favourite uncle a pathetic social outcast. He had resolved that he would never put himself at risk of suffering a similar fate.

He was different from his uncle, of course, he was a home grown celebrity, routinely appearing on local radio and, following his brief appearance on the national news he was beginning to find himself very much in demand; lucrative speaking engagements were starting to flood in and finally it seemed that the good times had arrived.

The loud knock on the door nearly made him jump out of his skin: quickly he logged off the computer, his fingers clumsily groping for the keys and, looking less than completely composed, he opened the door to admit Detective Inspector Hobson and Detective Sergeant. Nadin.

Without undue ceremony, Hobson briefly explained the purpose of the unexpected visit and then asked Winston how well he had known Virginia Brocklehurst.

"Hardly at all," said Winston, "I only met her once when her husband introduced us at a dinner. She seemed a pleasant enough woman, but I didn't really know her at all."

"That's not what we hear," said Alan Nadin, "We understood that there was a blazing row between you and her at the Royal Albert about twelve months ago and that you haven't spoken to her at all since that date. Would you care to enlighten us with the details?"

Winston began to look uneasy and Mark Hobson noted that despite the relatively cold temperatures of the room he was quite definitely beginning to sweat.

"It was nothing, just a silly difference of opinion, but she was a highly strung woman and she continued to bear a grudge."

"We believe Mrs Brocklehurst to have been a very intelligent and thoughtful person," said the Detective Inspector. "We don't think she was the type of woman to hold irrational prejudices. I think there is something that you're not telling us Mr Winston, and it would be better all-round if you did tell us what you know."

Winston was now looking very ill at ease, his deep rich voice sounded distinctly cracked, and there was the hint of a stammer as he spoke

"Can I tell you things in confidence?" he asked. Hobson shook his head. "If you've done nothing wrong," he said, "you've nothing to fear, and anything you tell us which is not criminal and not linked to this inquiry will be treated properly and will not be released to third parties. But any relevant information you provide will form part of my investigation and will have to be written down as such. Now what exactly do you wish to say to us?"

"I met Virginia a couple of times twenty years ago at my uncle's farm: it was winter time and I remember always being cold. She was a distant relative of his first wife who I think was a cousin to Virginia's mother. I was about twelve months younger than her and probably quite immature for my age. She was a very pretty girl and my uncle seemed particularly taken with her. There were other children of similar age who were at the farm as well, I don't know where they came from, but Uncle Crawford didn't seem at all interested in them or in me when Virginia was around and sometimes the two of them would just disappear together. I followed them once into the cow shed and they climbed a ladder and went into the hay loft. It was fun. I imagined myself to be a spy carrying out a dangerous mission. I was ever so quiet. Up amongst the bales it was nearly dark and my eyes took time to get used to the dim light. I saw Virginia remove her top, she did it quite willingly, and then my uncle started kissing her breasts. I'd never seen a naked breast before, except in magazines which were smuggled into school, and I was transfixed. My uncle ran his hands over her skin and it seemed to give her pleasure, she took everything off and so did he and they lay down together on his coat and she started to moan softly as he touched her body."

"The dust from the hay got into my throat and I couldn't stop myself from coughing. My uncle looked so startled and then so furious that I thought he was going to hit me and that I would be banished forever from the farm, but instead he became exceptionally kind to me and he asked me to treat the episode as our little secret. He promised me lots of presents and he kept his word and I remained a regular visitor to the farm, but Virginia didn't. I never saw her there again after that day. The next time I saw her was that time at the Royal Albert Hotel when her husband introduced her to me. I didn't recognise her, although there was something about her that looked familiar, but something I said to her must have unlocked her memory. She had been as nice as pie until that moment, but from that instant she changed completely. She asked me if I knew Hill Top Farm and I told her that I did. She looked me in the face with a look of complete contempt and she called me a voyeur, and she screamed at me. I was still only 13 when it happened and I didn't do anything wrong, but I thought she would tell the world that I was some kind of pervert: somehow Jack managed to calm her down, and after that we simply never spoke again, and thankfully she didn't make any further accusations about me."

"What were your feelings towards her after that incident?" asked Nadin, "Only I suspect that you hated her and that you saw her as a threat to your status and your good name. She was a ticking time bomb; did you have to take drastic action to prevent her from exploding?"

"I was frightened of what she might do, I admit that," said Winston, "and I wanted her to go away, but I swear I didn't kill her; do you really think a man like me could go about unnoticed in a small community like this? I also suffer from asthma; do you really believe that I would be physically capable of dragging a body half way up a hillside?"

"We don't yet know where she was killed, unless you can help us on that score," said Hobson tersely, "but you've just told us you wanted her out of town and I think it was your idea to organise the "Skemmety" ride."

"Skimmity ride," said Winston pedantically, much to Mark's irritation, "it's called a "Skimmity ride.""

"Skemmety, Skimmity, Stang," said Mark, "it doesn't matter a damn what you call it, but the whole charade was your idea wasn't it? You thought that if enough people joined in it would frighten her away; now isn't that the absolute truth?"

"There were others," said Winston "and the idea only came to me after Joe Broadbent had made the scarecrow. If that hadn't have been there for the taking I would never have thought about it. There was such a reservoir of ill feeling to tap into, it was so easy. The whole thing snowballed spectacularly; I was amazed and gratified to discover how much she was hated by so many people here. The fact that it happened was down to me, I admit that, I didn't realise how good I was. I aroused the whole town. When that ridiculous dummy was set on fire and the people cheered I felt like a hero. It was one of the best days of my life: if she'd heeded the warning and just gone away then she'd still be alive today."

"It felt that good did it?" asked Alan Nadin "If the destruction of the image excited you so much, how much better might it have felt to experience the destruction of the real thing?"

"Stop right there, you're not pinning anything on me. I've told you already that I had nothing whatsoever to do with the murder of Virginia Brocklehurst and you haven't got a scintilla of evidence to say that I have, because there simply isn't any."

"Then you won't object to us having a look around your house will you?" said Mark, "Do you mind if we start in the kitchen?"

Winston's face crumpled in terror, "Oh please, please stop. I'm telling you the truth; I swear to God, I don't know anything about Virginia's death. I did nothing to encourage anybody to harm her.

I abhor violence. I am one of Nature's cowards" and he said that with such feeling that both Hobson and Nadin felt that he was probably being honest, at least about that assertion!

"I'll ask you point blank," said Hobson. "Have you got a large knife, or any sort of sharply pointed implement in your kitchen, or your garden shed, or anywhere else in this house? Remember, I only need to convince a magistrate that I've got reasonable cause to suspect there are items in your home that may have been used in a murder to get a search warrant and I don't think I'd have much trouble doing that, would I Alan? I doubt if we could keep the fact of the search secret though, and, regrettably, I believe that gossip would spread like wildfire that you were a murder suspect, which I think could be pretty bad news for you."

Detective Sergeant Nadin nodded his head, "It'd be a piece of cake Boss; we've got ample grounds to justify making an application and not a snowball's chance in Hell of keeping it under wraps."

"Oh God," snivelled Winston, "Are you trying to ruin me? I promise you on my mother's life that there's nothing here except a bread knife." He led the officers into the kitchen and produced a very flexible, cheap knife with twin prongs and a serrated edge on either side.

Nadin looked at Hobson, and Hobson shook his head.

"Is that all you've got?" demanded Nadin and Winston, who

looked as if he was about to burst into tears, protested vehemently that there was nothing else.

"You'd better get us your class records for last term so that we can have a look at them," said Mark, and Winston was only too willing to oblige, hoping that once they had seen them his unwelcome visitors would then depart.

"Connor Tipping and Ben Rogers, those are names to play with," commented Alan Nadin. "Are toe rags like them your usual type of student?"

"Of course not," replied Winston. "But they found the course interesting and they weren't representative of the class as a whole. We had a retired librarian, two former teachers, a bank cashier, half a dozen middle aged ladies, and one of your detectives and his girlfriend also attended several of the lectures, only missing when his work prevented him from doing so: perhaps you should concentrate on him;" and John Winston risked a little smirk at this provocative suggestion.

"Don't push your luck," snapped Mark Hobson. "You are one of the prime suspects in a murder inquiry and until anything is proved to the contrary you will continue to be so."

Winston didn't answer, but resolved immediately not to antagonise the two police officers again.

Mark looked at Alan Nadin, I think that Mr Winston has got the message," he said. "Can you think of anything else that we need to put to him at this time?"

"No Boss." said the Detective Sergeant, and both officers stood up and started to leave the room. At the door Mark Hobson stopped and turned again to John Winston, who was beginning to feel relief that his ordeal was finally over.

"There's one more thing Mr Winston," he said. "If you know what's good for you keep your distance from my wife; if I hear that you've been trying to squeeze your body up close to hers again, I'll make you wish you'd never been born; is that clearly understood?"

Winston's newly found composure instantly evaporated; he turned bright scarlet and stammering he confirmed that the message was one which he had fully taken on board.

Chapter Thirteen

Whilst D.I. Hobson and D.S. Nadin had been interviewing John Winston, Paul Burgess had been instructed to speak to Rowena Kelper, the organiser of the Scarecrow Festival, and to follow up any leads that might flow from that conversation. He was not thrilled at the task; he had seen photographs of Ms Kelper in the Burrdale Advertiser and he had not liked what he had seen.

Paul had an eye for quality: he liked intelligent, fashionable, attractive women, of any age, but Rowena with her long flowing floral skirts, dyed crimson hair and silly costume jewellery didn't conform to any pattern that remotely appealed to him. She was also overweight and chaotic, qualities which didn't endear themselves to Paul; but she was a willing volunteer in almost any cause and was desperate to make a mark on her newly adopted home town. Earlier on in the year, a public meeting had been called by the Burrdale Amenity Society to find a new secretary for the current years Scarecrow Festival, and Rowena had been the only person to come forward. Although there had been quite a few misgivings, she had been appointed, and actually she had done surprisingly well, and had now been selected to run the next three festivals on the strength of her achievements to date.

Paul met her in a small untidy office at the Burrdale Town Hall; sheets of paper were scattered everywhere and photographs of scarecrows were either pinned to the walls or spread out across a trestle table in one corner of the room. Rowena was in the course of preparing a Scarecrow Website but was finding the job an exceedingly difficult one.

"It's good of you to see me Miss Kelper," he said, in clear, firm tones that sent a tingle down Rowena's ample spine.

"It's Ms Kelper," she said in an oddly childlike voice, which did nothing to cause Paul's perfectly proportioned backbone to react in any remotely similar manner, "but you may call me Rowena."

Paul forced himself to smile. He hated it when silly, impressionable women came on to him, but he was professional enough not to show his disdain to the spaniel like Scarecrow Festival Secretary

"Do you have a list of all the people who made and exhibited scarecrows?" he asked. "I'm particularly interested in the man or the woman who made the scarecrow of Virginia Brocklehurst."

"I knew it would cause problems," said Rowena. "I didn't want to accept the entry, but the Scarecrow Committee made it clear they wanted it included and, try as I might, I couldn't find any grounds to exclude it. There was supposed to be an explanatory notice telling people who she was and what she'd done, but I put my foot down at that; if we'd allowed that placard to stand I think the council and the festival organisers could have been sued for defamation of character and there was no way I could take that risk. With hindsight, I should have fought harder to keep it out, but what could I do? The festival committee were all against me."

"Who was the maker of the Scarecrow?" asked Paul," I need to speak to him or her as a matter of urgency."

Rowena reached into a desk drawer and produced a lever arch file which she opened. "His name is Joe Broadbent," she said, "and he lives at no. 15 Lower Burrdale Common; I have a telephone number. Do you want that as well?"

Paul indicated that he did, and he recorded all the details he had been given into his notebook. He firmly declined a cup of herbal tea, even though implored by Rowena to try one, and he didn't offer her any cause for optimism when she asked, somewhat plaintively, if it was likely that he might want to talk to her again.

Lower Burrdale Common was part of the council estate and it had mostly been built in the ten year period immediately following the end of the Second World War. Many of the houses were now privately owned and these were the ones with conservatories, PVC double glazing, hardwood doors, patios, garden fences and, in a very few cases even a scattering of garden gnomes. Joe Broadbent's home was not one of these. At some stage the original thorn hedge had been ripped out to allow access for the

Motorability car stood parked upon the scrubby unkempt grass. The hand rail at the side of the front steps indicated to Burgess that someone living at that address was disabled; the general state of the property didn't suggest that the occupant had any pretensions of affluence. He knocked loudly on the door and waited for a reply. He waited for a long time, and was on the point of giving up, when eventually he saw the shape of a person on the other side of the frosted glass upper panel. Finally the door to the house was opened by a large middle aged man who looked as if he hadn't shaved for several days and who walked with the aid of a walking stick. There was no flexibility in his right leg and it was clear that that limb owed nothing to nature; there was also a substantial degree of scarring visible on his face.

Paul produced his warrant card and without any sign of emotion, Joe Broadbent allowed him to enter the house and led him slowly to the sitting room where he invited him to take a seat. The contents of the room surprised Paul because he had expected to see so much less, given the exterior state of the property. There was a large flat screen T.V., a video player, a home computer and an amazingly powerful Hi-Fi system, all of which had been top of the range models in their day and, although they were now a few years old, it appeared that they had been well looked after and that they retained significant value. Around the room many photographs hung on the walls and various sporting trophies decorated the mantelpiece and the oak sideboard which dominated the whole room. One picture in particular caught Paul's attention. It showed Joe, dressed in whites, being presented with a silver cup by Jack Brocklehurst on the occasion of the Burrdale first eleven winning the Derbyshire and Cheshire Villages Cup final.

A sense of pity came over Paul; he was a little taken aback, he didn't normally feel pity.

"You know why I'm here, don't you, Mr Broadbent?" he said, "I'm investigating the murder of Mrs Virginia Brocklehurst and the circumstances surrounding her death and I need to ask you a few questions."

"Fire away, lad," said Joe, "I've got nothing better to do with my time, but don't expect me to shed any tears I am very, very glad that the bitch is dead and I don't care who knows it."

"You made the scarecrow didn't you?" said Paul

Joe nodded, "Of course I bloody did," he said, "and if I say so myself I made a pretty good job of it; a lot of people have commented how lifelike it was but to me it was a labour of love, and I had a lot of time to spend on it," and Paul noted the bitterness in Broadbent's voice when he said that.

"It cost money as well as time, that fact's pretty obvious," commented Paul. "I've spoken to a number of people who were present at Gibbet Field and it's only the fate of the coat that makes them feel uneasy. I don't think you paid 10p for that at a jumble sale."

"It cost me ninety two quid on E-bay it would have cost 6 times as much if new. I could have bought one cheaper but it wouldn't have had the right impact," said Joe, "and the impact had to be exactly right."

"I'm not being personal, I promise you," said Paul, "but I can see you have mobility problems, and £92 is a lot of money for...."

"Somebody claiming Disability Living Allowance to find," said Joe, completing the unfinished sentence. "Yes, it is, and I haven't got money to burn, although I suppose on this occasion it turned out that I had," and he laughed a strangely cold laugh that sounded to be utterly devoid of humour.

"Did you know in advance that the effigy would be destroyed? Was that the plan all along?" asked Paul, "And, if it was, who else was involved in organising the street protest. We know about John Winston but were there others involved in the planning as well?"

Joe Broadbent shook his head and then explained to Paul that he had no prior knowledge of the events which had subsequently taken place. He said that his intention had been to seat the scarecrow next to a comprehensive list of her sins, as he believed them to be, so that visitors to the town could learn how badly

Virginia had behaved; and he expressed his anger at not being allowed by the Scarecrow Festival Committee to place his carefully worded placard alongside his creation. At the end of the two week festival he had planned to remove the facsimile to his front lawn, where nobody could stop him from also displaying his lengthy indictment of her offences, and there she would have remained until Bonfire Night when she would have been given to the Rotary Club to sit astride the town bonfire, as rockets screamed skywards and the smell of wood smoke scented the air.

"So you did intend it would burn eventually?" said Paul.

"Yes I did," replied Joe, "But at a time and place of my choosing when its work of informing the public was done, not before it had hardly begun. To begin with I was pretty pissed off when the scarecrow was pinched although, given the level of publicity it subsequently attracted, I'm actually pretty well delighted now that events turned out as they did."

"I'm investigating a murder as I have already told you," said Paul. "You clearly loathed Virginia Brocklehurst. Would you like to tell me why you hated her so much? Just exactly what did she do to you to make you feel so bitter?"

"It's a long story," explained Joe, "but I've got all day to talk; have you got all day to listen?"

Paul indicated that he had.

"A long time ago, when I was young and fit, and earning good money as a class 1 H.G.V. long distance driver, I used to go to the clubs in Manchester on my weekends off, and one night I picked up this girl at a disco in Salford. I was 26 years old. I thought she was aged 18 or 19. I dated her a couple of times, and then I discovered she was only 15. I was a normal bloke, I'd already been a long way with her and on the night I found out how old she was we were in bed together and she was desperate for me to make love to her. She wasn't a virgin, I'd already discovered that, and I would have shagged her, there's no two ways about it. When I discovered that she was just a kid I shot from under the covers like a rat down a drain pipe. I called her "a dirty little tramp", and a lot more besides and I left her half naked begging for me to come back.

That girl was Virginia. I never saw her again until Jack brought her to Burrdale. I knew Jack from the cricket club and he was president when I was club captain; I topped the averages for both batting and bowling three times running in the late 1980's. Jack was a grand bloke and I liked him a lot and even after I stopped playing cricket we kept in touch. When I had my accident in 1995 he was absolutely superb. It was on the A6 at Whatstandwell in the early hours of a foggy morning. If I'm honest it was my own fault, I'd been with a few old mates from the cricket club and I'd had a bit to drink, which was very unusual for me. I wasn't legless or anything like that," Joe stopped in mid-sentence as the unfortunate choice of words hit home; "not like I am now," he continued in a flat voice that didn't conceal his self-loathing. "I ended up not getting much sleep. I ploughed right into the back of a broken down lorry and wrote off the wagon I was in. I had to be cut from the wreckage. I was so badly injured that the police couldn't breathalyse me, I had multiple fractures and they had to amputate my right leg to get me free. They told me later on I was lucky to be able to walk again. I told them at the time, and I've repeated it many times since, that I'd have been better off dead. I didn't get a huge compensation pay out because the accident was my fault and a lot of people thought I was a fool. My wife was one of them: she couldn't cope with living with a scar faced cripple and she discovered that the company of two legged, sweet faced heterosexual men was irresistible. We were divorced two years ago."

"Jack was different. He tried to help me in every way he could and he promised me a well-paid office job when I was fit enough to work. He told me about this amazing young woman who he'd met and he wanted me to meet her too. I didn't recognise Virginia, she was so well groomed and so sophisticated, but she recognised me straight away: Jack always said she had the best brain and the most fantastic memory of any person he'd ever met. She didn't say anything, of course, but I know that she worked behind the scenes to ensure that I didn't get the job that Jack had promised me. He was only human. He could only withstand so much pressure and the end result was that, because of her sustained intervention, I was deprived of the work that would have been my salvation. By doing that, she destroyed the last vestige of optimism that I had left to cling on to. She robbed me of the rest of my life, so you can see why I rejoice in the fact that the heartless bitch is dead. I tell you Sergeant, I've dreamed of killing her many times and I have prayed that somehow an opportunity would arise when I could make that dream real, but even in death, she got the better of me and one more hope that I had to keep me going has now crumbled into dust."

Chapter Fourteen

The arrival of Henry Osbourne at Burrdale police station was unexpected. Detective Inspector Hobson was busy studying the witness statements of the small number of people who believed that their memories had been jogged by the re-construction of Virginia Brocklehurst's last known walk. The response had been poor. One or two people remembered Virginia being followed by a man behaving oddly but that man himself had then turned up at the Inquiry desk to throw light on the situation. He was a retired tax inspector from Matlock who had been staying with his sister in Burrdale at the time of the public protest. Having seen photographs of the scarecrow in the Advertiser, he had instantly recognised Virginia when he saw her in the flesh. With nothing better to do he had thought that it might be interesting to follow the real life version of the person burned in effigy hoping that there might be some sort of public disorder. Nothing at all happened and he had become bored and returned in disappointment to the Stocks Cafe for a comforting mug of tea and a fried egg and bacon sandwich

Hobson already knew that he needed to talk to Osbourne and had planned that he would personally visit the newspaper editor at his office the following day. He would have much preferred to have stuck to that plan as he had found from long experience that people were often more ill at ease, and thus less mentally prepared to lie convincingly, when there was a risk that they might be overheard by friends, family or work colleagues. When a man or woman attends a police station voluntarily to keep a pre-arranged appointment, he or she is prepared for the ordeal to come. On those occasions they usually have had ample time to anticipate the sort of allegations the police will make against them and to plan their answers carefully in advance.

It was different of course when men or women who had never been questioned before had guilty secrets that they were desperate to keep hidden; they worried that their own lips would betray them. To the uninitiated the police interview room can be a frightening place, and over the years, many confessions have been freely given by suspects simply to bring to an end the ordeal of being detained in a room without windows and with no natural light. This doesn't apply to career criminals: they often regard the whole process as a game of bluff and double bluff and many of them excel at parrying probing questions and its then experienced detectives need all their skill and guile if they are going to achieve a positive outcome from the interviewing process.

Henry Osbourne was not a career criminal, at least as far as his antecedents suggested, but he appeared a master of self-control; exuding self-confidence from every pore. He was though a snob and a poser, but he was also indisputably a successful businessman, with a keenly developed sense of his own importance. Almost single-handedly he had changed the Burrdale Advertiser from being a failing newspaper into an award winning local journal; and this was by no means his only achievement in the field of publishing. He was a clever individual, and he took every opportunity to demonstrate that fact; although justifiably admired by many for his intellect and wit, his acid tongue could be vicious, cruel and hurtful when he wanted it to be, and his willingness to attack anyone who disagreed with his point of view didn't make him a front runner in any *Mr Popularity* competition He was short of stature, but what he lacked in height, he made up for in his sense of style. Superficially, he reminded Mark of his friend, Detective Superintendent Tim Gratton, in that both men were fastidious about their appearance. But there the similarity might end. Mark knew that Tim was a man of integrity and genuine depth; with Osbourne he couldn't tell. His first impression was that in his case this could be a triumph of style over substance and, despite his obvious sense of élan underneath all the show, he suspected, that there was little of real value to get your teeth into. There was another thing that didn't help the editor's cause: it was stupid, and Mark readily acknowledged that fact, but he had an irrational prejudice against men with goatee beards and Osbourne had the neatest, most well clipped facial hair he'd ever seen. Hobson was sure that it had been skillfully crafted to conceal the inherent weakness of the publisher's receding chin.

"Inspector Hobson," said Osbourne, "I believe that you're in charge of the investigation into Virginia Brocklehurst's death. I imagine you intend to come and see me at some time and, as I had a few moments to spare today, I thought that I would save you a journey."

"Why should I want to see you, Mr Osbourne?" asked Mark, a little ingenuously. "What is it that you've done that leads you to believe that I might want to interview you?"

"I'm not a stupid man Inspector Hobson," replied Osbourne, tetchily. "I know I made a fool of myself in the Bull's Head a few weeks ago, and I know that one of your young officers witnessed my stupidity; a man would have to be very silly indeed not to realise that, given the unnatural death of a person he has made inebriated threats to take revenge against, he has idiotically talked himself into the role of suspect in a murder enquiry."

"That's a pretty fair assessment of the situation, Mr Osbourne, so have you come here to make an admission?"

Osbourne looked at Mark in the way one might look at a slow witted incontinent and retorted very firmly, using exaggeratedly simple language that that was not the case. Mark didn't find himself warming to the pompous little egotist who stood before him.

"Come into my office, Mr Osbourne." he said, "In there you can tell me everything that you want to get off your chest."

Osbourne followed Mark into the small, unpretentious office and sat down on the seat that was offered to him.

"Virginia Brocklehurst was a very complex woman and a person of many different moods. Jack was 18 years older than she was and, although Virginia told me he was an extremely kind and able man, he was not capable of fulfilling all her needs to the extent that she wished them to be; but he could give her wealth and position and there was a bond of affection between them which I believe to have been completely genuine. Despite the real feelings that they had for each other Virginia needed other outlets, and she was also realistic enough to know that Jack would not be around forever: not many people knew this, but Jack had a serious circulatory problem. If he hadn't been killed in that car crash there's every possibility that he could have died within the next five years of natural causes.

He did nothing to help himself, of course. He didn't acknowledge to anyone, not even himself, that there was a weakness, and he kept up a punishing schedule of meetings and business trips that would have daunted a man half his age and in rude good health. Virginia needed the company of virile men. She had powerful basic instincts, but she demanded far more than just sexual gratification; she wanted intellect, sophistication and culture and I was able to provide all of that in abundance. I understand women you see Inspector; I give them what they want, and in me Virginia found a man who had all the attributes she needed packaged, although I say it myself, in a very presentable package."

"Then why did she dump you, Mr Osbourne?" asked Mark bluntly. "She can't have been all that impressed if the moment the opportunity arose to establish an open, complete full blown relationship with you, she drops you like a hot potato. I can't begin to imagine why a highly intelligent woman like her would discard an embodiment of perfection such as yourself at the very time that she could have had it all; it simply just doesn't add up!"

The sarcasm was not lost on Osbourne and it rankled.

"Look Inspector," he sniffed, "I came here to help you. If you think you can do without my assistance then I'll go." and Osbourne stood up and turned to leave the office.

"I'm sorry, Mr Osbourne; I didn't mean to be rude. I just wondered why, at the very moment when she could have had everything she appeared to want, she totally changed her mind about you and rejected completely everything that you could give her." said Mark.

"I've already told you that she had a very complex personality," explained Osbourne, "and it wasn't always possible to know what was going on in her head. I do know that she'd been very worried about something, and for quite a long time she hadn't been her usual self at all. She seemed unsure of what to do next which was completely unlike her, and she was definitely pre-occupied by some problem which she wouldn't talk about. Then, shortly before she died, everything changed, and she was liberated and free from anxiety: she was strong and assured once more and she convinced herself that she didn't need to be close to anyone. I don't mind telling you, Inspector, that it hurt when she turned against me; I thought that she had appreciated all that I'd done for her. I didn't deserve to be treated in the way that she treated me, hence my shock and anger, and my ill-advised comments in the local pub."

"Do you know what she was worried about?" asked Hobson.

Osbourne shook his head. "It was something from her past, but I don't know what it was. I have an inkling that it may have involved some sort of sexual abuse a long, long time ago, but I venture to suggest, Inspector, that if you can find the cause of her concern, you might also find the solution to the crime that you are investigating."

Mark nodded his head. "I think you may well be right, Mr Osbourne," he said, "I think you may well be right."

It was as Henry Osbourne was leaving the police station that the second interruption to Mark's afternoon schedule occurred.

Sounds of anger and protest rose up from the police station yard and these were accompanied by a banging of car doors and a clatter of heavy feet. It was not unusual to hear such noises at night when drunks were arrested for alcohol fuelled yobbishness, but it was unusual for such sounds to occur at 4pm on a quiet Thursday afternoon. Although Mark would not normally have wandered into the custody area unless requested to do so, on this occasion he was curious to discover what had taken place so early in the day, and so he took a break from his desk and made his way down to the cell block.

At the reception desk, red-faced and angry, stood a furious Councillor Tony Patterson, who kept interrupting Constable Jessica Wain as she tried to explain to the Custody Sergeant the reason for his arrest. Patterson only quietened down when the Custody Sergeant, who was an experienced and forceful man told him that if he didn't shut up and let P.C. Wain speak, he would find himself in a cell until such time as he calmed down and learnt how to control his temper. Mark noticed, with amusement how quickly Patterson's resistance crumbled when it became obvious that he couldn't browbeat his way out of his predicament.

Constable Wain explained that she and a colleague had been sent to a public meeting at Little Strawton Village Hall called to protest against the proposed closure of the primary school, which the County Council had threatened to shut as part of a grand plan to *rationalise* educational facilities in rural areas. Patterson had harangued the representative from the Education Department and had ended up calling him a great many uncomplimentary names. When he had refused to be silent, the headmaster of the school, who up until that point had seen Patterson as an ally, had been left with no other option but to call the police, and Jessica Wain had attended in response to his phone call. When she tried to reason with Patterson she had also met with personal abuse and, having failed to heed her warnings, Patterson had been arrested for using abusive words and behaviour likely to cause harassment, alarm or distress. At that point he had called her a "black bitch" and P.C. Wain now wanted him charged with a racially aggravated offence. Her parents were of mixed race, and she had taken his insult as an attack on her ethnicity.

Detective Inspector Hobson spoke to the Custody Sergeant and, after discussion, a decision was taken that Patterson should be warned, in the strongest possible terms about his future behaviour. On this occasion there would be no charge, an outcome that didn't please the arresting officer: but Mark had his reasons for wanting to see the case disposed of in this way, and Patterson, whose bravado had dwindled away to nothing, was now glad to accept a verbal caution..

After he had been severely lashed by the Custody Sergeant's

tongue, Detective Inspector Hobson invited the chastened town councillor, in a way that did not allow for the option of refusal, to join him in his office.

In the privacy of that office, Mark turned on the *Champion of the People*.

"At a recent Council meeting," he said "you described Virginia Brocklehurst as a "greedy cow", "a grasping hard faced bitch", "a corrupt stinking whore," and a whole lot more besides. The lady you so thoroughly abused is now dead. I'm wondering if the man who expressed such hatred and such venom might be the man who so brutally murdered her. I need to know exactly what you did a week ago yesterday, particularly between the hours of 1pm and 5 pm."

Patterson's lip began to tremble, and his complexion changed from crimson to grey, and when he spoke, he was no longer the tub-thumping rabble-rouser he normally portrayed himself to be.

"Jesus Christ!" he groaned, "This can't be happening to me," and he vehemently denied that he had anything whatsoever to do with the dramatic events that had culminated in murder, but even though repeatedly given the opportunity to do so, he couldn't put forward any evidence to support an alibi. But alibi or no alibi, he remained adamant that he was no way involved in Virginia's execution. The passion with which he protested his innocence was so intense that Mark suspected that it might be true, but at the same time he was clearly scared out of his wits about something, and the Detective Inspector had no doubt that in some way it was relevant to the crime he was investigating. Even though repeatedly pushed on this matter Patterson refused to say what it was that was worrying him. Although he remained suspicious, there wasn't a shred of actual evidence to link Patterson to the killing, and in the end Mark had no alternative but to let him leave the police station without charge; a braggart with a burst ego, and in a state of blind panic. One thing was beyond doubt; Tony Patterson would sleep badly in bed that night.

Chapter Fifteen

John Lomas had spent most of the last seven days fielding increasingly fanciful questions from journalists, and it had taken all his experience and skill to prevent some sections of the press rushing headlong into the realms of wild speculation.

"No, there wasn't a shred of evidence to suggest ritual slaughter."

"No, he didn't believe that the victim had been cursed."

"Yes, he did believe in evil, but people were evil, not places."

"Folk tales were fairy tales and should simply be treated as such," and he had made many other such pronouncements.

His considerable powers of persuasion were being stretched to the absolute limit: he needed hard facts to give him the opportunity to bring a semblance of reality into the bizarre world that some of the Fleet Street hacks were now starting to inhabit: he hoped Mark Hobson would be able to provide him with some of these rare commodities.

"What stage are we at now Mark?" he asked. "Are we any nearer at all to catching Mrs Brocklehurst's killer than we were a week ago?"

"Well, we are not as far advanced as I'd like to be, but we've made some useful progress. We know a great deal more about the deceased than we did, which has to be a plus, and we've identified a number of different people, all of whom may have had pretty decent motives for killing her, but I have to admit that we've still no tangible evidence to link any individual to the murder.

"Tell me more," said Lomas, and Mark then explained to his senior officer the state of the murder inquiry to date.

"We don't have any solid evidence as I've already said and I think we're very unlucky that we haven't. We could reasonably have expected to find D.N.A. on the victim. To strangle her with the force that was applied required a great deal of effort. I'd have thought that it was almost inevitable that the killer would have exhaled droplets of saliva on to her hair and on to her coat, but there just isn't a trace of any. The body being dumped in dirty water didn't help, of course, but, even so, I'd have expected some vestiges of D.N.A. to remain. The degree of force with which the knife was plunged into her chest was also very great, and again we would have predicted there would be trace D.N.A. to her front but, again, we have absolutely nothing. It's almost as if the killer fully understood the potential to leave D.N.A. and went to extraordinary lengths to ensure that he didn't do so, which, if that were true would make him quite a rare specimen. Phone checks have been carried out on Mrs Brocklehurst's land line and we know that the phone call she received shortly before she went out for the last time was made from the call box next to the Post

Office on the Market Place. A mobile phone was recovered from her raincoat pocket, but it was completely waterlogged and is utterly useless to our inquiry. The hunt for the weapon used to inflict the after death wounds goes on, but so far without success and, although we still don't know where exactly Virginia was killed, my enquiries have revealed that her body was recovered from the same pool that twenty years ago was the place where an eight year old boy drowned," and Mark told the Detective Superintendent about Lucas Norton, and also about his suspicion that Virginia Brocklehurst might have been the young girl mentioned at the inquest.

"We know that she was in the Burrdale area at the time of that incident," he said, "and we think she may have been the victim of child abuse. If that's correct it is highly likely that that experience left her emotionally scarred. She seems to have been sexually active and picking up older men in Manchester clubs from at least the age of fifteen onwards and, although she obviously turned her life around, we've no idea what lasting effect all those experiences had upon her."

"You mentioned a number of people who could have decent motives for killing Virginia; tell me about them."

"I'll start with Richard Norton," said Mark. "He's the father of the dead boy and he took his death incredibly badly. I went to his house. He was drunk when I saw him but he's not a quivering wreck, far from it. He's a very powerful, intense man, and of all the people the police have seen so far, he's the one who has the strength of body and of will to be able to commit this crime. If we could prove Virginia was the girl whose actions caused Lucas's death, then he'd definitely be my number one suspect, but there's a problem. If his daughter is telling the truth, he has an alibi, and if she's lying we have an added complication because she's the girlfriend of Paul Burgess, which could make things very difficult."

"Who else is in the frame?"

"Well, there is your *friend* John Winston for starters. We know his uncle was a convicted sex offender, and Winston himself has told us how he spied on his uncle and Virginia having a sexual encounter. When she returned to Burrdale nearly twenty years later Virginia recognised him and there was a blazing row; he was terrified that she'd try to damage his reputation. He dreamed up the idea of the "Skimmity ride" to drive her out of town and, although I am pretty certain he hasn't got the bottle to do the act himself, he's a powerful speaker when he chooses to be, and I've no doubt that he is capable of inspiring others to do things on his behalf."

"Any more?" asked Lomas, and Mark nodded.

"There are three other contenders at present," he said, and Mark told Lomas about the other people who had been interviewed so far.

"Joe Broadbent was spoken to by Paul Burgess. He's got really good grounds for hating Virginia because she took from him his last chance of employment." and Mark explained the history Paul Burgess had uncovered. "Like Richard Norton, I think Joe's got the guts to carry out the act, but he was so badly injured in the road traffic accident that I don't think that he's got the physical strength to do it. It's possible that somebody could have helped him and, if he'd had the chance to vent his rage on the corpse, it is quite possible that he would have done so to try to purge his demons by one symbolic act: unless that sounds too crazy to even contemplate.

Henry Osbourne had a short lived sexual relationship with the deceased and was shell shocked when she dumped him. His ego took a massive hit and, since then he has made specific threats to take revenge. He's not the sort of bloke to get his hands dirty though and, in any event, I don't believe that he has the backbone for such a task, although like John Winston, it's possible that he might have been able to persuade or pay others to do his bidding. I don't doubt that he's a man who would bear grudges and he undoubtedly felt devalued when Virginia cast him aside. He did tell us something useful though; he told us that she'd been very worried about something for a considerable period of time, but that an event happened recently, he didn't know what it was, that seemed to have lifted the worry from her shoulders."

"Could it have been blackmail?" asked Lomas, "Possibly a threat to expose details of her past life."

"It could well have been," said Mark, "but, if it was, we don't know who the blackmailer is and, if it was blackmail, then for some reason or other the threat seems to have lost its potency shortly before Virginia died.

The last contender is Tony Patterson, who I interviewed here at the station. He's made all sorts of abusive comments about the deceased, both verbally and in print but, if you'll pardon the expression, I think he's all "piss and wind" and that he totally lacks the courage to do anything himself. Despite his high opinion of his own standing, I don't believe he's got either the money or the powers of persuasion to tempt other people to do his dirty work for him. He's also basically thick, and the elaborate window dressing this crime possesses would be quite beyond his mental capabilities: but he's excessively scared about something and it's certainly possible that he may know a great deal more about this crime than he's letting on at present. He denies any sort of connection with Virginia Brocklehurst, and I think he's worried that our investigation into her past could cause him problems, but that's just a gut feeling, I could be a million miles away from the mark."

"We just have to keep digging," said Lomas. "It remains

imperative that we find the missing weapon and that we establish beyond doubt the exact spot where Mrs Brocklehurst was killed. I agree with you that Richard Norton has to be our number one target; put some pressure on his daughter to see if the alibi she gives her father really holds up, and keep Paul Burgess away from this aspect of the investigation. If he has really fallen for the girl, and all the signs are that he has, he's bound to experience a conflict of loyalties, and it would be a tragedy to see the future of a very bright young officer destroyed because he couldn't disentangle his personal feelings from his professional duties as a police officer. We can't allow him to become compromised, it's not fair on him, and it also puts at risk a successful outcome to the entire police investigation. There are plenty of other suspects to be worked upon. Let him concentrate on them, and you keep a gentle eye on him Mark: let me know the moment you see the first signs of any problem developing."

Chapter Sixteen

It was late afternoon and it had been a good day. Becky had been shopping in Manchester, and in the city centre department stores and the high fashion retail outlets she had come alive, and felt a sense of freedom that she could never experience in her own home town. She had spent an awful lot of money, but her dad always ensured that money was no object and everything she had bought was eye-catching and attractive. She knew when she wore the clothes in Burrdale, people would be jealous, and that some of them would be spiteful and mean spirited, but she didn't care; she'd got used to their envy and, deep down, she understood that all the girls who said nasty things about her, would secretly give their eye teeth to look like she looked, and to be able to afford even just one of the beautiful dresses she had purchased today. Paul would love them, he liked nice things: when they went out they would make a dazzling couple, and she smiled as she looked forward to the romantic dinner for two that lay ahead.

It was only as she approached the flat over the shop which had been home for the last twenty years that the sense of euphoria began to fade; instinctively she knew that all was not well with her father. She had only herself to blame, of course. She was much later getting back than she had said she would be, and that had given him the opportunity to brood. Mentally she kicked herself for allowing him the time to remember, but she resented his inability to resist the temptation to wallow in self-pity and, although she would never have dared say so to her father, she was now finding herself hating her dead brother with almost as much hatred as the hatred that had been instilled in her to feel for his killer.

When she opened the door to the flat her worst fears were met. Her father was clearly drunk, photographs of Lucas were strewn across the dining table, and the sacred box containing his precious memorabilia lay open on the floor. The only thing that stopped her running from the room in dismay were the tears in her father's eyes and the fact that, this time, he had also clearly been thinking about her as well as about Lucas: school photographs, graduation certificates and even some holiday snaps, which seemed to suggest that there had been times, now long forgotten, when they must have been happy, were spread out on the settee upon which her father sat. A sense of pity replaced the feelings of resentment and Becky sat down next to him, and put her arms around him in an attempt to comfort her father.

"Oh Dad, Dad," she said, and she could feel the tears in her own eyes as she spoke, "It's all so long ago, this grief and anger is killing you Dad."

Richard did not look up. "I died twenty years ago," he responded, and Becky felt the pain of rejection as he spoke.

"What about me Dad? What about me? Don't I count for anything? You had two children Dad and this one is still alive. Can't you find just a little comfort in my existence?"

They were both in tears now, and Richard held his daughter and, sobbing loudly, protested that she meant everything to him; neither of them heard Paul Burgess knock, or saw him come into the room. Becky noticed him first and was glad that he was present, Richard felt his daughter pull away from him and, when he finally understood that another person had entered their private world, he was angry at the intrusion; if he had been alone he would have screamed at Burgess to get out but, even in his drunken state, he knew he couldn't allow himself to give vent to his true feelings. He said nothing, but there was a chill in the atmosphere which was palpable, and Paul felt very uncomfortable.

"Is it the usual…?" he asked Becky; Becky nodded her head.

"Speak to him Paul. Convince him that it's over, the rage is destroying him piece by piece, and it's destroying me too; we can't carry on like this. He needs help, but he won't listen to me; he's got to move on. Lucas's death has all but ruined his life and it's ruining my life too." The desperation in her voice was all too easy to detect.

"Richard," said Paul to the morose, sullen figure who now sitting alone on the settee, "this isn't helping. Can't you see the harm you're doing to yourself and how corrosive this obsession with the past has become? People all over town are beginning to talk, they're saying you're an alcoholic: my landlady, for one, has stopped coming into your shop because she finds the whole experience so depressing. You used to be the best butcher for miles around, but you're letting your business go to the dogs, and, if it does, what good will that do you or Becky? You can't bring back the dead. You had your vengeance a long, long time ago. Shane Chadwick is dead; he died of a heroin overdose in 1993. They found his body in a filthy squat; it had lain undiscovered for over three weeks, it was badly decomposed. He was never able to find work, he never found happiness and all his life he was tormented by the terrible memories of Lucas's death and your fury. Can't you let it be? He couldn't have suffered more than he did, no one possibly could have done."

Richard staggered to his feet and, for a second Paul thought he was about to hit him, he was so angry. "Don't you dare measure his suffering against mine! Every minute of every hour of every day I live with the memory of my murdered child; do you think it consoles me to know that his killer died a miserable death? If I could spit on Chadwick's grave every morning, it might help just a little but nothing can ease my distress. I don't know if Chadwick's parents are alive or dead, and I can't remember now if he had brothers or sisters or cousins or half cousins; but I tell you this, if he did they are all the filth of the universe and, until the world is rid of that verminous breed," and Richard noticeably slurred his words as he spoke, "I can never be at peace."

"So you feel that way, even about innocent members of his family who may not have been born or who were little more than babes in arms at the time of your tragedy?" asked Paul; who, even if he hadn't known it before, knew now that Richard Norton could never be rational in his attitude towards that cursed and tortured tribe.

"There are no innocent members of that fucking clan," snorted Norton.

Becky grabbed her father and shook him. "Don't Dad, don't." she pleaded, "Paul's only trying to help. Can't you see you are making life unbearable? Sometimes you make me wish I'd never been born; this is driving such a wedge between us, don't you understand that? You're driving me away from you, I can't cope with this situation for much longer; I've got to get away."

"Then go Rebecca, go, and take your pretty gobshite policeman with you; and don't bother to come back!"

"Dad!" cried Becky, and the tears once more burst from her eyes in an unstoppable outpouring of grief.

"Oh Becky, Becky, my Becky, I'm sorry, I'm so sorry, I didn't mean that, you know I didn't. If you went away, then there'd be no point to anything else. You're the only precious thing I've got left in the world. Please, please stop crying, I'll never speak to you like that again. Go out and enjoy yourself with Paul but, for the love of God, please come back home afterwards. Don't leave me alone; oh dear God, please don't ever leave me alone."

Very gradually both father and daughter regained a degree of self-control. Becky left her father and boyfriend together as she went to change her clothes: there was no more overt anger, and even a forced attempt at casualness, which neither party managed to pull off with any great distinction. When Becky finally returned she looked sensational and, despite his inner anguish, when Richard saw her looking so radiant, he felt an immense pride in his daughter: Paul could not believe how lucky he was to be dating this staggeringly beautiful, fantastic young woman.

At the Bistro he knew they would be watched, and he was sure that there wouldn't be a man in the place who didn't envy him the company of this bright, vivacious, lovely girl who would light up the room with her glamour and her charm.

And it was true; when they entered the restaurant heads turned to look at them and Paul knew it was her beauty and not his appearance that attracted the attention. They dined on pheasant, ripe and tasty, cooked in Calvados, and seasoned with cinnamon and black pepper and talked of many things and Becky apologised to Paul for her father's behaviour. "He really can't help it." she said. "Sometimes it is worse than others, and this ghastly murder, and the endless news coverage that there has been of it seems to have really got to him: ever since it happened he's done nothing but drink and remember Lucas, I'm just hoping that when you catch the killer and the story fades into the mists of time, he can get back on to some sort of even keel. I dread to think what the future holds for him and for all of us if he doesn't."

"He'll never lose his bitterness though, will he?" said Paul.

Rebecca shook her head. "I can't blame him," she said, "and I realise this sounds awful, and it makes me appear very hard, but I share most of his feelings. I know Shane Chadwick was just a young child when he killed Lucas, and I know that somebody who was older and wiser encouraged him, but he pushed Lucas into the pool, and the image of a little boy forever encased in a block of ice has been part of my nightmares for as long as I can remember. Maybe Shane Chadwick didn't mean to cause harm, maybe it was a spontaneous act, and maybe he, too, was a victim, but, intentional or not, he not only killed my brother, he broke my parents marriage, he drove my father nearly insane and even today, twenty years on, he continues to overshadow my life. He's robbed me of so many things girls should be able to take for granted: a happy home, a loving family, joy and laughter and so very much more. I'm glad he's dead, I'm glad he died in sorrow and in loneliness and, God forbid! I hate him and I hate his family just as much as Dad does, but I'm able to keep my hatred under much tighter control than he is able to do."

Chapter Seventeen

Henry Osbourne's revelation that Virginia Brocklehurst had been a worried woman for several weeks prior to her death had to be treated seriously. At the outset of the inquiry Mark had wondered if she might have been the target of a hate campaign, but neither her computer, nor her correspondence had contained any evidence of a vendetta, and the pattern of phone calls to and from the house had been largely unremarkable. Largely, but not completely: three calls had been made to, and two calls had been received from the same public phone box and, most intriguingly of all, one of them was the last phone call that Virginia Brocklehurst ever received. What the content of these calls were nobody could say, but since his meeting with Detective Superintendent Lomas a new theory was gaining precedence in Mark's mind. Hate mail now seemed less likely, but given what the police had discovered about Virginia's past, and the specific events described by John Winston and Joe Broadbent, the possibility of blackmail now loomed a great deal larger. Thus far the police had been looking for poison pen letters, now they needed to switch their attention to her diaries and personal papers, including bank and building society pass books, to see if any of them could give support to this alternative theory. A further visit to the victim's home was essential and, the Spanish housekeeper, and anyone else who had been in Virginia's employ, needed to be spoken to in case their mistress had unwittingly said something to them which might help to point a finger towards any particular individual. It was a big task, and more than one officer would be needed to perform it. Mark wanted to set the ball rolling himself, and then to hand the job on to another detective. Mindful of John Lomas's instructions that Paul Burgess should not be placed in any situation where he could face a conflict of loyalty, and also that a gentle eye should be kept on the young officer, it seemed abundantly clear that he was the best man to accompany him to begin with, and thereafter take complete charge of the reins. He was also an extremely bright detective and Mark had no doubt that his contribution to the venture would be valuable.

However, before the morning briefing, and the subsequent allocation of jobs, Mark had something that he needed to do. So far, he had thought that the large amount of cash in Virginia's purse was just a small example of her obvious wealth, but what if she had intended to make a cash payment (perhaps one of many) to a blackmailer? Inside his own wallet Mark knew he carried three photographs of Helena, a variable amount of cash, a variety of credit, debit and cash cards, crumpled up Switch receipts, invoices and various other bits of paper with random jottings thereon and he was sure that, if he had lost that wallet and it had subsequently been recovered by the police, the entire contents of it wouldn't have been individually catalogued: only the more significant items would have been listed. He wondered if this might have happened with Virginia's purse, and whether there could be something still inside it, perhaps even an address or a phone number, which might prove to be highly useful to the murder inquiry.

As it happened, he was largely disappointed; Virginia had obviously been a much tidier person than he was, a fact that he would have had no trouble whatsoever of convincing Helena of, but still the re-examination of the contents was not without benefit. It was the single photograph that excited Mark. It was of a young boy of pre-secondary school age and it looked as if it had been cut from a larger group photograph, possibly a school or class photograph. It was not possible to work out when it had been taken, but it certainly wasn't recently. What really grabbed Mark's attention was the face and the facial expression; he was sure that he had seen a very similar photograph somewhere before.

His immediate thought was that the boy might be the young Lucas Norton: there had been so many pictures of him scattered around Richard's flat that it was very probable that one of them might well have caught his eye, but he was by no means certain that this would turn out to be the case. If it was Lucas Norton, it begged the question why Virginia was carrying his image in her purse and, if it wasn't him, then it was imperative to find out who it was, and then to ask the same question as to why the picture was being carried. Mark didn't return the photo to the purse but, instead, took it with him, and arranged for it to be copied in time for it to be shown to the officers at the morning briefing in the hope that somebody might be able to shed some light on the child's identity.

As it happened, nobody present in the briefing room recognised the picture, although Paul Burgess was able to state, with apparent certainty, that it was NOT Lucas Norton: but he did concede there were some similarities between Lucas and the unknown boy. Mark allocated the tasks for the day and then, after a short conversation with Paul Burges, he and the Detective Sergeant then set off for the late Mrs Brocklehurst's home.

It was twenty past eleven when they arrived at the house: the two men had walked the half mile distance from the police station, the weather had been dry, and neither officer had wanted to take a car. As they strode out together they had further discussed the case, and Mark had repeated his belief that somehow the current events had historic links to the events that had happened twenty years before. Paul was unconvinced, he expressed scepticism, and

Mark had been forced to acknowledge that he didn't have an iota of proof to support his strongly held, but totally unsubstantiated theory.

As they approached the house they were met with the sounds of loud music, the windows were wide open and there was not a mourning drape to be seen. Emelina was evidently enjoying herself and was clearly not remotely distressed at the permanent departure of her unlamented mistress. Mark knocked loudly on the door, and eventually the drumming of his fist overwhelmed the rock band and, more than a touch grumpily, Emelina finally opened the front door.

On entering the living room, the first thing that Mark noticed was the chaos on show there; glossy magazines were strewn everywhere, the television was switched on but with the sound turned right down and the Hi-Fi was set to full volume; it was only turned off, reluctantly, when Mark insisted that this be done. Since Virginia's death Emelina had done very little work, and that was the way she intended it to stay until such time as the house was sold and the administrator of Virginia's estate ordered her to leave. Until that time she had more or less *carte blanche* to do as she pleased, the administrator rationalising that it was cheaper by far to continue to pay her a monthly salary rather than employ a security firm, at exorbitant expense, to guard the premises.

The second thing that Mark noticed was that there were no family photographs at all, in this the main reception room of the house. He asked Emelina if she had taken down any pictures, and the Spanish housekeeper vehemently denied that that was the case.

There had been, "menee photographs," she said, but Virginia had taken them down, as she had done all over the house. In the room that had been Jack's private study she had apparently been particularly ruthless, and images of his children and grandchildren had been removed, as had framed newspaper cuttings showing Jack handing over cheques to High Peak charities, or awarding trophies at local sports clubs; and various shields, plates and tankards, bearing inscriptions to mark occasions when Jack had been honoured by a wide range of Burrdale groups and societies had all been crated up and relegated to a packing case in a damp cellar, where they now lay tarnishing and gathering dust. It seemed very strange therefore, that Virginia, who was clearly not in the least bit sentimental, should carry the image of a little boy in her wallet; Mark rationalised that it was unlikely that she kept it with her for any nostalgic or affectionate reason.

He produced a copy of the picture taken from Virginia's purse and asked Emelina if she had any idea at all as to who the child might be. Emelina replied disinterestedly that she "deed not ave a clue," so far as she was aware, she "deedn't" think that Virginia had any close relatives; she believed there may have been step-brothers or step-sisters, but, if they existed, Virginia had definitely not keep in touch with them. When Jack had been alive, his children and grandchildren had been frequent visitors to the house, and had often stayed overnight, but all that had changed with his death. Emelina delighted in telling Mark about an angry scene which had taken place involving Jack's eldest daughter and Virginia, who the girl accused of being a cheat and a fraud. She had struck her step-mother with such force that the noise of the slap had echoed and re-echoed throughout the entire household. Virginia hadn't flinched even though the slap had left an angry red mark: she had laughed at the girl, whose hand stung so painfully that she nearly burst into tears, and had ordered her to get out of the house. Ever since that day, not a single member of Jack's family had set foot inside the building, and the only communication between Virginia and any of them had been carried on through solicitors at arm's length, Jack's children seeking to restrain Virginia from disposing of any of his property until a legal challenge to the will could be mounted, and Virginia's solicitor totally refuting that they had any claim to the property at all. Emelina was anxious to tell Mark that she was not a "bizzee boddee", but that she had "accidentallee" overheard Virginia's solicitor telling his client he was convinced that she had very little to fear, and that he was "completelee" confidant any court case would "bee resol-ved" in her favour.

Whilst Mark was talking to Emelina, who was by now enjoying herself immensely, having warmed to her task of listing Virginia's many iniquities, and elevating her own importance to the police inquiry to unassailable heights, at a nod from Mark, Paul Burgess had slipped into Jack's study. The contents of an antique oak bureau, which was the principal piece of furniture in that room, would need to be examined, but before he commenced that task Paul observed that, if in nothing else, at least in the matter of photographs Emelina had told the absolute truth. No pictures or artefacts that related to Jack were anywhere on display, and Paul wondered how Jack would have felt if he could have seen how thoroughly his wife had expunged every memory of him from this his inner sanctum.

As well as the bureau, the room contained a comfortable leather chair, a small oak table and a bookcase, which was now filled only with books that interested Virginia. Piled on the floor were some lever arch files which seemed to be relics of Virginia's past professional life, but a quick glance at them revealed them to have no evidential value. Paul turned his attention to the bureau. Inside, he discovered a number of ledgers, notebooks and diaries, all compiled by Virginia herself. Paul was struck by the neatness of the script. A handwriting expert might well have commented on the extraordinary self- control the writer had exhibited; there were no variations of touch, no blotches, no errors, no crossings out and, there was only one entry in one of the diaries which bucked the trend in that the letters were larger and more exuberant than anywhere else. It had been made just over a fortnight before Virginia died; it simply read "Now I know for sure" and Virginia had emphasised the importance she gave to that statement by following it with three dramatic exclamation marks which soared exultantly towards the top of the page.

It was as Paul was holding this diary that Mark entered the room having finally extricated himself from the clutches of the ever more garrulous Emelina. Paul hesitated for a second and then handed the book to Mark, who then studied the pages with great care. The elation that Virginia felt when she wrote those words was obvious, even to a layman, and perhaps provided proof that she had indeed discovered something very dramatic as Henry Osbourne had already suggested might have been the case. It profoundly irritated Mark that the conceited editor had been right, but what irritated him still more was the realisation that he would need to enlist his help again. From his lengthy conversation with Emelina Mark was now convinced that none of the people who had worked for Virginia in the recent past had any greater knowledge of her family history or private life than the maid herself possessed; and that was precious little; it seemed to be a racing certainty that none of them would be able give much assistance to the investigation. It was imperative the police discovered who the boy in the photograph was. The involvement of the local press was unavoidable, and Mark now knew he would have to go cap in hand to the self-opinionated newspaper man and ask him to publish the picture in the Burrdale Advertiser: the prospect of begging a favour from Osbourne held no appeal for him whatsoever.

Nothing else of interest was unearthed, but it still took the two C.I.D. officers another twenty minutes to disentangle themselves from the unstoppable Emelina. It was nearly two o'clock; neither man had eaten since breakfast so Mark suggested grabbing a bite to eat before returning to the police station. The Royal Albert had a good lunchtime menu and was noted for the quality of its beer. Once there had been a time when the combination of wholesome food and real ale or, perhaps, just the ale alone, would have guaranteed Mark Hobson's late return to the office, but things had changed radically in the last few years and now it was very rare for him to drink during the day, and never more than one pint with a meal. The two officers entered the pub and ordered their food, Burgess selecting a Tuna salad and Mark settling for home made leek and potato soup and a freshly baked bread roll; Mark drank draught bitter, Paul chose a bottle of lager: as they ate they talked about the case.

"I know we're not supposed to have feelings about cases," said

Paul, "but sometimes you can't help but get involved. When a crime disgusts or appals you and you can't get the image of the victim out of your head, and the suffering that he or she has endured makes you feel sick, then you pull out all the stops to make sure that somebody pays. You're desperate for the brutality of the offence to be punished, maybe even avenged, and you can think of nothing else but catching the bastard who did it. You want more than just an arrest, you want to see the offender pilloried, and, if he or she is a terrorist, a sadist or a child molester you want them to feel the fear their victims felt. If later you read in the papers that they have been attacked in prison and badly injured you feel no sympathy, and perhaps even a sense of satisfaction that they've been made to suffer. But there are other cases where your sympathies lie with the offender, you know the type of thing I mean; killings where a devoted wife helps a terminally ill husband to commit suicide or those poor sad bastards who, after a lifetime of being bullied or abused, finally snap and batter their tormentor to death with a rolling pin or a car jack. You know what you've got to do and you do it because there's no other choice, but you don't go for the jugular, and you put in a good word where you can, in the hope that the court will show leniency. Well, I feel that way about Virginia Brocklehurst's killer. What good did she ever do? I can't see that she had a single redeeming feature. To me she seems to have been an arrogant, heartless, bitch. If your theory is right, and I'm sorry I can't accept that it is, but if she was the cause of Lucas Norton's death, then she was displaying savage, sadistic tendencies even as a young girl. She proved herself to be petty and vengeful and, once crossed, she never forgot the slight and she bore grudges for years and years. She deliberately ruined what little was left of Joe Broadbent's life, by denying him the chance to regain his self esteem through work, and she obviously cared nothing for her husband, or his reputation, otherwise she'd have honoured his memory and carried out his wishes instead of doing everything in her power to delete him from the pages of history. I bet you, if we ever find the man, or the woman, responsible for killing her, then he or she will turn out to have had good cause for acting in the way that they did, and we'll discover just one more person who has been damaged by the spiteful life of a very spiteful person. Don't you think that that's a very likely outcome?"

The Detective Inspector looked at his younger colleague. "Good speech that Paul," he said, "and I agree with a lot of what you've just said. There have been times when I've felt all those emotions, and I can remember occasions when I've deliberately wound up some nasty little yobbo to take a pop at me so that I could have the pleasure of smacking him in the face, but I really don't agree with you about Virginia. She was an incredible woman, who probably could have been just about anything she chose to be if life had treated her differently. She'd no home life that we know of and, so far as we're aware, she had a mother who cared nothing for her, and who palmed her off on various distant relatives, so that she could go and enjoy uninhibited sex, with whomever her current boyfriend happened to be at the time. The poor kid was left to cope alone. Is it any surprise that she seems to have become the victim of child abuse, and that later she was allowed to run riot, in the fleshpots of Manchester? Do you know what usually happens to girls with that sort of history Paul? Well, I'll tell you, they end up as smack heads working the streets of Salford or Sheffield, or any town or city you care to name, and they die premature deaths, sometimes in the most squalid circumstances you could ever imagine. Did that happen to Virginia? Did it heck! At some point she took hold of her own life by the scruff of the neck and she turned it right around; that took bravery and incredible determination, and I doubt if one person in a thousand could have pulled it off. Jack Brocklehurst wasn't a fool and he wouldn't have married Virginia if there'd been no substance to her; and one thing's certain, Virginia wasn't an actress, I think her outburst when she recognised John Winston clearly demonstrates that fact. I think she had courage and a great deal of spirit and unlike you I believe there was real affection between her and Jack, just as Henry Osbourne has claimed. Undoubtedly she was scarred by her experiences, and she was definitely capable of being ruthless and vindictive, but there was another side to her. Did you notice the books in the study that she chose to read? There were novels by Conrad and Hardy, as well as authors like Hemmingway and F. Scott Fitzgerald; and those books have got real depth. Somehow, in the most difficult circumstances possible, she got herself to university and managed to qualify as an accountant. She was living well, even before she met Jack, and she did it all off her own bat. I think she's got to be admired for all that. The fact that she took down Jack's photographs I don't think was an expression of indifference but rather a recognition that she had to move on, and that she had to do that by herself in a largely hostile world. She may have ruined people's lives, but just look what people did to her. She was a truly remarkable woman Paul, and if we forget that fact, we do so at our peril."

"If you say so, Boss," muttered Paul, but Mark could see he wasn't convinced, and he sensed a certain awkwardness, perhaps because the young officer was uneasy about taking a diametrically opposed stance to the one adopted by his more experienced senior colleague.

"If we can't agree about the victim, let's see if we're any closer in our thoughts about the murderer," suggested Mark.

"I honestly don't know where to start," responded Paul. "We've got a good number of suspects, it could be any one of them, and it's just as possible that it might be somebody we haven't even thought of yet. I know you think that Virginia Brocklehurst's murder is in some way connected to Lucas Norton's death but, for all we know, there could have been dozens of people in Salford and in Manchester who had their own scores to settle and, maybe one of them did just that."

"I was thinking more of a profile than a person." commented Mark. "Have you any thoughts as to the sort of man or woman who could have done this?"

"It could be anyone. It could even be a contract killing. Who knows the type of person we're looking for?"

"Of one thing I am convinced," replied Mark, "we're not looking for just an ordinary thug. Our man or woman, and I think it's almost certain to be a man who did the deed, is clever, well read, creative and resourceful. I have no doubt that his motive is highly personal, and that the killer at the time of the murder felt real anger, and perhaps real pain too. I told you, Paul, that I thought Virginia was a remarkable woman; I think her killer will turn out to be a remarkable person too."

It was a telephone call from Helena which finally interrupted Mark's speculation. She had received a phone message from her sister Jenny to tell her that their father had now been given a date for his heart by-pass operation. It was to be in nine weeks time. There was a very real danger that it could clash with the birth of his first grandchild, if that child happened to be born early. Anxiety was not doing either his wife or her father any good. Although she had tried hard not to show it, Mark could tell that Helena was worried and that this worry was just one more complication to add to an already stressful pregnancy that she could well do without. He promised her that he would try to get home early and he would have given anything at that moment just to be able to put his arms around her and hold her close to him until the fear in her subsided.

As it happened, for once Mark was able to be as good as his word and his promptness surprised and pleased Helena; he had also brought flowers, and she remembered the first time he had brought her flowers, looking so uncomfortable and so unsure of himself as he had entered the room He had often brought her flowers since because she loved to see them about the house; but the most beautiful flowers he had given her had been the wild flowers of England, which he had introduced her to and, she now thought the scents of honeysuckle and of meadowsweet to be the most glorious fragrances in the world. Mark held his wife in an embrace and she allowed herself to melt into his tenderness, and to feel secure, as she always did in her husband's arms.

"It will be alright, Love, I know it will. Your dad isn't going to pass up the chance of being a granddad for anything in the world. Twelve months from now he'll be buying his grandson his first England football shirt and spoiling him rotten. We'll have to keep a strict eye on him to make certain he doesn't totally undermine our authority"

Helena smiled, Mark had always been able to make her feel better, and she had implicit trust in him.

Mark told her about the photograph and the visit to Virginia Brocklehurst's house, and the note in the diary, and lunch with Paul Burgess, and Paul's reservations, and the fact that he was going to have to enlist the help of Henry Osbourne, and Helena noted with amusement his grimace when he mentioned that man's name.

"Paul Burgess is pretty sure that the photograph is not of Lucas Norton, isn't he?" she said, "and he's likely to be right about that so you must have seen the picture somewhere other than Richard Norton's flat; do you think it could have been in our mystery box?"

"There is only one way to find out." replied Mark and he went and got the box from its place of storage and together he and Helena re-examined the contents, using a magnifying glass where necessary to look at some of the smaller photographs that had filled the pages of the various scrap books.

The quality of definition in the newspaper pictures was not good, but a face in a school photograph from 1977 seemed to bear a very close resemblance to the face on Virginia's picture. It wasn't identical, the child in the photograph was younger and his hair looked different, but there was certainly a distinct possibility that Virginia's image was of the same boy, maybe taken two or three years later. Mark realised that, as well as the single photograph which he was going to have to ask Henry Osbourne to publish, he was also going to have to request that the paper re-publish the group photograph which had first seen the light of day twenty two years before.

Chapter Eighteen

Like every other human being, Mark Hobson is not without faults although, unlike some people, he is mostly aware of his; he also has the advantage of having a sensible wife, who cares a great deal about him, and who will always try to tell him if he is making a mistake.

One of Mark's occasional faults is a tendency to anticipate trouble where none exists and to plan in advance how to respond to situations which in fact are unlikely ever to arise. His meeting with Henry Osbourne was one of those occasions. He had visited the offices of the Burrdale Advertiser expecting resistance, but instead he had met with total cooperation. Osbourne told him that the paper would be pleased to publish both photographs and that it would do so prominently; in addition, he promised to write a column explaining the significance of the pictures, and urging his readers to assist the police in any way that they could. He of course had compelling reasons for his constructive attitude, the story would do nothing whatsoever to harm the circulation of the newspaper, and in due course, if an arrest or arrests were made, much good publicity would flow from the assistance that the paper and its readers had given the authorities. There was also the possibility lurking in the back of Mark's mind that this whole hearted demonstration of support might be intended to divert attention away from any possible role that the newspaper editor might have had in Virginia's death; but for whatever reason there had been no conflict and Mark had left the meeting, feeling somehow slightly cheated that there hadn't been a battle of wills.

After his visitor had left, with impressive haste, the editor set about completely re-modelling the layout of the front page of the paper, and also re-jigging the contents of some of the inside pages to take into account the late change of lead story. The end result was far more than Mark could have hoped for and also far quicker. When he had arrived at the office he had expected that the police would have to wait a week before they would see the photographs widely publicised and perhaps it would be a few days after that before there was a public response. Osbourne had promised him that within twenty four hours the newspaper would be on the streets and that he was sure that, minutes after it went on sale, the first telephone calls would be received.

Back at the office there had also been positive developments. Alan Nadin had received a telephone call from a local farmer. David Wright owned about seven hundred acres of pasture and moorland on which he grazed both sheep and beef cattle. Because the farm was so large, he habitually used a quad bike and trailer to get to the more outlying parts of it; he also used it to carry fodder and cattle cake to feed his livestock in winter and to transport tools and fencing material when he needed to repair collapsed dry stone walls.

The story had been a rambling one. Mr Wright had banged on about the damage thoughtless hikers caused to boundary walls when they tried to clamber over them, rather than seeking out the proper stiles, and he had explained at length how much worse, he thought the problem would become if the Right to Roam Bill ever became law and every *Tom, Dick and Harry* had the belief that they could go anywhere they wanted to go without hindrance or restriction. At times Sergeant Nadin had struggled to keep him to the point, and it was only after much sympathetic "tutting" that he had managed to get him back on track. Eventually the farmer had returned to his tale. He had explained that the quad bike was old and of little value. The key to the ignition had been lost a long time ago, and now a screwdriver permanently jammed into the lock formed the starting mechanism: he also explained that the pin that secured the draw bar of the trailer to the coupling mechanism was badly corroded and that for many years now it had not been possible to decouple the trailer.

He told Alan that the quad was normally kept in an old barn that stood alongside a footpath that leads directly to the Pennine Way because there it was nearer to his sheep, but that did mean that it was left a fair way away from his house. Nothing else of any worth was stored there but there were a few bales of hay, one or two rolls of sheep netting and some very old tools: one reason why nothing worth taking was left there was that the barn itself had no doors, so access was unrestricted, and it was not unusual for walkers to shelter inside it if caught out by a heavy downpour. When he finally got to the point of the phone call, it turned out that the news that he had to give was news that the police had been had been waiting to hear for a long time.

He had gone to the barn to collect a couple of posts and some wire to mend yet another broken wall and, whilst he had been throwing tools into the trailer, he had discovered amidst the dirt and hayseeds on the flat bed a pearl ear stud. It couldn't have been casually lost, and it hadn't been deliberately hidden, and David, who was an intelligent man and who read the national and local papers, suspected that it might be Virginia Brocklehurst's missing ear stud. Alan Nadin, who was sure of his source, was also convinced that this would turn out to be the case, and was confident that at last the police had found out how the body of Virginia had been taken to the pool. There was still an unanswered question, however. David's barn was a good two and a half miles away from the place where the purse had been found and, up until this new development, the police had believed that if there had been any sort of struggle, it must have taken place there and that almost certainly the murder itself must have been committed nearby: it was also at that location that the extensive search for the missing weapon had been concentrated. This new discovery cast grave doubt on the accuracy of both those assumptions.

When Mark returned to the C.I.D. office, Alan told him of the phone call, and of how confident he felt that this was the break through the police had been looking for. On the assumption that this was likely to be correct, a small team of Scientific Support Officers was assembled quickly; if it was the missing ear stud, barn, bike and trailer would need to be microscopically examined for fingerprints, fibres and D.N.A., and a thorough search of the area surrounding the barn would need to be carried out.

Alan then voiced the concern that he was feeling; "There's just one thing I can't understand," he said, "and that's why the purse was found so far away from the barn if as now seems probable the barn was the place where the murder took place. Maybe it could be the case that it was somehow just lost after all, but I still find that proposition hard to accept."

"Speak to your witness again." instructed Mark, "You never know, he might have made a mistake: if he's sure that he hasn't then I suppose we'll have to track the whole way from the purse to the barn to see what, if anything, can be discovered en route."

Twenty minutes later, Alan returned to the room, he was nearly exploding with anger. "He's a lying little twat! He's just told me now that he actually found the purse on the footpath next to the barn: he took it to the police station because he hoped there'd be a reward. When he discovered there wasn't one that really pissed him off, and he then couldn't be arsed to take me all the way back to the barn. He said he couldn't wait to get out of the nick. He told me a complete pack of lies so he could get on his way. I think we should charge the bloody moron with Obstructing the Police, or Wasting Police Time."

Mark shook his head, "It's not worth it Alan, and in any event he didn't realise that there'd be any significance in pinpointing the exact location where he found the purse; give him a verbal bollocking and then get another witness statement from him, this time clearly stating where he actually found it and why he said something different to us first time around. When you've got that all set up, then we'll get straight over to the farm."

It was a little over an hour later when Mark and Alan travelled in Alan*'s* car to meet David Wright and to see for themselves what he had recovered. As they drove down the pot-holed drive that leads to the centuries old farmstead, on the other side of the valley they saw lurchers and terriers running free, criss-crossing a field, apparently in search of rabbits: following behind them, urging on the dogs were two men. Alan's car was well known in the area: as the vehicle got nearer to them the men turned to stare at it and then, as if resentful at the intrusion, they gathered in their dogs and strolled defiantly into the distance.

Alan turned to Mark. "They're bad news those two, particularly Mike Skinner, especially when he's got a couple of drinks inside him. He comes from a long line of villains, he's got a list of convictions as long as your arm, and he's twice done time for assault. His shotgun certificate was revoked years ago. We know he's still got a gun, but catching him out with it has been a bit of a problem. The other chap is Bob Leather, he's just big and daft, but an out and out poacher, and both of 'em seem to have no understanding whatsoever of the concept of private land. Most of the local farmers turn a blind eye to what they're doing, but if they're caught by the gamekeepers on the Coverdale Estate, they mete out their own kind of justice; we don't get involved, it's always been that way."

"How very medieval!" commented Mark.

"Burrdale's that kind of place, Boss," retorted Alan, and both men laughed out loud at the comment.

When they arrived at the farm they were met by David Wright. "I suppose I should have left it where it was," he said, "but by the time I'd picked it up to see what it was, I figured it was too late to worry and I didn't want to leave it unprotected in case somebody wandered into the barn and took it. I put it into a sandwich bag and brought it away with me," and he then produced the bag from the pocket of his jeans for the officers to look at. When they saw the ear stud both detectives felt sure it was what they had been looking for; it appeared identical to the one removed by the pathologist from Virginia's right ear, and later forensic examination would reveal traces of D.N.A. to confirm that it was indeed hers. Immediately, the police Scientific Support Team, which had followed the two detectives to the farm, commenced the slow job of examining the barn and its contents in their search for more evidence.

As it was now known that the purse had been dropped close to the barn, and very possibly that the murder had taken place there too, it was obvious that a thorough search of the surrounding area would need to be undertaken. The pieces were beginning to fit into place. One thing that had always puzzled Mark, when he had thought that the murder had taken place where the purse had allegedly been lost, was why the killer had risked striking there, when both he and his victim would have been highly visible to passing ramblers: the secluded barn was easy to find, and would have been an ideal meeting place for people who didn't want to be seen. It was also the perfect place for butchery. Mark wondered if there had been any discussion between Virginia and her assassin before he took her life: maybe she had taken out her purse to pay him money, or perhaps more likely, to produce the photograph to prove to him some point. Had there a shouting match? Did Virginia at some time turn around to storm out of the building, maybe to expose her attacker to the outside world, not realising that he already held the knotted cord in his hand? His actions would have been sudden and savage and, given the force with which he had tightened the ligature around her neck, Mark doubted if Virginia had even been able to cry out; the end must have been swift and the terror unimaginable.

Using the land line in the farm house, as there was no signal for his mobile, Mark telephoned John Lomas to alert him of these developments and the Detective Superintendent quickly dispatched teams of officers to the barn. Straight away they began the task of combing through the grass and mud that surrounded the building on three sides looking for clues, some of them cursing their bad luck at being called out so late in the afternoon when a quiet evening at home, or a noisy one in the pub, had seemed to be on the cards

In a small ditch, the banks of which had been trodden down by the cattle and liberally coated with khaki cow pats which made everywhere slippery underfoot and therefore difficult to walk on, a find was ultimately made. Officers had squelched through the filth and bovine excrement and had made many loud comments about the nature of the foul task they were performing but, in the course of protesting, one man had tripped over a hidden boulder and, to prevent himself from falling face first into the stinking watercourse, he had extended both his arms which had sunk elbow deep into the mire. His fingers touched something hard and metallic, he seized the object and with a little effort pulled out what appeared to be a large rusty chef's or butcher's knife: the tip of the implement was pointed and, despite its discolouration, the edge on the blade was still very sharp. The find was produced to Detective Sergeant Nadin, who very carefully bagged it up. Within the space of four hours, it looked as if both the missing ear stud and the missing weapon had finally been found!

Chapter Nineteen

Of the 28 children who had formed the class of 1977 at Burrdale Primary School, 3 were now dead, 10 others had moved away from Burrdale, although a majority of them had retained family links with the town, and 15 of them still lived and worked within a 10 mile radius of the homes they had grown up in. The most popular jobs for the boys had been driving H.G.V'S, and working in the building trade: 4 of the girls were hairdressers, 3 more were secretaries, and 2 had actually made it to university.

The local newspaper usually hit the streets in the early afternoon; by 7pm on that first day 6 people had telephoned the Burrdale Advertiser and another 14 had contacted the police directly. There was unanimity that the boy in the group photograph, who had been specifically highlighted by the newspaper, was Shane Chadwick, and 70% of the people who replied were either sure, or strongly of the opinion, that the boy in the single photograph was also Shane Chadwick, although 25% of those who replied were not certain one way or the other, and 5% were adamant that it was not him, but none of these could suggest any alternative identification. Over the next four or five days, further responses were received and the same proportion of certainty to doubt was repeated many times over. The results were good enough for Mark Hobson: until evidence to support an alternative identification was forthcoming, he would work on the basis that the single photograph carried by Virginia Brocklehurst was of Shane Chadwick, but still he could not completely banish the little niggle of doubt that occupied the deepest recesses of his mind, and that disconcerted him.

Of all the persons who had been spoken to so far, Dick Norton was the man on whom the life of Shane Chadwick had made the biggest impact and consequently, if he hadn't been before, he now definitely had to be regarded as the prime suspect in the Brocklehurst murder inquiry. If, somehow, he had found out that it was Virginia who was the girl at the pool side, and if for some reason she had met him in the barn, and taunted him with the picture of Shane Chadwick, Richard Norton couldn't have maintained his self-control. It was easy to imagine how he would have exploded with anger and, in that instant, destroyed the person who had wrecked his life and, out of all the suspects, there was no doubt that he was the only one for whom the remote dark pool had any symbolic significance; but for him the significance could hardly have been greater. Perhaps the Burrdale butcher believed that, by returning the body of the woman he now knew to have been responsible for causing his personal tragedy, to the place where that tragedy had begun all those years ago, it would bring him closure in a way that virtually no other action could ever begin to do. The only problems were that there was no way of proving that Richard Norton knew what Virginia might have done, there was no physical evidence whatsoever to link him to her murder, the murder of Mrs Brocklehurst was not spontaneous and, most problematic of all, if his daughter was telling the truth there was also the small matter of the alibi to consider. There was plenty of suspicion, that was undeniable, but nowhere near enough solid facts to justify an arrest and, unless and until something else emerged, the police could not properly bring him in for questioning.

The examination of the knife recovered from the ditch didn't give Mark the grounds he was looking for. The Forensic Pathologist was able to confirm that this was the weapon that had been driven into Virginia's chest; the size and shape of the blade matched exactly the size of the puncture wound, and later when minute fibres clinging to it were microscopically and chemically examined, they matched exactly the fibres of the Burberry coat. Frustratingly, however, no fingerprints were found on the hilt, and no D.N.A. or other forensic evidence was discovered to indicate who had used the sharp implement to such savage effect.

"The killer's almost certainly got to be local." said Mark. "He seems to know this area like the back of his hand and, at some stage he must have sussed out the barn prior to the murder and, common sense dictates he has to have started up the quad bike to make sure it worked. He may also have walked the paths and tracks up to the pool, to find out if they were driveable unless, of course, he was already totally familiar with them, as I'm sure Dick Norton would have been. I'd be willing to bet a king's ransom that he's been up and down those paths a million times in his mind; one of our top priorities has got be to find out if there have been any sightings of him near to or even in the barn."

"So you're convinced that once the clandestine meeting was arranged the final outcome was never going to be in doubt, and there wasn't any chance that Virginia would leave the barn alive?" asked Alan Nadin

"I'm totally convinced. Our murderer is either a driven man, or someone who was terrified that Virginia would expose aspects of his life that he was desperate to keep hidden; in either case there was only one result which would possibly satisfy him"

"I'm not sure you're right that the killer has to be local." commented Paul Burgess. "This is an area of outstanding natural beauty which is visited by tens of thousands of people every year, and many of them come back again and again. Some of those people know about tracks, trails and paths that most people from round here don't even realise exist. I've done a fair bit of walking in the last few months, and I've seen the same faces time and time again. Some ramblers are pretty odd looking specimens, they stand out from the crowd and I'll bet a pound to a penny that a few of them know more about these hills and moors than ninety nine point nine percent of the local population could ever hope to do."

"Point taken; but none of them would appear to have a motive to kill Mrs Brocklehurst would they? If we were looking at a rape or a robbery, as I've said before, it might well have been a case of being in the wrong place at the wrong time, but this was a pre-arranged meeting; there's nothing unplanned about this killing, the roots of this murder grow very deep. There's one thing that bothers me though; I know the barn gave the killer a private place to carry out his crime, but wasn't there still a risk that he could be interrupted by David Wright or one of his workers? He's got to be a man on a mission to be prepared to run that risk, and what about the risk of being noticed when he took the body up to the pool? Doesn't all that seem again to point at Richard Norton? Nobody could want vengeance more than he did could they? He might be prepared to take more chances than anyone else."

"I think I can answer that one Boss. We know it was a fortnight yesterday that Virginia left home for the last time, and the pathologist now thinks it most likely that she died on the same day she was last seen alive. David Wright and his family would have been at a family wedding that day and after the service there was a slap up wedding reception, nobody would have been working on the farm. Anybody who lives locally would have known that. It isn't as if he were a dairy farmer with afternoon milking to take care of, barring emergencies nobody would have been about that afternoon and, if the killer is a local man, he'd have known that for a fact, therefore the level of actual risk would have been very low. The pool isn't close to any of the main paths, quad bikes and trailers are common sights, most hill farmers use them nowadays and, if the body was in the trailer covered with some sacking, or maybe even with some hay, anyone who saw the rig wouldn't have given it a second glance. The only real danger would have arisen when the corpse was chucked into the water, and I think if the killer had good eyesight he had a 95% chance of spotting anyone who might have been on the horizon; given what you say about him, and I completely agree with you, I think he'd have gladly taken those odds. His only mistakes, so far as I can see, seem to be the fact that he failed to pick up the purse, although he had a bit of luck there in that it was later found by a lying little scroat who pissed us about, and the fact that he failed to notice that the ear stud had been ripped out; but for those two small errors we'd still be trying to work out where Virginia was killed, and how her body was taken to the spot where it was dumped."

There then followed a sometimes animated discussion with Paul still arguing that a stranger could have been the killer, and Mark and Alan maintaining that that was probably unlikely. After that debate had raged without resolution Mark went to see John

Lomas and, in private, he updated him on all the recent events and recounted the conversations he had had with his two colleagues: he pointed out that Paul still seemed keen to divert suspicion away from local inhabitants and towards an unknown stranger but that both he and D.S. Nadin had a different view. John Lomas considered carefully the information Mark laid before him, and took no issue with his evaluation of the state of the inquiry to date. He agreed with Mark that a number of factors pointed directly towards the killer being a resident of Burrdale and he concurred with his Detective Inspector's assessment that, despite the considerable degree of suspicion, the police didn't have enough real evidence to bring any individual person in for questioning.

"If you can put Richard Norton in or near the barn I'll sanction an arrest," he said, "and obviously if we find any prints or forensic to link him to the deceased you can pull him in straight away; also if you can establish he's lied, particularly as regards his alleged alibi, I'll be more than happy to see him downstairs in an interview room. Go and see his daughter again, and take Alan, or any other officer you want except Paul Burgess with you, and put some serious pressure on her: if the alibi cracks arrest her for Attempting to Pervert the course of Justice, and then while she's still in custody arrest Norton on suspicion of murder. I fancy if there's ever going to be a confession in this case it will be made to us while he believes his daughter to be at risk; and if one is made then, it's Bingo! Job done! It will damage your relationship with Paul because he'll resent any rough handling of his girlfriend, and the future working relationship between the two of you could be destroyed. If things do get bad I'll arrange for him to be transferred, which I'm sure won't go down well, but in the end it may be that'll be the only solution; however it might not come to that, and things could improve if we don't actually charge the girl, which to be honest, I've no real wish to do so. She's in a bloody terrible position, and if she has lied she's only done what any normal person would have done in the circumstances. Whatever the law may or may not say, it is human nature to try to protect the people we love, and it's very hard to criminalize anybody for doing that when they've been under as much pressure as that poor girl has been for most of her unhappy life."

Chapter Twenty

As well as the phone calls which were responses to the photographs and the article, which appealed to readers to help identify the boys in the pictures, the renewed publicity seemed to re-awaken general interest in the case and several calls were received from people claiming to have information about the killing itself. Some of these people even nominated persons they thought may have been responsible. The name of Richard Norton came up three times, and Tony Patterson was also put forward as a possible suspect, but all these suspicions seemed to be based upon their public utterances rather than any actual knowledge possessed by the caller: despite that fact, however, each call was carefully logged and diligently followed up, even though many of them from the outset appeared to lack any real substance. Some of the people who telephoned left full contact details, others did not. P.C. Ollerenshaw was the man most of the callers wanted to talk to, but there were persons who would only speak to Alan Nadin, and there was one particularly impatient man, phoning from a public call box, who was insistent that he would say what he had to say to Detective Sergeant Paul Burgess and to nobody else.

It was after P.C Ollerenshaw had spent the best part of one

afternoon with Mary McKendrick, a retired care worker who now augmented her income by doing a part time job cleaning at the Health Centre, that he came to speak to Mark Hobson. Mrs McKendrick had been a customer of Richard Norton for nearly twenty five years. She didn't like him as a man, she found him rude and arrogant, but he had always sold the best meat, and she infinitely preferred his produce to that available at any of the local supermarkets. Very recently, however, she had noticed a dramatic falling off in quality and, perhaps even more strikingly, the standard of service he provided for his customers had plummeted. Whatever had been the turmoil in Richard's life, in the past, he had always been dependable, but three times in the last fortnight he had suddenly walked out of the shop without notice, leaving a queue of people waiting to be served and a harassed part time shop assistant at her wits end. He had told nobody where he was going nor had he given any indication when he would be back, but Mary had a friend who had told her that, at least once, he had returned angry and frustrated and had screamed at the beleaguered assistant for forgetting to put some cooked meat back in the cold room and overlooking a small amount of change that should have been placed in the till. His conduct had been totally unreasonable, and the whole episode had been shameful to watch, as well as being grossly unfair to the poor girl, who had tried her best to cope in the difficult circumstances he had left her with.

"Where did he go?" wondered Mark, "and what was so pressing that it couldn't wait?" He instructed P.C. Ollerenshaw to speak to all his many contacts to see if any of them might be able to throw some light on the butcher's strange and unpredictable behaviour.

It was after Ollerenshaw had left that Mark telephoned Rebecca Norton and asked if he could come and talk to her. Rebecca was not keen on a meeting. She tried to explain that she had things to do and that it would be very inconvenient for her to have to alter her plans. However Mark was insistent that the matter couldn't be delayed and effectively left her no option other than to agree to see him, but he arranged the meeting for the early afternoon, ostensibly to allow her a couple of hours to re-organise her day, but actually to give her plenty of time to worry about the further questions the police might put to her. He was about to call in Alan to ask him to go with him to see Rebecca, when the door to his office was flung open, and in stormed Paul Burgess. He was almost shaking with anger, his normal calm and slightly withdrawn manner had completely deserted him.

"I've just had Becky on the phone." he yelled, "She was in floods of tears, just what the bloody hell's going on?"

Mark jumped to his feet; he found the manner of his subordinate to be insolent and unreasonable.

"Hold it right there Sergeant. You don't speak to me like that, not unless you want to find yourself up before Superintendent Lomas! Remember, you're a bloody police officer and try to behave like one. Rebecca Norton is going to be interviewed again as a witness; her father is the prime suspect in a murder investigation, and I'm doing everything in my power to find a killer. There are no "No Go" areas. If you ever behave towards me again in the way you just did, I promise you your feet won't touch the fucking ground. I think it would be in your best interest get out of this office right now and not come back until you've got an apology for me; and don't go talking to Rebecca Norton again today until after I've finished with her otherwise you might find yourself on a charge of obstructing a police officer acting in the execution of his duty. Do I make myself clear! I should remove you completely from this inquiry as of now and, if there's the remotest sign of a repeat performance, then I'll do exactly that; but I'm going to stick my neck out for you and give you a chance to prove to me you can still make a valuable contribution to this investigation. Now, go and cool down and think about what I've just said and only come back and see me when you're in a different frame of mind."

Resentment showed in every line on Paul's face but, even in the intensity of his rage, he had the residual common sense to realise that his Inspector held all the cards and that he could also expect the unconditional support of senior officers.

"I'm going, Boss," he said through gritted teeth, "I've got some real work to do meeting a potential informant, not bullying innocent young women and trying to twist facts to fit some crackpot theory." and with that he turned his back on Mark and left the room, slamming the door behind him as he went. Mark didn't call him back, but at that moment made up his mind that without a sincere and radical change of attitude there was no further place for Paul Burgess as part of his team.

A few seconds later there was a knock on the door and in walked Alan Nadin. "What was all the about, Boss?" he asked, "Only I've just passed Paul on his way to the car park and he had a face like thunder; I wouldn't want to get on the wrong side of him, the mood he's in at the moment."

"Oh, it's nothing," said Mark, "he's just a little annoyed that I'm going to question his girlfriend again. It'll soon blow over. I want you to come with me when I do so, if that's O.K. with you. and if you've got the time to accompany me this afternoon."

"Gladly," said Alan, "I've just got a couple of phone calls to make and then I'm yours any time you wish."

While D.S. Nadin made his calls and sorted out one or two bits of paperwork, Mark re-read the notes that he had made after his first meeting with Rebecca, in particular trying to memorise specific details she had given in answers to specific questions. Times, places, actions and conduct were all important. If Rebecca was able to give the same answers today as she had given before, it would be a powerful indicator that she had told the truth; if she couldn't remember or gave incompatible answers, then she had probably lied, and would then have to be further interviewed under caution at the police station about her reasons for giving misleading information to the police. He was fully prepared by the time Alan Nadin rejoined him.

When they arrived at the flat Rebecca was alone, and she looked nervous. Richard was downstairs in the shop. He had wanted to be with her when the police came, but she had insisted that he wasn't there: the last thing she needed to contend with was one of her father's outbursts, which would have totally wrecked her composure. Rebecca didn't really know why it was so vital, but she knew that she had to keep all her wits about her. Her Dad's melodramatic posturing could easily scatter them to the four winds.

Inspector Hobson and his colleague were very polite and professional; they both declined the cups of tea they were offered, and Mark then began to seek clarification from her about the things she had told him before. Despite her best efforts her mind was suffocating in a black fog of uncertainty. He asked her simple questions about what they had eaten for lunch, which had not seemed remotely relevant when she had replayed the first interview in her mind whilst waiting for the police to arrive: she couldn't remember. He asked other easy questions about the precise time of the meal: she couldn't recall. He asked her whether they had watched television and whether they had talked and she couldn't recollect, and all the time the one officer plied her with questions, his partner wrote down every detail of her answers in his pocket notebook. Without the remotest possibility of being able to control it Rebecca began to blush, and the more she struggled to respond the deeper the blush became; she felt hot and uncomfortable, and she wished the policemen would go away. Eventually the probing ceased.

"You've lied throughout this interview, haven't you Rebecca: and the more you've wriggled the deeper the pit you've dug for yourself. Now isn't that the plain and simple truth?" Becky nodded her head and sank back into her chair in total distress.

"You're going to have to come with us so that we can interview you properly at the Police Station," said the Detective Inspector, and the Detective Sergeant then arrested the now distraught girl and led her, gently but firmly, to the waiting police car parked outside. There was no fuss, and mercifully handcuffs were not applied: few, if any, persons actually saw her depart with the officers.

At the Police Station, after the embarrassing experience of being booked in as a suspect, Rebecca was interviewed under caution; she declined the assistance of a solicitor, and in the interview room it was a very frightened and chastened young woman who tried her best to answer questions correctly.

She told the officers that it was not true that she had been with her father all afternoon, as she had claimed; she had in fact for a large part of the time been waiting in the Stocks Cafe for her boyfriend Paul to come, but he'd been late arriving. She was pretty certain that her father had been receiving telephone calls which, she suspected, related to Virginia Brocklehurst, but she had no idea at all as to why that might be. When Virginia Brocklehurst died, her father had reacted very oddly: he had been frantic to learn about the killing, and his sole topic of conversation had been about her death. Rebecca had seen him bad before, but this time he'd seemed almost wild in his obsession with the news. She had begun to fear that he might have known something about the murder itself and, when she found the police at the flat already questioning him when she arrived back home, she had been afraid that he would be arrested, and spontaneously she had lied to protect him. At the finish of the interview both Hobson and Nadin felt sure she was now telling them as much of the truth as she could honestly remember.

In an unusually considerate move Hobson didn't order Becky to be placed in the cells whilst D.S. Nadin took pre-charge advice from the C.P.S. but instead allowed her to remain in the interview room watched over by a sympathetic female detective officer. There was no such consideration extended to her father. Mark dispatched two powerfully built experienced policemen to go and arrest Richard on suspicion of murder and, whilst they were gone, he briefed John Lomas on the events of the day. Detective Sergeant Paul Burgess had still not returned to the police station and, by and large, Mark felt there were fewer complications if, for the moment at least, it stayed that way.

Richard Norton was almost beside himself with fury when the police came for him, but he wanted to be at the Police Station where his daughter was and, although he swore and shouted, he didn't struggle with the officers, even when they put him in handcuffs before placing him in the rear of the police car. Although it appears nowhere in any records of the journey, and would be strenuously denied by every police officer involved in this case, Richard was given food for thought as he was taken the short distance to the station; it may never officially have been said, but somehow he got the distinct impression that if he cooperated with the police and told them everything they wanted to know, there was a fair chance that no further action would be taken against Rebecca: if he did not then …!

The interview with him was never going to be easy. Mark had

refused point blank to answer any of his questions about Rebecca, and Richard didn't know that the police were already considering releasing her without charge. He didn't want to talk to them, he didn't want to give them the time of day; but in his mind he saw his beautiful daughter, tearful, terrified and alone in an uncomfortable police cell, so he curbed his natural inclination towards stubbornness, and gradually began to reveal information about the case to the interviewing officers. He admitted he had received phone calls from a person he refused to name. He said that that person had told him that he knew facts about Lucas's death that would profoundly interest him; he also hinted that this knowledge could be dynamite in the current climate that existed in Burrdale: but it all came at a price. He said he had arranged to meet the man, but that on two occasions he had been let down by him. On the third occasion they had finally met and, after being paid £200, the man had told him he had proof that Virginia Brocklehurst was the girl who had stage managed the incident in which his son Lucas had died. The man had also claimed to have evidence, at greatly increased cost, which would reveal her true character to such an extent that her life in Burrdale would be totally destroyed by its publication. He didn't say what this evidence consisted of. Richard claimed that he was sceptical about these claims but, if they were true, and he could punish Virginia both for killing his son and for damaging the reputation of her late husband, who he had admired, then that was something he'd waited nearly half a lifetime to achieve. Detective Inspector Hobson wanted a name, Richard wanted to keep the name secret, but the thought of Becky, distraught and frightened was more than he could bear and finally he revealed that the person he had met and paid the money to was Mike Skinner.

Richard denied that he had had any involvement in Virginia's death; indeed he claimed to have been devastated when it happened because it robbed him of his opportunity to take revenge. He said he had intended to make her an object of scorn and contempt and to try to condemn her to a life of abuse and ridicule and, most of all, he wanted her to feel tormented, as he had felt tormented for so many years. Fate had denied him even that inadequate compensation and he had watched the developing news, and read the papers in bitterness and in frustration, cursing the fact that she hadn't been brought down by his hand.

On that sour note the interview ended. Mark and Alan were both left thinking that this account of events could be credible. They were not convinced that Norton was an innocent man but, they realised that, without a confession ,if they went to the C.P.S. for advice at this stage, they would be told that there was insufficient evidence to charge the suspect with any offence and that there were no clear grounds to seek a remand in custody. Norton was therefore bailed without charge pending further inquiries, and only at that time did Mark tell him that his daughter had been released, and was already at home, with no further police action being contemplated against her.

As Norton left the police station, Paul Burgess returned to it. He had obviously been home because he had changed his clothing and had showered and washed his hair: some of his previous passion had also seemed to have been washed away. He now realised for the sake of his career that he had to apologise to his inspector, which he fully intended to do. He had rehearsed the words in his mind and they would satisfy the need; his thoughts and feelings were less clear but, so long as he kept them to himself there shouldn't be a problem. The two men looked at each other as they passed. They didn't speak, but Paul knew instinctively that the already cool relationship that existed between them had now become degrees colder, and he understood that there was very little hope of any improvement ever being achieved. The future for him and for Becky didn't look bright, and that intensely saddened him.

Chapter Twenty One

For the group of ramblers now seeking *Absolution* in the lounge bar of the Coverdale Arms, the day had just got a whole lot better. The beer was strong and very drinkable, and the food they had eaten in the ancient inn had been well prepared, generously portioned and extremely tasty. The log fire that burned brightly in the Inglenook fireplace was refusing to let them leave without a struggle, and tired limbs were relaxing in its glow, bodies being warmed by the heat of the flames and the steak and ale pies that had been wolfed down at break neck speed. Conversation now flowed easily; the respective demerits of City and United were being passionately debated, the qualities of various performance cars vigorously discussed, the virtue of *Real Ale* universally extolled and a state of contentment was settling upon the sixteen men assembled together in the room.

Not that the day had started off badly. The weather had looked promising; everybody had arrived at Piccadilly Station in good time; the train hadn't been delayed, and all the omens had seemed to foretell an incident free day out.

The failure of the veteran diesel's engine midway between Marple and New Mills had thrown a major spanner in the works, and it had taken the best part of two hours for the breakdown to be repaired. Nobody had been permitted to disembark the increasingly cold carriages, and tempers had started to fray. Eventually the fault had been fixed, and the train had limped into Chinley Station two and a quarter hours late, at precisely the time that the party of men had been scheduled to sit down and eat their pre-ordered meal at the Coverdale Inn. Several miles of upland Derbyshire stood between them and their destination, so instead of the leisurely stroll everyone had anticipated, with plenty of time to stop and look at interesting flora and fauna, or take photographs of the panoramic views from the hilltops, a route march, at double quick time had been the order of the day. The sheer pleasure of being out and about in glorious countryside had been ground underfoot by boots ordered to "Press on lads, press on" by the leaders of the party.

The relaxed mood which now prevailed started to dissolve into the dregs of beer glasses when twenty minutes later the order rang out "Drink up lads we must get going, we've a few more miles to cover before we reach Edale." For a little while it seemed as if mutiny would be on the cards, and in gestures of defiance two members of the group decided to grab "swift halves" as a sign of protest but ultimately common sense prevailed. Six miles stood between them and their final destination, and time was not on their side.

By the time they reluctantly trooped out of the pub it was well past four o'clock: steep paths and heavy bellies made it unlikely that their further progress would be quick and, even if everything now went without a hitch, it was probable that they would not reach their final destination until after 6pm, when the sun would be low down in the sky. If there were any more hold ups en route that time could extend to nearer 7pm, by which time daylight would have completely vanished. Darkness gives the moors mystic qualities and, many people seek the quietness and the solitude that it offers, but it heightens the dangers weary travellers have to face, and the leaders of the ramblers fervently hoped they could complete the remainder of their cross country hike before the last rays of sunlight disappeared over the horizon. It was as they were striding across the peaty uplands above Burrdale, continually being urged to make haste by the anxious organisers, that one of the hikers noticed several dogs in a distant meadow. Long legged lurchers were running aimlessly around the field, and terriers were sniffing and pawing at a dark object lying on the grass. The hiker couldn't work out what the object was, it was too big for a sheep, and it seemed to be too skinny to be one of the black and white belted cattle that grazed the lower pastures. He had kept dogs himself, and he knew this behaviour was not normal; breaking away from the other members of the group, ignoring commands to stay together, he descended the slope, to find out for himself what it was that had so unsettled these excited animals.

He had approached to within forty feet of the thing before he realized that he was looking at a man. He recoiled in horror. He had seen death before and it had never unnerved him, and in his time he had shot and killed game birds and even foxes and had not been moved or sickened by their death throes; but this was different. This was a man, whose life had been savagely taken, and whose body lay contorted in agony on the hard earth. There is no dignity in dying, but the final image of this human being was repellent. The man wore a Barbour jacket, the pockets misshapen through over use, which was so crumpled and scuffed that in places the wax had worn thin. Lead shot had now shredded the fibres of the coat before blowing a gaping hole in the man's stomach and abdomen; his once red blood had already congealed and turned to black treacle. The grotesque finality of the scene laid out before him caused the hiker to scream out in alarm: his cries echoed and re-echoed around the valley until the half digested contents of his stomach spewed from his mouth, smothering the sound of his wailing with his own vomit.

His companions rushed from the hillside to join him: they too were appalled by what they saw. There was just sufficient signal to permit a 999 telephone call to the police and so a garbled message was sent. One man, made of sterner stuff than the rest, managed to capture the now exhausted dogs and to tether them to a tree stump. Nobody touched the double barrelled 12 bore shotgun that lay just out of reach of the man's right hand, that would be evidence and should be left well alone; and nobody strayed too close to the body because the prospect was too abhorrent. In near silence and in the ever deepening gloom, this now dispirited party of friends waited for the police to arrive and to take charge of the terrible situation that they found themselves to be in; their fun day out with friends had now hit rock bottom

Chapter Twenty Two

A few minutes after Richard Norton left the police station there was a gentle tap on Mark Hobson's door: so little force was used that the sound did not impact on his consciousness, and a second, louder, knock had to be made before it succeeded in attracting his attention. On being invited to enter the office, and after a noticeable hesitation, in walked a shame faced Paul Burgess. The anger and pent up emotion that had so characterised their meeting earlier that day had dissipated, and it was an awkward, self-conscious man who now stood before his senior officer. Sometimes struggling to find the right words he apologised for his attitude and his lack of respect, and he accepted unreservedly that he had been wrong and that Mark had had no choice other than to speak to him as forcefully as he had done so. It was clearly an ordeal for Paul to admit his faults and Mark recognised that fact: he was happy to take the apology at face value, and even began to feel some sympathy for his hot headed young colleague.

"Apology accepted Paul and that's an end to the matter. I was a bit harsh on you too, and I'm sorry I came down on you so heavily. Believe me; I do know what it's like to care for somebody in difficult circumstances. A few years ago now, when

I was a disillusioned D.S. whose career was going nowhere rapidly, I met the woman who was to become my wife. She was lying in a hospital bed having been badly injured by a car bomb that had blown her employer to bits and, if you'd told me about love at first sight, I'd have laughed in your face and called you stark staring bonkers; but believe me it happened to me, even though I didn't fully realise it at the time, and it was a bolt from the blue. She was the victim of violent crime in need of psychological support, she was also a witness to a murder who should have received expert handling and, later on, she became the target of a vicious campaign of harassment: any one of those classifications should have meant that the investigating officer remained professionally detached. I didn't do that and, if my boss had known how much I was breaking police rules by commencing a relationship with Helena, my career would have been down the pan. I couldn't help myself. There were many times when things happened which I should have told my superiors about, and I didn't do that. With hindsight, maybe sometimes my efforts to protect Helena actually exposed her to greater risk and it very nearly ended in tragedy but, thank God it didn't do so. Don't make the same mistakes I made by keeping everything bottled up inside yourself; talk to me if things get difficult. I promise I'll do everything I can do to try and help."

"Thanks, Boss," said Paul, "I'll remember that." Mark sensed that there was genuine appreciation in his response.

"So far as I am concerned, and I hope that this may help to put your mind at rest, I now believe that Becky's done her best to tell us everything she knows about the case: there won't be any charges, not even a formal caution, so nothing goes on her record and, with a bit of help from you, I think she'll soon be able to put her short lived ordeal behind her. You might also be right about her father, I think he found himself forced to give us far more information than he ever wanted to. I'm still not a hundred percent sure that we've got the whole picture, and remember he does remain a prime suspect, but some of what he's said sounds pretty credible, and it wouldn't entirely surprise me if it turned out that he had told us the complete truth. Once we've got this case wrapped up, it's possible that Dick Norton may start to see things in a very different light, and many of his objections to you might melt away into thin air."

"I don't hold out much chance of that. He's always been suspicious of me from the word go. After today he'll see me even more as part of the enemy than he did before. He's the most stupid, stubborn man I've ever met; I can't envisage him ever changing his mind."

"Give it time Paul, give it time, it is the great healer, or so many people say. Incidentally, talking about time, how could you leave that beautiful young woman of yours all by herself in a café for over two hours, anybody who didn't know you better might think that you weren't really interested in seeing her?"

Some small, but discernible portion of colour seemed to drain from Paul's face, and Mark saw that this attempt at levity had landed well wide of the mark.

"I was ill," protested Paul. "I went off sick the following day, and as my record shows I never take time off work. It was just about all I could do to get out of bed that day, I'm sure Becky would tell you that she thought I looked ghastly when we did finally meet."

"It was a flippant remark, Paul, not a criticism." said Mark and, changing the subject he asked Paul whether he had gained anything useful from his informant.

"He didn't show, and after I'd worn a groove in the Market Square walking up and down it a few dozen times, I went home to think, and to have a shower, and to work out what to say to you when I next met you."

It was at that point that there was another knock on the door, and D.S. Nadin entered the office to join Mark and Paul.

"Sorry, Boss, am I interrupting something? It's not really important; I can come back later if you'd like me to."

"No, it's fine Alan; we've more or less exhausted our topics of conversation. What is it that you want to say to me?"

"I've been thinking about the evidence of Henry Osbourne," said

Alan, "and I have come to the conclusion that we may have got one or two things wrong." and he then proceeded to explain his concerns to his Detective Inspector and his fellow Detective Sergeant.

"From what Osbourne's told us it's clear that Virginia Brocklehurst had been very worried about something up until just a couple of weeks before her death, and then it all changed. She was calling the shots, and I think it's likely that she would have dictated terms to the killer and not vice versa. That means she probably selected the meeting place, which means that the killer didn't have the opportunity to check out the barn or the quad bike. It also means that it could be anybody. He doesn't have to be local: all he had to do was follow instructions, and perhaps have the basic ability to read an Ordnance Survey map." Although he didn't speak, Paul Burgess nodded his head in agreement with this assessment of the situation.

Mark listened carefully to the experienced detective, "It's a good point, Alan," he said, "a very good point. Either the murderer has been incredibly lucky in that he found inside the barn everything he needed to carry away the body, and I simply can't buy that or, and here I don't know how it could have been done, somehow he's manipulated the situation to make Virginia believe that she was in charge when in fact she wasn't and, somehow, he's been able to implant in her mind the idea of the barn, when in reality it was his choice of venue all along."

"So our killer will turn out to be a hypnotist," commented Paul, and behind the humour Mark sensed a moment of exasperation; nothing more was said on the subject and Detective Sergeant Burgess didn't set himself upon another collision course with his senior officer.

"Things like that do happen. I've told you before Paul that I think our murderer will turn out to be an extraordinary person; nothing has occurred since then to make me want to change my mind in any way."

The 999 call to police Divisional Headquarters, relayed minutes later to the officers at Burrdale dramatically interrupted the musings of the three detectives.

"There's been a fatal shooting at Blackdale Meadows," said Mark. "A group of ramblers have found the body of a man with half his stomach shot away. It looks like murder," and with that he took immediate steps to ensure that the well rehearsed procedures required to be followed in the event of a major incident were put into practice.

Detective Superintendent Lomas was already at the scene by the time Mark arrived. A lighting rig had been set in place and another one was on its way. The area around the body had been cordoned off and the party of ramblers had been moved beyond the cordon. Their personal details were being taken by uniform police officers. Scientific Support Officers from Buxton and Chesterfield were expected to arrive soon, as was the *Grim Reaper*. The shotgun hadn't been touched and the dead man hadn't yet been covered up. Light drizzle was beginning to fall and soon a tent would be erected to shield the corpse from the rain and from prying eyes. The grass around the scene had been trampled down: whether this had been done by heavy booted ramblers or whether the flattened vegetation was the sign of some sort of struggle was at this stage unclear. What was already certain was that it was a physical impossibility for the dead man to have shot himself without first removing a boot so that, theoretically, he could have reached the trigger of the weapon with his toe. That had not occurred; unless it was that he had somehow mastered the technique of replacing his socks and shoes after he was dead and tightly tying up his shoe laces! He could have used a stick to push the trigger down, but that hadn't happened either, because had he done that, the stick would have fallen near to the body and self-evidently there was no stick anywhere to be seen

It was when Alan Nadin joined the other officers that the identity of the dead man was established.

"Finally we've got him in possession of a bloody gun, and we can't charge him with a sodding thing: the one thing I never expected was for him to be shot by his own 12 bore. Being knifed in a pub brawl might well have been on the cards, but I never thought he'd come to grief out here. We ain't going to be bringing Mike Skinner in for questioning Boss, dead men don't fucking talk."

Chapter Twenty Three

It had become one of those contrary autumn nights that look forward with no enthusiasm to the forthcoming November gloom, rather than backwards with nostalgia to the heady days of glorious summer. It was grey and murky and, by the time the *Grim Reaper* attended the crime scene, light drizzle had turned into cold rain.

Doc Grimshawe was in a foul mood. The telephone call from the police had been received at the Grimshawe residence only minutes before the first of several invited guests had been due to arrive; it was not good news for the Home Office Pathologist. Gerald Grimshawe had left his house with the protestations of his wife ringing in his ears: terrible disasters would engulf him if he didn't get back to the dinner table by the time the soup was ready to be served.

"Why do you buggers always call me out when I'm just about to sit down to a meal?" he grumbled. "It's a bloody conspiracy to force me to lose weight. There's no God given law that says that stupid sods like this must pick the most inconvenient times to die, but I suppose that even if he'd been more accommodating you lot would still have sat on your arses until my wife was ready to dish up the sodding sprouts before calling me out!"

The examination was brief. In answers to questions put to him by John Lomas and Mark Hobson the Doc was almost monosyllabic. The cause of death was "bleedin obvious", the time of death was probably between 3pm-5pm, but he couldn't say for sure and a detailed report would only be provided after the full post mortem examination had been carried out. It wasn't much, but it was the best that could be hoped for given the circumstances and, by and by, a comprehensive, thorough, professional document would be prepared, which past experience had demonstrated would be of high quality. Two things however were already clear; firstly suicide and accidental death could both probably be ruled out and, secondly, if the presumed time of death was accurate, Dick Norton couldn't have been the man who fired the fatal shot as he had been in custody at Burrdale police station throughout the entire relevant period. It could not yet be said with certainty that he had no involvement in the killing, but both Hobson and Lomas knew that it was impossible for him to have been in two places at once and neither police officer believed him to be the type of man who would pay others to do his gory work for him.

The meeting with the dead man's widow had to be the next item on the agenda. It was not a task Mark Hobson relished; no matter how bad a person may have been, and Mike Skinner had at times been very bad indeed, it was always difficult dealing with distraught relatives, shocked by the sudden violent death of a loved one. In a strangely perverse way it was often those wives or girlfriends who had suffered domestic violence or abuse at the hands of their partners who were the most inconsolable. Jackie Skinner was not one of those women, she had never been physically beaten but, never-the-less, Alan Nadin said that there had been times when Mike had treated her badly and that many a woman would not have put up with some of the things he had done. On two or three occasions, according to police files, he had smashed up the house when in drink and there had been countless *one night stands* with local girls, some of which had sparked off trouble. It was well known in the town that Mike Skinner would shag anything in a skirt under the age of sixty five, provided it hadn't got the pox and weighed less than twenty five stone. It was also well known that he had done little or nothing to help his wife bring up their three small children.

Accompanied by a policewoman, Mark drove to Skinner's address. The dogs that had been running loose in the fields were now back in their compounds and, when the security lights fitted to the side of the house were activated by the arrival of the police officers, the terriers snapped and barked at them from behind the wire netting fence: broken children's toys littered the footpath, and the tax on the 1988 Rover 214 that stood rusting away on the muddy front lawn had long since expired. Mark rang the doorbell: the newly widowed Mrs Skinner opened the door, it was clear to see that she had been crying. She was about ten years older than her fashion sense, and a dozen or so pounds bigger than her dress size, yet underneath the now blotchy make up was quite a pretty, gentle face. Although by no means an intellectual giant, she was bright enough and she had done her best to look after her man, and to bring up three overactive kids in very difficult circumstances. Now she was alone, the predictable routines of her life had been wrenched away from her: she was confused, upset and very, very scared.

"I'm so sorry to have to trouble you at a time like this," began Mark, "and I promise I'll take up as little of your time as I possibly can, but we must find the person who killed your husband. I know it's very difficult, but do you think you could answer a few of my questions?" Jackie Skinner didn't speak, but between sobs nodded her head and indicated she would try to help the police in any way she could.

Her husband had his faults, what man hadn't? Sometimes, she said, those faults had led to real trouble. There had been times in the past when angry husbands or boyfriends of girls Mike had "played around" with had come looking for him with violent intent, but that had been a long while ago and Jackie told Mark that she knew of nobody who currently wished him harm. They had just lived through a time of comparative harmony and Mike had seemed more settled than he had been for many years. Money had been also less of a problem of late. Casual work with a builder in Glossop had been in ready supply, and there had been a two thousand pound windfall that Mike had said was the result of having had a bit of luck on the horses. In addition to all of that, one afternoon, when he hadn't been working, he'd gone out for a walk and returned home with a thick wad of banknotes saying that "Good times were just around the corner" and that soon they would be able to "spend, spend, and spend!" She had asked him where that money had come from, and he had touched his nose with his forefinger and had said that that was his little secret; but he had promised her on his life that none of the cash was nicked. He had also made it clear that in his opinion there was "plenty more to come" and he had revelled in having "several irons in the fire." He'd talked about buying a decent car, and he'd promised her new clothes and a holiday in Tenerife with the kids, and Jackie's face crumpled and her voice cracked when the thought struck home that none of this could ever happen now. Mark let her weep and the female officer made a cup of tea, and only after Jackie had regained a degree of composure did he continue with his questioning.

Mike had been by nature a *chancer,* and a *wheeler dealer*. He kept his cards close to his chest, except sometimes when drink loosened his tongue, and of late that had not been as big a problem as it once had been. Jackie had no idea why his fortunes seemed to have changed, and didn't have a clue where all the promised money was going to come from. Mike had talked about "more than one source", but he had named no names and she couldn't begin to guess as to what or who those sources might be. Mark asked Mrs Skinner if she had any idea when her husband's good fortune commenced. She didn't know for sure, but she wondered if somehow it was connected to his father's death and to some letters and photographs which had been found inside a biscuit tin stuffed away in a chest of drawers in a spare bedroom, which he had discovered when the house was being cleared. Her mother-in-law had been a waste of space and she had left all the funeral arrangements to Mike and to her, and Jackie was suddenly overwhelmed by the realisation that it would be she who would have to deal with the hysterical grief all over again, but this time completely on her own.

She was by now too distressed to carry on and too confused to start looking for the tin, but she did promise that she would let the police have the box and contents as soon as she could bring herself to carry out a search for it. Mark was desperate to get his hands this material, but there was so much sadness in the house that he knew he couldn't demand that she look for it immediately. He begged Jackie to let him have the box as soon as she possibly could stressing that it was his view that there was every likelihood that important clues in the hunt for the killer of her husband might lie hidden amongst the paper work. Mark ended his conversation with Jackie by asking her if there was anybody else who might know some of Mike's secrets who he could talk to whilst she was trying to come to terms with her loss. Jackie answered that if anybody might know his inner most thoughts it would be Bob Leather, his friend and partner in crime, for more than thirty years.

The final brief questions concerned the gun, Jackie knew that Mike still had the shotgun, he had kept the cartridges in his bedside table, but she didn't know where he had stored the weapon. She didn't like to have guns in the house, they frightened her and she feared for her children's safety, but hunting and shooting had been a way of life to Mike, and he could not be tamed or hemmed in. She had never tried to stop him when he had said he was going out, even though many times she would have preferred it if he hadn't gone. Every day when he wasn't working and every evening, whether or not there was work to go to the following day, he would just take off into the hills and return, hours later, with a couple of pheasants, a rabbit or a hare. She hadn't complained, and had dutifully plucked, gutted and cooked the birds and animals he had brought home with him, even though she didn't like doing it, and despite the fact the kids often wouldn't eat the meal that was set before them, which sometimes led to noisy family arguments.

Grieving relatives began to arrive in numbers. Mike's hysterical mother was first on the scene, and then came various sisters, nephews, nieces and cousins: Mike's brother's widow was particularly distraught; having watched her husband die slowly of cancer, only eight months before, and the need for the family to be left in peace to grieve and to remember was paramount. Mark and the police woman again offered their condolences and, leaving Jackie to the support and concern of her extended family, they went. After the police had gone, and sorrows conceived in memory and baptised in drink, had overwhelmed the persons present, there were rifts, recriminations and bitter reproaches, but these were not police matters and nobody in authority witnessed them or saw how truly by herself Jackie Skinner really was.

One person who hadn't been amongst the early mourners was Bob Leather and that had surprised Mark, so, despite the lateness of the hour, he decided to seek him out. He went by himself to the scruffy stone cottage that was Leather's home, having sent the police woman back to the station to carry out other duties, and there he was met by Bob's notorious mother. She was a thin, hard faced, bony woman, who hated the police with a passion. She was reputed to rule her over large son with a rod of iron and, from all reports; the idea of motherly love was a completely alien concept so far as she was concerned. She had a numerous criminal convictions for shop lifting, benefit fraud, Public Order offences and recently she had added dealing in cannabis to her litany of offences. Other than to tell Mark her son was out, she was not prepared to give the Detective Inspector the time of day.

A phone call to Alan Nadin brought better results, and a short while later he joined his boss and together the two men drove to Elmton Clough, which lies a couple of miles out of town, where Alan said he believed that they might possibly find Leather. It was pitch black, but the powerful torch taken from the police car enabled the officers to carry out a search.

D.S. Nadin's instincts proved to be correct; Bob was sitting in the dark on a large boulder, staring blankly into space, while his two dogs ran around the field, completely ignored by their preoccupied master.

"Hello Bob," said Alan, "this is Detective Inspector Hobson; he wants to ask you a few questions."

"I know who he fucking is," snapped Leather, "I don't want to talk to anyone, so you two buggers might just as well piss off."

"Can't do that Bob." said Alan. "I thought Mike Skinner was a mate of yours, and that you'd want to catch the bastard who killed him. It wasn't clean, he didn't die instantly and he'd have been in terrible pain. You wouldn't let a rat suffer in the way that he did in his last moments on earth. Now are you going to sit there moping or are you going to help us to put the inhuman sod that put a two foot hole in your pal's belly behind bars?"

Bob Leather was quite a simple man, his size concealed many self doubts, and the picture the detective painted opened the floodgates. He had lost his best mate, his mentor, his guiding light and he was looking forward towards a life without direction. Mike had made the plans, Mike had decided what they did and where they went, and he had always deferred to him. Now he was no more. In many ways, at that moment, Bob was like a scrapped car, its engine removed and its wheels taken away, an empty shell incapable of going anywhere under its own steam.

He wiped a tear from his eye with a grimy hand. *Real men don't cry, you brainless pillock.* The harsh words of his mother rattled round his brain like a pinball, and at that moment, had she been within reach, he would have smashed her head onto the rock where he had been sitting, splintering her skull, and leaving blood, skin, hair and shards of bone coating the outer surface; but she was well out of harm's way and so no tragedy occurred. Some day in the future she might push too hard, or goad him just once too often, and the result would be catastrophic, but today the rage was impotent and could cause no injury. The fight inside him had gone. "What do yer wanna know?" he said in a voice that was strangely devoid of any emotion.

"I've been speaking to Jackie," said Mark, "and she's told me

Mike recently came into a bit of cash, and he told her he thought there'd be plenty more where that came from. She hasn't the foggiest idea what he was talking about. You were his best mate. Did he ever say anything to you about this money, and is there anything you can tell us about it?"

"There's now't much. Mike only ever told you things he wanted yer to hear. I think he met some bugger on a footpath outside town, and that that bloke paid him some cash; he showed me a bundle of notes, he didn't tell me how much there were. I ain't got a clue why he give Mike the money; it might have had sommat to do with a photograph he'd found which he seemed all fired up about. It was of his elder brother Alfred, we all called him Freddie and it were took a long time ago. There were a couple of older blokes in the picture, one was Crawford Winston, the dirty sod who got chucked into gaol for touching up little girls, I don't know who the other one were, and I think there were little lad inth' picture who were Crawford's nephew John. At the time that snap were taken nobody knew that Crawford was a bloody paedophile; otherwise Freddie's dad wouldn't ha let him go anywhere near th' fucking farm. They all thowt that he were a bit of a soft touch, who were stupid wih money, and that if they played their cards reet they could fleece 'im out of a bob or two: brass were always tight in that family. So fer as I knows there were some letters as well, which Mike believed to be valuable.

He found 'em amongst his dad's private papers, they nearly ended up inth' fucking skip, but Mike saw 'em and rescued 'em and in his mind he seemed to think that they could be worth a small fortune. Jackie's got 'em now. She'll give 'em to you if you ask her for 'em."

"We know that," said Mark, "and we'll get them from her as soon as she is in a fit state to give them to us. You've been a great help. I've just one more question for you. Do you know anything about where Mike kept his gun?"

Bob Leather shook his head. "I don't know owt about that." he said. Mark interrupted him. "Look Bob," he said, "I'm not remotely interested in trying to convict anyone on firearms charges. I just need to know where the gun was stored and who knew that it might be there."

Bob took a long while to answer "If I tell you I won't end up in the shit?" he asked: Mark gave him his word.

"I looked after it for him." he said, "It was a ropey owd thing that his Dad give 'im when he were a kid, it weren't worth nowt, but Mike liked it, and he must have killed shed loads of game wih it in his time. After he got banned he kept it in a cupboard at our 'ouse; the last time I saw it were early this afternoon when Mike called to pick it up: I don't bloody imagine it'll ever come back to our place agin now will it Inspector?"

Chapter Twenty Four

It was sometime after ten o'clock the following morning when Jackie Skinner arrived at the police station carrying a tartan biscuit tin. It was still less than twenty four hours since she had become a widow, and Mark Hobson recognised the supreme effort she had made, at a time of overwhelming personal crisis, to do what she knew to be right.

Understandably, she had slept badly, black rings encircled both of her eyes and she had not tried to hide them. Her three children accompanied her; no relative or friend had been prepared to look after them, and they were tiny, shell-shocked specimens of humanity, with not a spark of vitality between them. The picture this pathetic little group presented was a painfully disturbing one. Life wasn't fair. Mark couldn't help liking Jackie, she deserved far better than this, but Fate had dealt her an unquestionably shitty hand and seemed to have allowed for no possibility that her luck might one day improve. Just for a moment Mark wondered how the person who had murdered Mike Skinner would feel if he could witness firsthand the impact that his ruthless act of slaughter had had on innocent lives. It was pointless conjecture of course; Mark knew in reality he would feel absolutely nothing. Whoever the killer was he had a tunnel-visioned view of life;

wrongs had to be put right, people had to be punished, and whatever collateral damage was caused in the process of doing so mattered not a jot: nothing could not be permitted to stand in the way of him achieving his goal: oblivious to everything other than the dark forces that drove him on, the avenger didn't care who he hurt, or who he sacrificed on the altar of his revenge. The only thing that was important was the outcome, and if innocent people were destroyed en route that was a minor detail: a pretty, uncomplicated, hard working woman like Jacqueline was of no consequence whatsoever.

She didn't really say much, there was nothing much she could say, and she didn't want to stay long at the police station. Mark's genuinely made offers of help went almost unheard, and his promise to keep her informed of events as they unfolded barely seemed to register. Mark watched with feelings of anger and pity as this poor woman and her bewildered brood left the police station in dejection to return to a world of struggle and uncertainty

It took a little time for the Detective Inspector to shake off his emotional response to the personal tragedy that had all but crushed one struggling member of the human race. Perhaps he was getting old, perhaps it was having a wife who cared, perhaps it was the prospect of fatherhood, but it was no longer as easy as it once had been, to remain detached from the plight of the blameless victims of crime. Eventually he forced himself to act. He picked up the tin and carefully removed the lid. It was full of photographs and hand written notes, some of which had been bound together with elastic bands and all of which first saw the light of day at least one generation back in time.

The box contained a large number of old love letters, from a variety of teenage girls, all addressed to "Freddie" Skinner, who self evidently had had no problem in attracting female admiration. The box also contained picture postcards from mates and random notes from various sources reminding him about sports fixtures and other planned activities. There were also one or two birthday cards from relatives which had once enclosed gifts of money to mark eighteenth and twenty first birthdays, and on some of these Freddie had scrawled unkind words like "stingy" and "scrooge" and on one of them he had added the whinging comment "Crawford would have done much more for me than this." There were photographs too, and when Mark examined them they turned out to be a pretty eclectic mix. There were pictures of local football and cricket teams, snaps of a motley collection of drinking pals, and there were a great many of young women and girls, some of which had writing on them. Phrases like "All My Love" and "Eternally Yours" were scribbled across some of the eager young unthinking faces.

The particular print that Bob Leather had mentioned, and the one that Hobson was most eager to find was not difficult to pick out, and Leather's description of it proved to be spot on. As well as the people mentioned by Bob, the print showed that two other persons had been present. They were two young girls: one was unmistakably the teenage Virginia Brocklehurst; the other was a slightly younger girl who looked tense and uncomfortable on this fading pictorial record. Fortunately for the police, somebody had written, in a very neat hand, an endorsement on the reverse side of the photograph. The endorsement read "Taken at Hill Top farm—February 12th 1979". For the first time the police now had clear, indisputable evidence that Virginia had been in the Peak District, at more or less exactly the same time that Lucas Norton died.

There was one final letter which caught Mark's attention. So far as it was possible to tell it had been written just a few days after the photograph had been taken. It was addressed to "My Gorgeous Freddie" and had obviously been composed by somebody very young and unhappy as at times the writer appeared to be almost hysterical. In the letter she told Alfred that she was being sent away in disgrace and that she might never see him again, and she blamed "nasty little John" for spoiling everything. There was bitterness, anguish and painful immaturity, and also a great number of swear words, which seemed quite shocking coming from the mouth of one so young. The writer expressed her undying hatred of the pathetic snivelling John, and a detestation of "horrid little children everywhere." She begged Freddie to run away with her, and there were a many protestations of love and fidelity. The foot of the page was smothered in kisses and the writer had drawn a heart with an arrow through it and printed the words "Ginny loves Freddie" in capital letters. The more he thought about it, the more Mark became convinced that "Ginny could only be "Virginia" and, for the first time, he understood the motive for her aggressive behaviour two decades before. A sexually abused and emotionally disturbed child, used as a sex toy by a sick minded pervert for his own gratification and then cast to one side whenever it suited him, could very easily have been attracted to a good looking, shallow teenager, and imagined herself to be in love with him. If she had then been expelled from the community that she thought she would always belong to when her only crime was to be a victim and, if the catalyst for this cruel action had been the prying eyes of a childish little boy, then it was not surprising that she would feel anger and bitterness not only towards him, but also towards anybody else who she thought came out of the same mould.

In Mark Hobson's eyes the photograph and the letter strongly suggested that the murders of Virginia Brocklehurst and Mike

Skinner were linked, even though, as yet, he had no evidence at all to establish any connection between the two victims. They had moved in very different circles and, however similar their origins might have been, they had ended up inhabiting different social spheres. Had they been seen together, and in a small town like Burrdale they would have been seen if they were together, people would have talked, but mouths had remained tightly closed; there had been no knowing gossip that he was aware of, but that said, even the best *bush telegraph* in Derbyshire couldn't know everything. Secret meetings away from prying eyes could have occurred and communication by phone or other means could have taken place, and there were a number of lines of inquiry that the police still had to pursue. Was it possible that Skinner had used the documents he had found to extort money from Virginia? Certainly the £2000 that Mike had told Jackie he had won on the horses would have been little more than small change to her, but Mike still had the picture and the letter and Virginia would have insisted on having them in return for any payment she made to him. It would also have been a dangerous game for her to play. She could never be sure that Skinner hadn't taken copies, indeed even a moronic blackmailer would have done so, and these could be used to cause future embarrassment or to squeeze additional payments from her. There was also no way of knowing if there was any more material somewhere in the pipeline. It was perfectly possible that the only photograph that existed with the potential to harm Virginia was the one that lay on Mark Hobson's desk, but it was equally possible there could be other photographs: Mike Skinner had been a street-wise, devious man who could well have spirited away items for later use. Virginia Brocklehurst, if she was being blackmailed, must have feared that was the case and thus, perhaps, had the strongest of motives to wish him dead, but she had been killed a fortnight before Mike died, and death had given her the perfect alibi. It was of course conceivable that she had paid somebody to do the job for her. She had had ample means to do so, and life in certain areas of Manchester came pretty cheaply, but, given the publicity her own bizarre and brutal murder had received, Mark reasoned that a contract killer would simply have taken the money and run. He wouldn't have risked detection by continuing with the crime when the intended victim meant nothing to him and there was not the slightest need to carry on with the contract because the woman who had paid him would never know if he chose not to do so. In addition, the manner of Mike's death didn't bear any of the hallmarks of a professional hit.

The other person who certainly had paid money to Mike Skinner was Richard Norton. He was a man haunted by memories of a twenty year old tragedy and everybody in Burrdale knew that fact. If Skinner had been drip feeding information to him, piece by piece, with a hefty price tag attached to every small snippet that was revealed, it would have been easy money. If Mike had become greedy and had withheld the most damning evidence to increase the cash payments he obtained, it was not difficult to imagine Norton losing his temper and perhaps threatening Skinner with his own gun, which could even have gone off accidentally. The fundamental flaw to this thesis was that Norton had been in police custody at the time of the death and could not possibly have committed the murder unless the *Grim Reaper's* estimates of time had been catastrophically off the mark.

If not Virginia (dead) or Norton (in a police cell), then who else could it be? Mark sought the input of the two Detective Sergeants to see if either of them had a theory to place upon the table. There was a divergence of opinion between the two men. Paul pointed out that the death of Virginia was almost theatrical in its conception, a piece of pure melodrama, a link in death between modern history and ancient folklore; whereas the murder of Skinner had no style at all, and could even have been unpremeditated. He felt that this incident might well turn out to be a stand alone killing. Alan disagreed: he felt that although the level of thought that had gone into the second murder was considerably less than that which had gone into the first, that was possibly because the murderer had had to react to events, rather than choreograph the whole grisly pantomime. It was at this point that the three officers were joined by Detective Superintendent John Lomas and Deputy Chief Constable Terry Goddard.

Mr Goddard was nearing retirement. He had thirty five years service under his belt and, when time permitted he was now embarked upon a sort of valedictory tour of outlying police stations to say his farewells. He had started off his long career at nearby Buxton and had always retained a particular interest in events that happened in the High Peak. The debate between the officers intrigued him. Goddard was an affable man with a great deal of experience behind him and, at this stage of his career, an understandable tendency, on occasions, to reminisce.

"How would you commit the perfect murder?" he asked, "and, more importantly, how would you cover your tracks to throw the police off the scent?" The question was not one that demanded an answer as the D.C.C. was already launching himself into a story.

"A long time ago," he said, "when I was a young Detective Sergeant, I dealt with the most ghastly murder it's possible to imagine. The victim was a young woman, an attractive girl, who worked as a legal secretary for a well established law firm. On her way home from the office, on a cold winter's evening, she was attacked and killed. I have never seen so much blood either before or since. Her skull had been fragmented by repeated blows with a heavy iron bar, leaving her face unrecognisable: even her own father didn't know who she was, and for years afterwards he suffered terrible nightmares. The frenzy of the attack was beyond comprehension. Robbery was put forward as a probable motive because her purse was missing and everybody, including me, thought that the killer was likely to be some deranged lunatic, high on heroin or LSD.

We were all wrong, although I had changed my opinion by the time an arrest was made. The killer turned out to be her husband. He was a brilliant accountant and the most immaculate, fastidious, well organised, self-controlled and logical person you could ever hope to meet. He had begun an affair with a work colleague of his wife's, who wasn't particularly beautiful as I recall it, and his wife had found out. The night before the killing she'd told him that she was going to sue for divorce, which would have been at a terrific cost to him, but she hadn't taken any steps to instruct a solicitor, nor had she told anyone of her plans as her parents were on holiday and she hadn't wanted to spoil their holiday for them. She'd thought things could wait until they returned home. In that belief she was tragically mistaken.

Her husband coldly and clinically planned her death: he had reasoned, with good cause, that the police would be searching for a maniac, not a member of the Rotary Club. His plan almost worked, but he was such an arrogant sod that he made the hackles on the back of my neck stand up and that was an unwise thing to do." Mr Goddard smiled a self satisfied smile as he continued to tell the story. "Whilst everybody else was looking for an outsider, I started to look for evidence to pin the crime on him. Eventually, it came in the form of minute specks of blood found on one of his shoes. He was also dropped in it by his new girlfriend who became frightened of him and some of the things he said to her in the heat of love making. A decade or so before and he would have hanged, and that would have been the best thing that could have happened to him. The point of this story gentlemen is that the most unlikely people are capable of doing absolutely anything so don't be surprised if there aren't a lot more twists and turns left in this inquiry before it's complete."

Mr Goddard then told one further story. When he was barely out of his probationary period, in the summer of 1975, there had been a vicious knife attack in Burrdale, when a twenty one year old man had been targeted because some of the local residents believed him to be *queer*. The first stab wound had been to the small of the back as the victim had tried to walk away from trouble, and there had been at least another six blows with a carving knife before his attackers had fled. They had worn masks and the injured man, who nearly died from his horrific injuries, had been unable to identify them and, although arrests were made, with no eye witness testimony and no forensic evidence on which to build a case, no charges were ever brought.

Two local children had seen the incident and had named names, but, at the ages of 5 and 7 respectively, it had been felt by the prosecuting authorities that they were too young to give evidence at a trial. It might have been different today with video evidence and Special Measures being available, but none of that applied then and, as a consequence, two guilty men went free and later even gloated about the brutal assault. The two boys, as Goddard recalled it, were inseparable companions; the elder one was Mike Skinner, the younger one was Shane Chadwick, and Mark rued the fact that he hadn't known this earlier. It was likely that Skinner of all people could have given the definitive answer as to whether the boy in the photograph really was Shane Chadwick although Mark had to accept that in all probability he would have refused to say anything to the police at all.

The conversation then turned briefly to matters personal. Mr Goddard asked Mark how he was keeping and Mark joked about being knackered and how much worse he might feel when Helena had the baby. He didn't say anything about Helena's health, but it was common knowledge at the nick that his wife's pregnancy was turning out to be a very difficult one.

Chapter Twenty Five

The murder of Mike Skinner, coming on top of the murder of Virginia Brocklehurst as it did, was playing havoc with Mark's home life. The pattern of the last five days had been long periods of work, interspersed with short periods of rest, and the time he valued most, the time he spent with Helena, hearing her voice, watching her face, dreaming, planning, supporting, listening and learning had almost ceased to exist; he deeply regretted that fact. Although they were inching towards a date when the baby would arrive, progress often seemed to be painfully slow. These were hard times for Helena. Mark wondered if things would have been so bad if she hadn't lost their first child. He didn't know, and there was no way of telling, but, in his heart of hearts, he was sure that they wouldn't be. She could not lie comfortably in bed, she couldn't get enough sleep, and she was still feeling sick every single day. She worried about losing this baby and she worried about her father's pending operation, and all that anxiety did nothing to help her blood pressure: although she didn't say so, she also worried about Mark every time he went to work, particularly when he was investigating bloody and violent crime. She was a bright, lovely, intelligent woman, who loved her husband, as he loved her, and she had qualities of gentleness and goodness which he adored but which made her vulnerable, and certainly unable to develop the thick skin of detachment that so many policemen's wives were able to grow for their own protection.

Because she slept so little during the night, she tended to sleep in fits and starts during the day, and this further reduced the time that she and Mark could talk to each other. As she slept on the sofa, Mark sat and gazed at her as she slumbered. More than anything else in the world, he just wanted her to be alright, and for them to have the strong and healthy baby they both longed for. His mother had said to him many times during his childhood "What you never have you never miss", but that was only partly true. For years before he met Helena, even during the disastrous years when he had been married to Annabel, he had never thought about parenthood and, certainly with the bitterness and recriminations which followed Annabel's death that had been the last thing on his mind. If, even for a second, he had considered fatherhood, whilst anaesthetising his feelings in smoky Islay malt, he would have perceived a child to be an impediment, a millstone and a source of untold problems.

He had never been a father, but for eleven glorious weeks he had thought he was going to become one and everything had seemed set fair. Until Helena miscarried life had been wonderful, and he had allowed himself to dream and, when that dream had shattered it had left a great void. A new dream had begun when Helena became pregnant again, a harder, less certain, more disturbing dream, although still with the promise of a new beginning, but this time only if a difficult and dangerous journey could be completed.

Helena had now carried the new baby for twenty eight weeks, and there were moments when Mark told himself that, if anything happened and the baby had to be born quickly, medical advances would give their son a realistic chance of survival but, if he ever voiced such thoughts to Helena, she would remind him of the inherent dangers involved with premature birth and express her determination to deliver the child full term to give him the best possible basis for a healthy, normal start to life.

Mark remembered the desolation that Helena had felt when she lost their first baby and, although he had tried to heal the distress, for the first time in his life that hadn't been easy to do. What had really upset him was the knowledge that she believed herself to be a failure, and that she had somehow let him down by not being able to perform one of the most fundamental tasks of Nature, essential for the continuance of any species. He had held her and loved her, and told her that she was so precious and so special, and that she would always be the very best in his eyes, and he had promised her that things would come right again. Eventually she had allowed herself to hope afresh, but now that hope was always tinged with fear and Mark dreaded what might happen if this second child was lost or damaged: it would destroy Helena and if she were destroyed, then he was undone. There was nothing else worth living for; it was as simple and as stark as that.

Briefly, his thoughts turned to Jacqueline Skinner. She had three healthy children and, so far as Mark was aware, had never experienced the difficulties and setbacks in pregnancy that Helena was now experiencing; but in her household tonight anxiety and uncertainty were in command, and there was no strong reliable figure to advise, assist and re-assure that poor, distraught woman. Without intending to, Mark groaned as the sadness of that family overwhelmed him, and that noise, although not loud, broke through Helena's blanket of sleep and pulled her back into the realm of consciousness.

"Oh, I've been asleep again, I'm so sorry," she said. "I'm afraid I'm not much company for you at the moment. You've had a busy day. The last thing you need is to come home and find me asleep; I do so much want to know what you've been doing, and I know that you need to talk about things just to unwind but, instead, you're met with this silent, silly, senseless woman," and she reached for her husband and her eyes started to fill with tears. Mark held her very tight and put a gentle finger on her lips,

"Don't talk like that Helena," he said. "Just the fact that we're together makes me feel strong. I'll never be able to tell you exactly how much you mean to me but it's everything, and the thought that you are going to be the mother of my son is awesome. Waking or sleeping, it doesn't matter a jot. Being here, being mine are the only things that count and I wouldn't change that situation for the whole world."

"I love you, Mark," said Helena. "I love you so much that sometimes I dream about you, and when I wake up and you're here I have to pinch myself to make sure I'm still not dreaming; but sometimes I dream that I've lost you and that you're never coming back to me, and I wake up terrified that that dream will come true. You mean so much to me."

"I'm going nowhere, my Darling," said Mark. "You're stuck with me until Hell freezes over and then some; give me a smile and a cuddle and I'll make us both a coffee and you can tell me about your day."

As they drank, they talked about many things. They talked about the baby and about the future and about their lives together and about how much things had changed for the two of them, even in the comparatively short time since they moved to Burrdale.

"I'm still adjusting every day," said Mark. "For a small town with half a dozen pubs, three churches and a few shops it's a surprisingly difficult place to get the feel of. Maybe I need large housing estates, maybe that's what I'm suited to. I can feel the pulse of a city with much greater ease than I can understand the moods of this infuriating little town. You've got to have lived here six generations at least before you're regarded as local but, when you're accepted, then I think the place gets under your skin and into your blood and you develop a mind set, an understanding, a way of looking at things and a way of doing things that is peculiar to here. I'm sure if I had that mindset now, the Virginia Brocklehurst case would be a great deal easier to solve. People round here talk about the "Street" and the "Consti" and it means nothing to me. "The Jubilee" pub is universally referred to as the "Drum", which was the former name of the inn in Victorian days, there hasn't been a Massey at Massey's Farm since the end of World War 1, and there hasn't been a gibbet in Gibbet Field for over two centuries; and that's only the beginning!

The locals refer quite glibly to "Scoop" or "Bobcat" and expect me to know who they're talking about. Alan Nadin is often called "Slogger" because of his ability to smash cricket balls all over the ground when he was a young man. I know three teenage lads called Ross, two of whom have the nickname "Rusty" because of their red hair, and it doesn't help that they're both related to each other! Gypsies and tinkers frequently give children names identical to their fathers, and they swap identities at the drop of a hat, but that's deliberately done to confuse the authorities. It isn't like that here. It's just that everybody takes it for granted that everyone knows what everybody else is talking about and if you're a Wainwright, a Bagshawe, a Skinner, a Leather or a Norton, and that covers virtually two thirds the entire population of the town aged over fifty, then they're probably right!"

Helena smiled as she listened to Mark's litany of complaints. "Poor you," she said, "but it must be the same for every newcomer, and I'm sure you're a lot better at remembering names and working out the location of places than most of the recent arrivals here."

Mark shook his head, "Paul Burgess is far better at it than me, but, then again, he's a card carrying member of the same club, so I suppose it comes naturally to him."

"What do you mean by that?" asked Helena, looking more than a little perplexed at Mark's enigmatic statement.

"He doesn't talk much about himself does Paul, and sometimes he's quite touchy when people ask him about his personal life, but he once mentioned in passing that he had an Auntie, I think he said her name was Jill but I'm not entirely sure, who family and friends alike referred to as Auntie "Jenny" because her maiden name had been Wren. In the end she used that Christian name herself and most of her husband's family never knew or suspected that she had an entirely different name on her birth certificate. So, you see love, he knows all about things not being what they seem, and people not being who or what they appear to be. Do you know, Paul came here only six months before we did, but he's mastered the local geography and the local history, and seems to have a crystal clear understanding of who is related to whom, and how this bloody contrary little place ticks? As you know darling, we asked the public to contact the police, if they had any information about the Virginia Brocklehurst killing. Ollerenshaw and Nadin both received dozens of phone calls, which is not surprising because they've both been here since the dawn of time and have put down roots. Paul Burgess got a call, admittedly it turned out to be a wild goose chase, but that's not the point. Do you know how many calls I got? I'll tell you! Zero, zilch, nil points, sweet F.A!"

"You're just jealous," teased Helena. "If you were as young and as good looking as Paul then you might have received a bucket full of calls yourself."

"Are you saying that I'm not as handsome as Paul?" laughed Mark. "Then, in that case, I'm deeply hurt and I withdraw all the nice things I said about you before. You're just a bad person, with a totally distorted view of humanity."

Helena was giggling now and her smile illuminated the darkest recesses of Mark's mind.

"He's a bright lad," he said, "a very bright lad. He'll go a long, long way, and maybe he'll take a very glamorous young woman with him, although that remains to be seen, but he'll never be as lucky as me. Even if he rises to the rank of Chief Constable, he'll not have the success in his life that you've given me in mine;" and he kissed his wife and they both lay together on the settee, in each other's arms.

Chapter Twenty Six

The Vixen and Cubs Inn is a forty minute car journey from Burrdale and, as such, is seldom visited by any of the townspeople. Once, it had enjoyed a great reputation for exciting and adventurous cooking and, for a short while, had been the *in place to go;* but several changes of chef, and a succession of short term landlords and temporary managers had put paid to all that. Its reputation had plummeted. Determined efforts were now being made to turn things around, and some success was being achieved, but it was still a long way away from re-capturing its former glory, and certainly it didn't appear in the *Egon Ronay Guide* or feature on any list of places that Paul Burgess would have chosen to dine.

He had wanted to take Becky to the famous Red Grouse Restaurant, which consistently topped the *Derbyshire Good Food Guide's* lists of places to eat, and frequently earned high praise in regional and national food magazines. It was very, very expensive, much more than he could really afford, but she needed something to help her put her ordeal at the hands of the police behind her so he had decided to splash out. When he had told her of his plans he had expected her to be overjoyed, but, instead of being excited, she had refused point blank to go. He had cancelled the booking with more than a little loss of face, and he had then suggested that the Burrdale Bistro, or the Royal Albert, both of which were highly recommended, would be nice places to eat, but she had rejected them both out of hand. For a long while it had seemed as if she would decline to go out with him altogether, and he had wracked his brains to think of some way to make her change her mind. Eventually he had hit upon The Vixen and Cubs and she has agreed to go there, and, on the basis that anywhere was better than nowhere, he had jumped at the chance. So it was they sat together, just one of three couples, in a large dining room waiting for their starters of moules marinieres and grilled goats cheese with cherry tomatoes and salad, to arrive, chosen principally because neither dish gave too much scope for total disaster if the new chef turned out to be no better than some of his unlamented predecessors had been

Becky was not relaxed, which meant that Paul was also tense, and there were long periods of silence briefly interrupted by odd moments of strained conversation. The contentious subject of Becky's arrest was studiously avoided. Eventually Paul couldn't take any more. "Honest to God Becky, I've tried. I've told Hobson that he's barking up the wrong tree, and almost flushed my career down the pan in the process of doing so. Nobody could have done more, I've stuck up for you, I love you, I believe in you, so why are you giving me such a hard time?" he asked.

"Oh, you think you're having a hard time do you? Have you got a father cursing and swearing one minute, then breaking down in tears at the next? Is anybody spreading rumours about you? No, I didn't think so! Do you know that I'm supposed to have been dragged, kicking and screaming and thrown into a police riot van? Are people saying that you're about to be charged with being an accessory to a murder? Is anybody predicting the sort of vile things that will happen to you when you end up in prison?" bristled Becky, barely managing to control her emotions as she spoke.

"But none of that is true, is it?" cried Paul; "Hobson told me himself that you'd been released without charge and under no threat of further investigation."

"Of course it's not true, but can't you see that doesn't matter in the slightest? It's what people think is true that counts and, right now, I rank somewhere between Ruth Ellis and Myra Hindley in the league table of wicked women of the world, in a lot of peoples' minds."

"So that's why you wouldn't let me show you off and we've ended up in this dump." blurted out Paul, just as the waiter arrived to remove empty plates from the table. He was not best pleased to overhear this unflattering judgment delivered on his place of work, and the routine inquiry about the acceptability of the meal so far, which he had always been taught to make, was left sullenly unsaid. His comments in the kitchen, out of the earshot of the paying customers were somewhat less than complimentary.

"How can I possibly go out in Burrdale when a lot of people believe I'm about to follow in the footsteps of Jonathan Aitken? Some people have always resented the fact that my dad tried to give me every advantage in life. Now it's payback time and all because twenty years ago, my eight year old brother was killed by a stupid little moron, egged on by an evil little tart."

"It wasn't deliberate," said Paul. "It wasn't planned. It was a tragedy that happened before you were born, and I can't have been more than five years old, but it is still ruining lives, even after all this time. Surely we have to move on? You've said so yourself, and you've pleaded with me to try to convince your dad that should be the case."

"And I was wrong wasn't I? I know that now. It's impossible. Round here we don't forget, and we certainly don't forgive. I remember when I was nine or ten years old, when Crawford Winston was being tried for child abuse, half the town was scared witless about what he would disclose, and the other half was busy churning out sordid stories about events that happened thirty, forty, even fifty years before. My dad can never change, and I can't change my dad and none of us can change the past. When

I'm eighty, if I get to live that long, people will still point a finger at me and say "She was once arrested on suspicion of being involved in a murder. Nothing was ever proved, but..." and, for a second time, Paul felt that Becky was about to get up and run from the restaurant.

"Becky, don't leave! For Christ's sake, this is madness! Don't torture yourself with your dad's bitterness! Come away with me, we could go tomorrow, start a new life somewhere, anywhere together, and never worry about this bloody place and its bloody people ever again!"

Rebecca shook her head "It isn't that easy Paul," she said. "Don't you think I haven't thought about doing that, but how can I? If I left him it would kill him, and I couldn't live with that on my conscience. You must understand that!"

"But why is he so bad now?" asked Paul. "Shane Chadwick is dead, Virginia is dead, and if she was the person who caused everything, surely the manner of her death and the way her body was treated after death is sufficient punishment even to satisfy the demands of your father. It would certainly be enough to satisfy me."

"You don't understand the half of it. Your Inspector Hobson thinks the deaths of Virginia and Mike Skinner are linked. That's good enough for my dad and he's not going to settle now until all the facts are known. There's another thing as well. He believes

Mike Skinner knew far more than has come out so far. He certainly seems to have told dad that he had information that would be devastating if it was known, but he wanted a lot of money before he'd divulge it. Dad's now convinced that out there something is hidden which could dramatically change our lives, and he can't rest now until he finds it,"

"Your dad's insane," snapped Paul then, seeing the anger on Rebecca's face and sensing the movement of her chair, he immediately recanted.

"I'm sorry, Love," he said. "I didn't mean to say that, but he's wrong and it's all down to Hobson's obsession. Just consider the facts for a moment. Suppose Virginia was the mystery girl, and it's looking increasingly likely that she was, who would have had a motive for killing her? There is only one person I can think of and that's your dad. Nobody else would want vengeance after all this time would they? Given your dad's obvious frustration at her death I don't think he killed her, and we know that he couldn't possibly have killed Skinner, so it has to be someone else. The police know next to nothing about Virginia's early life, but she seems to have succeeded against all the odds. God knows how many people she might have stepped upon on her way to the top. If somebody hated her enough, and knew some of her past secrets, how easy would it have been to lay a false trail? All you would need would be a lot of bottle, a bit of luck and a gullible detective inspector and you could commit murder and escape scot free."

"I don't think that Hobson's gullible" said Becky, "I'm sure he's pretty clued up. He certainly wouldn't have terrified me as much as he did if he'd been rushing around like a headless chicken, but let's drop the subject. The whole thing is just too depressing. I can't see any way out of the mess we're in and I really don't want to think about it anymore."

At that point the rest of the meal arrived: it didn't inspire, but it did provide them with a reason to stop talking so both Paul and Becky took refuge in their own thoughts, and finished their food in near silence, and without any sense of pleasure or enjoyment.

Chapter Twenty Seven

The police file on Richard Norton had been destroyed in 1989. For logistical and other reasons it had been common practice in the 1970's and 1980's for police forces to keep closed files for no longer than ten years. Murder files were treated differently, of course. They were retained in perpetuity. Dick Norton had not killed anyone nor had he caused physical harm to any individual: but mental scars, they were a different matter, and his uncontrolled fury had left indelible marks that had permanently damaged lives. The fact that there was no paper work didn't surprise Detective Inspector Hobson and in reality it didn't make a great deal of difference

He knew in broad terms what the case file would have contained. The eye witness accounts of Mr and Mrs Chadwick would have described the amount of damage done and the level of fear they experienced. A monetary value would have been put upon the shattered and splintered objects and some indication would have been given as to their feelings about the ordeal they had undergone, although there would be no formal Victim Impact Statement as had become the norm in later years. In addition to the evidence of the civilian witnesses, the police officers who attended the scene would have recounted what they saw, and no doubt would have emphasised how violent and how difficult Norton had been when he was arrested. Finally, there would have been the record of the police interview, which in this case had been a full and frank, not to say boastful, admission, followed in due course by an early guilty plea. Mark felt that it was likely that there was nothing in any of that which would have significantly advanced his inquiry. Had the Unused Material still existed, that might have been a different matter, and things not relevant in 1979 could potentially be crucial twenty years on; but all that had been destroyed and there was nothing he or anyone else could do about that.

The Coroner's file dealing with the death of Lucas Norton should have been a richer seam of information, but a fire in 1994 had destroyed all the records between 1962 and that date. It had been caused by an electrical fault and was not in any way suspicious, but it did mean that another source of material that could have assisted the police was no longer available to them. All that really remained intact for Mark to study were the back editions of the local newspapers.

Crawford Winston's case file, although it post-dated that of Richard Norton by almost ten years, was caught up by the same difficulties. Because his crimes had been those of Indecent Assault and Gross Indecency there would be a Scotland Yard record of the conviction and his fingerprints would also have been preserved (these days there would also have been D.N.A. samples which would have gone onto the police national data base; but that was not the case then, and Mark Hobson couldn't help but consider how much the whole process of crime detection had changed during the currency of his police service). Once again though, it meant that the only available sources of contemporary eye witness accounts left open to him were the archives of the *Burrdale Advertiser,* and perhaps also the *Derbyshire Times,* the *Glossop Chronicle* and the *Matlock Mercury* if they had covered aspects of the story.

Once upon a time, a trawl through past editions of newspapers had been a fairly unattractive job. Mark remembered occasions in South Yorkshire and in London when he had spent hours in gloomy, dusty cellars painstakingly reading yellowing broadsheets and laboriously making long hand notes of any fragment of information that appeared to have the remotest relevance to the inquiry in hand. Sometimes that process had had to be repeated and repeated because there was more than one newspaper circulating in the area where the crime had taken place. It was all very different now: a trip to the library, a bright and airy room, a computer screen, a printer, and cups of coffee virtually on demand to sustain the researcher in his task. This was one area where progress came without baggage, and was not in fierce competition with nostalgia.

Despite the comfortable surroundings, however, it was still a daunting task. As soon as Mark started to open up the pages of the newspaper it became evident that the little box hidden in his loft only told a small fragment of the whole story. When Lucas Norton had disappeared the search for him had involved not only the police, but also hundreds of local volunteers, who had braved sub zero temperatures, howling winds and near horizontal snow to look for the little boy; that much was already known. What Mark hadn't known about were the problems that had beset the search. Frozen diesel had made vehicles almost impossible to start, broken power lines had interrupted the supply of electricity and, misery and frustration had been caused because many country roads had become impassable because of the ever deepening snowdrifts. His scrap books had not concerned themselves with the mechanics of the search.

When the small body of Lucas was finally discovered, there had been an outpouring of public sympathy and the funeral of the child, held after a post mortem had confirmed the cause of death to be drowning and discovered no other injuries or suspicious circumstances, had been attended by hundreds of mourners despite the bitterly cold weather conditions.

Richard Norton had been insistent on a burial; the idea of flames consuming the earthly remains of his precious child had both sickened and appalled him. Maybe he had still prayed for a miracle, maybe he had hoped beyond reason that, somehow, like Lazarus, Lucas would breathe again. Try as the vicar and the undertaker might to persuade him that cremation was a better option, given the rock hard ground and the Arctic temperatures he had not given an inch. With extreme difficulty, and with the aid of large braziers to soften the frozen soil, which were kept burning for three days, a trench had been dug, the grave diggers cursing with every thrust of their spades Richard Norton's obduracy and pig-headedness.

The dramatic actions of Norton when he learnt about the events that immediately preceded his son's death had also been widely reported; indeed the press had had a feeding frenzy. Pictures of the wrecked house had been published in more than one newspaper. It wasn't the scattered debris of the wrecked television set, or the slashed furniture, or even the smashed windows and doors that grabbed the attention: it was the family photograph of a smiling six year old little boy lying amid splinters and shards of glass that was the most haunting image. The picture had been ground under foot, crushed and stamped upon in fury and in loathing, and the photographs of its destruction had the most unforgettable impact.

From big stories little of value is often found. A long time ago Mark Hobson had learned from a battle scarred detective sergeant that it is the small, seemingly irrelevant footnotes to the main narrative that often hold the key. He had read all the accounts of a historic crime in the local papers and had then reported to his senior officer that nothing of value could be discovered. The sergeant had thrown his report, the product of many hours of work, into the waste paper bin and had told him to go back and examine the letter pages of the various journals that circulated in the area of the crime. By careful reading and with meticulous attention to detail and this time in full command of his brief, Mark had eventually discovered a letter which attacked the police for incompetence and insensitivity and which contained information about the crime which was strikingly accurate, but had only become known to the police with the benefit of hindsight and with recent scientific re-examination. As a result of that discovery a twelve year old crime had ultimately been solved and a brutal sexual predator had been locked away behind bars for the rest of his life.

Cheered by memories of that success Mark turned his attention to the musings of the good citizens of Burrdale about the circumstances that surrounded the crimes he was currently investigating.

The start was not a promising one; the letters which were published during the period that Lucas remained missing turned out to be either simple expressions of sympathy or unthinking attacks on Local Authority and other workers for not gritting the roads or repairing the power lines, and holding them responsible if some terrible tragedy should befall a lonely frightened little boy. The letters that immediately followed the confirmation of the death were in a similar vein, and apart from showing the extent, to which a very local tragedy had touched the whole community, did nothing at all to assist Mark in his investigation.

The reaction to Richard Norton's violent attack on the Chadwick household largely fell into two categories. There were some people, although in a minority, who called for "restraint" and "forgiveness." These were mainly members of the various churches, but their letters were full of Christian platitudes and, for the most part, lacked real depth and genuine understanding, and there seemed to be an absence of true compassion which made some of them appear very superficial. The other category of letters was more strident, blaming society, television and bad parenting for the actions of Shane Chadwick and almost endorsing the cruelty and anger of Richard Norton. The number of these letters multiplied considerably after Richard Norton's Crown Court hearing, helped no doubt by the fact that the day before his appearance for sentence, he had been photographed in the church yard, now bright with daffodils and bathed in sunlight, standing alone and inconsolable next to the gravestone of his lost child whilst all around him new life blossomed.

There was one letter, however that was different from the rest. It was intelligent, articulate, caring, understanding and packed with sound common sense. The writer, a Mrs C.L. Hambleton had chosen her words carefully. She asked for tolerance and understanding and her letter contained genuine pity for Richard Norton and also for Mr and Mrs Chadwick: the writer clearly had personal knowledge of all the parties concerned and her words resonated across the page in a way that no other correspondent's letter had managed to achieve. It was the sort of letter Mark knew Helena might have written in the circumstances and which would have been entirely beyond him; there was a fundamental decency about the piece that struck him, and when he later discussed the letter with Alan Nadin and Paul Burgess, they both agreed with his assessment, and Paul added that he believed she had always been the same.

The opinions expressed after the trial of Crawford Winston were universally hostile towards him. The court had branded him a "paedophile" and a "sexual deviant", and the judge had used words like "loathsome" and "abhorrent" to describe the man in the dock when passing sentence.

Almost every single reader agreed with the judge's assessment, and many of the letters bemoaned the fact that the sentence hadn't been harsher. Had some of the more extreme scribes been able to impose their will, castration, flogging, branding and mutilation would all have been considered to be appropriate penalties. The revulsion felt towards Winston seemed to extend towards other members of his family. His wife had been spat at and manhandled, his children had been ostracised and vandalism had been directed towards his home and his car. There had been the danger of a "lynch mob" mentality developing, and the ineffectual bleating of the then vicar and his favoured flock had done nothing to calm the turbulent emotions which were threatening to engulf the town.

Amidst all the hysteria one voice spoke out yet again: it was Mrs Hambleton, and her heartfelt plea that the innocent shouldn't be punished along with the guilty was well argued, thoughtful, convincing and compelling. She seemed to be the sole voice of sanity in a disturbed and manic world and Mark thought that of all the opinions that had been expressed, hers were the only ones that were really worth listening to. The contrast between her intelligent humanity and the bellicose stupidity of so many other contributors was stark. The image of Tony Patterson floated into his mind, it wasn't a welcome sight, but it caused Mark to wonder how often this self-opinionated bag of wind had been reported in the local paper; he presumed it must have been thousands of times. As a brief distraction from his primary task he typed Patterson's name into his computer and instructed it to search against it. It was as he suspected, he had featured many times, mostly as a councillor or a political activist, but also for a brief time as a judge in a photographic competition run by the *Advertiser* for young people up to the age of 16 years. He had been scathing in his comments; no allowance had been made for youth. His brutal assessment of the children's work had angered many readers; the competition had become an annual event, but Patterson had never been asked to judge it again.

As Mark read with amusement a surprisingly good character assassination of the arrogant judge by a 13 year old competitor with a nice line in humorous invective, his attention was drawn to a photograph on the same page of the newspaper. The article in which it appeared was headed "Bangkok or bust!" and immediately Mark thought the story would be about an endurance race or some sort of charity event. He was completely wrong. The picture was of a group of local businessmen about to set out on a business trip to India and then to South East Asia. The thing that was unusual about the photograph was the unmistakable presence of Tony Patterson. He wasn't employed by any manufacturing firm in the High Peak, he was an avowed enemy of capitalism, and Mark was sure he entirely lacked the knowledge and self control to ever be an effective salesman. He seemed the last person anyone would want to have on a sales and marketing trip, but there he was, as bold as brass; there had to be a reason for that.

The only other snippet of news that made Mark wonder was a very short piece in an edition of the paper from 11 years ago. There had been an incident in the Wellington Inn. A woman had been involved in a violent argument. She had grabbed a dart from the dartboard and hurled it at Tony Patterson, scratching his ample belly but doing no serious harm. A bystander, Mike Skinner, had grabbed her and calmed her down. Patterson had declined to call the police. The woman had been asked to leave the pub, and order had been restored. What it was that sparked the row the paper didn't say, and what was behind Paterson's unusual magnanimity in deciding not to prosecute Mark didn't know. It was food for thought, but not now. Mark had already been sitting at the computer desk for over three hours.

Before his eyes completely succumbed to the strain the computer screen had subjected them to, Mark briefly jumped back in time to the vicious assault Mike Skinner and Shane Chadwick had witnessed so many years before. There was widespread dissatisfaction that no charges had ever been made to stick and letters had appeared condemning the wall of silence that had protected the guilty parties. One or two of the persons who contributed their views on this unsolved crime were people who had also written to the *Advertiser* on later occasions. Like it or not, accept it or not, it was clear to Mark that, despite some loose threads, past, present and future were beginning to weave a single tapestry. It hadn't always been obvious but Mark now knew that one line of investigation had to involve Shane Chadwick, another strand to the inquiry had to focus on the victims of Crawford Winston and, even though others might disagree, Mark was sure long undisturbed stones needed to be overturned to find out just exactly what secrets would crawl from underneath them when exposed to the glaring light of day.

Chapter Twenty Eight

Mark's meeting with John Lomas had been friendly. There had been no carping or criticism, but both the detective superintendent and his inspector had known from the outset that progress had to be made quickly, and that they were now beginning to run out of time. If a trail becomes cold, the task of following it becomes immeasurably more difficult, the public mood hardens, the level of support for the police falls away and the media become increasingly critical and antagonistic.

The two men had analysed the current state of the evidence and Mark had informed his boss of the new lines of inquiry he was hoping to initiate. John Lomas had endorsed his D.I.'s reasoning and had asked to sit in on discussions Mark intended to hold with Paul Burgess and Alan Nadin, prior to briefing all the officers attached to this double murder investigation: so it was that four policemen of different rank and with very diverse opinions were closeted together in a small office assessing the health of the inquiry to date.

"Let me ask you all the same question." said Mark. "Who is the one person who connects Mike Skinner, Lucas Norton, Richard Norton and, so far as we are aware, Virginia Brocklehurst? Let me give you my answer. I think the only person who fits the bill is Shane Chadwick. I know I may be barking up the wrong tree, but just run with me on this one for a few moments and let me explain. Virginia Brocklehurst by her actions ruined the lives of Shane Chadwick and his parents and also shattered and distorted the life of Richard Norton. Until now we have all believed that the entire Chadwick family fled Burrdale in 1979, never to return, but just consider for one second the possibility that Shane could have come back. Nobody would recognise him after all this time would they, except maybe somebody who had been his best friend as a child. Suppose Shane killed Virginia in revenge for causing him a lifetime of misery, suppose he then dumped her body into the very pool in which Lucas Norton died after first taking his revenge on her corpse. That would have given him the satisfaction that he must have yearned for all his life, and it would have had the added bonus that it made Richard Norton, who is the other person he could blame for causing his unhappiness, the prime suspect in the murder inquiry which would inevitably follow. If somebody realised who he was, put two and two together and, then tried to blackmail him that would create a situation where he would have to kill again; the most likely person to have suspected his true identity would have been be Mike Skinner, I know this is all pure conjecture, but doesn't it fit all the known facts?"

The faces in the room expressed contrasting emotions. John

Lomas was open-minded but not completely persuaded, Alan Nadin obviously agreed with what he had heard, but Paul Burgess was profoundly unconvinced.

"It's not a bad theory, Boss, as theories go," he said, "but there is just one teeny weenie little fact that drives a coach and horses through this clever little bit of logic. Shane Chadwick is dead. He died six years ago in a squalid, rat infested squat; unless the dead really can walk, and he was so crippled by heroin in life that he could hardly even move then, I don't see any way how he could possibly be our killer."

Mark felt both deflated and ridiculous. "How long have you known that? I admit I should have checked up yesterday, but I had other things on my mind. I take my hat off to you Paul, I really do. You'll be sitting in this chair before nightfall, and you'll be vying with Mr Lomas for his seat within the next couple of months!"

"Oh several weeks ago." said Paul. "I didn't tell you because I didn't think" (he nearly added the words "you'd be daft enough to suspect Shane" but wisely prevented himself from doing so in the nick of time) and instead completed his sentence with the words "it was relevant."

Alan Nadin interrupted at this point. "Is it possible that he may have had a pal or somebody close to him who could have wanted to avenge a soul mate? I know that sounds stupid, but people round here are like bloody elephants, they stick together, they fight each other's battles and they never bloody forget!"

The look on Burgess's face was scornful and incredulous. "Perhaps he had a flipping pen friend or perhaps this is entirely the wrong direction to be going in, and just maybe we might be better employed checking out the past life of the victim herself, rather than trying to find ways of charging a ghost! But I've said all this before and it doesn't seem to make a blind bit of difference."

"We're doing that Paul," said Mark. "It's just that so far none of the officers looking into her background have come up with the tiniest scrap of evidence to point towards a possible killer and, even if her death was in some way linked to her single minded determination to succeed at all costs, there's certainly absolutely nothing to suggest her assassin either knew, or had even heard of, Mike Skinner. I'm still convinced that those two deaths are linked. I think Alan's got a point and that we should keep that option on the table."

"It's your shout Boss," said Paul, but in a manner that was far from enthusiastic.

"You have another slant on the investigation too don't you Mark?" interjected John Lomas.

"Yes Sir, I do. I've been reading all about the trial of Crawford

Winston and, although she wasn't a witness at that trial, we know that Virginia was one of his victims and I think it is more than possible she could have known some of the other victims. She wasn't actually in Derbyshire for very long, but it was long enough for her to become infatuated with Freddie Skinner and it's not beyond the realms of possibility that there were others who she also took a fancy to. Perhaps even more likely is the possibility that she was abused by more than one single person. The Winston trial didn't make much headway in discovering if there'd been a child sex ring operating, certainly nobody else was ever charged with any offence, but rumour and gossip suggested that that may have been the case. Virginia Brocklehurst remembered John Winston from way back and she also had no difficulty in recognising Joe Broadbent. Becky Norton recalls half the adult male population of Burrdale being on tenterhooks during the trial: if Virginia recognised somebody else and wanted to make him pay for his twisted obsessions, especially if outwardly that person was now a respectable family man of some position, he'd be in constant fear of being exposed. Even if that was not her intention, he'd have no way of knowing that, and the only way he could feel safe would be by eliminating the risk altogether. Here again there is also a connection to Mike Skinner through Freddie, which fits in quite nicely with the thesis that our two murders were committed by the same person."

This time there were no unwelcome rabbits pulled from a hat to undermine Mark's conjecture and even Paul Burgess accepted that this could be a legitimate line of enquiry; later this theory did form the main basis of the full scale briefing.

Before that briefing took place however Mark did have a little time to reflect and to prepare. He was angry with himself and he felt a fool; if Paul Burgess could find out about Shane Chadwick then he should have been able to find out as well. Paul should have told him of course, it would have been the proper thing to do, but he should have checked. Mark knew why he hadn't done so and his reasons were understandable but also unacceptable. Helena hadn't slept well for the third night in a row. He'd wanted her to see the doctor to ask him for something to help her sleep, but she was reluctant to take any drugs that could possibly harm the baby. Her blood pressure was also too high and she was continually suffering from headaches; she was being closely monitored and there was an ever present risk that she could be taken in to hospital at any time. Last night they had talked; Mark had spent so little time with her lately that he felt he was neglecting her. He had just wanted to be with her, to be there for her, and to help her through the next few days and weeks. He should have spent the evening at his desk on the computer, but instead he had gone home; no doubt had he stayed and searched the records they would have confirmed that Chadwick was dead, and had he done so he would have avoided the embarrassment of appearing ill-prepared and inept, but that had never been an option. Even with the benefit of hindsight he would have done the same again, although with hindsight he would certainly have asked Burgess and Nadin if they knew anything about the current whereabouts of Shane Chadwick before launching into his ill-fated theory. Mark also felt just a little hurt. He had so recently offered Paul his support and he had thought that Paul had welcomed it, but there had been something triumphant about the way Paul had shot down the theory in flames. He was obviously a very capable officer, and highly ambitious, but, for the first time, Mark wondered just exactly how far he would go to fulfil that ambition, and whether qualities of friendship and loyalty were already being sacrificed to a self obsessed desire to succeed. There was talk at the police station that things were not going well between Paul and his girlfriend: maybe, thought Mark that could explain the emergence of a colder, angrier, more ruthless person.

It was the personal phone call after the briefing that dramatically altered all Mark's thought processes. It was from Helena. She never telephoned him at work unless it was really important and this time she was barely able to speak, she was sobbing so much, and she sounded terrified. Dropping everything, Mark rushed straight home not knowing what to expect, and dreading that he might be told some terrible news about Helena or the baby's health, and praying that things would not be as bad as he feared.

When he got to the house the doors were locked, which sent his anxiety into overdrive because they were never normally secured except at night. He turned the key, but the door was bolted, and wouldn't open, which unnerved him even more. He banged frantically upon it, terrified that there'd be no answer, and mentally preparing himself to force an entry into the house in case there was none. With relief he heard Helena shout "Who's there?" and, when he replied, the door was flung open and there was Helena, almost shaking with fear, and with tears pouring down her face.

He held her so tight to him, and kissed her repeatedly and tried to calm her down, and slowly in the safety of his arms she began to regain just a little self control. "I'm sorry. I'm so sorry to have dragged you from your work," she said, "but when I opened the parcel it was so horrid and so evil I just lost all reason. I couldn't help myself Mark, I really couldn't. It was like the nightmare was beginning all over again." and once more Helena began to weep.

"What parcel, Love, what parcel?" cried Mark. "Where is it? Let me see, let me see!"

Helena stood rooted to the spot. "It's in there," she sobbed, "on the kitchen table. I'm not going in there while it's in there. Just get it out Mark. Please, please just get it out of the house."

It wasn't a big package. It was about the size of a shoe box, and quite rigid. It had been wrapped in brown paper and the name "Mrs H. Hobson" and the address had been neatly printed by a computer on a label, and it had been posted in Manchester. When Mark looked inside it, even he recoiled in disgust. It contained the body of a dead magpie, which was starting to decompose, although the smell had been masked by strong scented pot pourri to obscure the stench of decay. A rusty nail had been forced through its rotting flesh, and the bird was pinned to a roughly made wooden crucifix. There was also a card with three words written tauntingly in red upon it. "One, for sorrow." they said prophetically: there was no promise of anything else; "gold", "silver" and especially "joy", were clearly not options in the sender's malignant imagination

For any woman to receive such a *gift* it would be distressing enough, and for any pregnant woman the level of distress would be greater still, but for Helena the effect was cataclysmic. It wasn't just the immediate shock that had caused so much dread, it was the long buried memories of the cruel and slanderous campaign of vilification that she had been subjected to by a deranged and dangerous woman that came flooding back to haunt her. In her mind she recalled every vicious attack on her character and the months and months of fearing the arrival of the postman. And there had been much worse: tied to a wooden grille in a dilapidated stone barn she had been threatened with disfigurement and a slow death. Her nostrils almost smelt the sulphuric acid as she had smelt it when her tormentor had approached her, intent on throwing the contents of the jug of acid into her beautiful tear-stained face. She had been told that her attacker would rejoice in her pain and that, when she had heard enough screams, the barn would be set alight and that she would burn to death in agony and in terror. She heard the sound of the door bursting open, the sound of Mark's voice, and then the gunfire and she remembered the total despair she had felt after he had been shot and she thought that he was dying.

It was all too much to bear. She started to shake again, her face drained of its colour, and then there was an intense pain in her womb. Her legs buckled and she almost sank to the floor. Mark was frantic, the 999 call was garbled and would never have been used as an object lesson on how to contact the emergency services, but the message was received and the urgency of the situation was understood. Within minutes Helena was being rushed to hospital by ambulance with Mark at her side. Suppose she was to lose the baby now? Suppose she was to die? Mark was beside himself with worry; his only thoughts were for the safety of his wife and their unborn child.

Chapter Twenty Nine

The hospital said that Helena's blood pressure was dangerously high. They said it was vital that it came down quickly, and that the next 24-36 hours were critical. A number of possible interventions had been explained to Mark, and he had struggled to take in everything that was said to him, but his mind could only focus on Helena.

Most of what the doctors told him had just been a jumble of sound, with the odd medical term leaping from the confused Babel of noise to imprint itself on his memory. He had heard the words "Pre-Eclampsia" and "Gestational Hypertension" which he had barely understood. He had better understood it when the doctors talked about the risk of kidney damage and of seizures, and had taken on board the fact that in serious cases inducing the baby was the only option; but Helena was only just over 29 weeks pregnant, and that was not an option the doctors wanted to take if it could be avoided. The immediate requirement was bed rest and the avoidance of all stress, and so it was that Helena lay, mildly sedated on a hospital bed, her heart beat, and that of the baby's being constantly monitored, looking utterly helpless and very, very vulnerable.

Mark detested hospitals; they always made him feel trapped and uneasy. His first meeting with Helena had been when she lay on a hospital bed, bloody and bruised after surviving a car bomb attack that had blown her then employer to bits. The terrible, terrible thought that now entered his head was what if his last meeting with her should also be in a hospital bed? He tried to convince himself that he was being over-dramatic, that she was in good hands, that everything would be alright. But, because he so desperately wanted that to be the case with every fibre of his being, a nagging voice inside his brain kept telling him that in real life there were very few happy endings, and for some reason he could only see images of loss and desolation. He remembered the death of his grandmother in a depressing geriatric ward. He had been quite young when she passed away; he had watched his cousin, to whom the old lady was particularly close, praying with tears in her eyes that she would get better and he had realised the futility of it all. If he could have prayed, he would have prayed for her quick end but, as he had so little faith, he had done nothing and waited in silence for the inevitable outcome.

He remembered watching his father being eaten away by cancer and his last horrible weeks when he had been wracked with pain. There had been times when the temptation to intervene to put an end to his suffering had been very great, and it was only the certain knowledge that to do so would have cost him his job and, in all likelihood dependant on the charge that was brought, also his liberty that had prevented him from doing so. He had to be in a position to support his mother in her sadness; he couldn't have burdened her with further heartache.

When grown men cry, they hold back their tears, they look away, they avoid eye contact, but the shuddering frame gives them away, and the bowed head reveals their inner grief.

The young nurse was very kind; she brought him tea and tried to comfort him. She told him Dr Khan was the best in his field, that if anyone could help Helena he could, and that she had seen similar situations many times before in which both the mother and the baby had survived and thrived. She didn't tell Mark of the other occasions when the unborn child had been lost and rarely, but not uniquely, the mother had also died. She said there was nothing more that Mark could do at the hospital, that he should go home and try to rest, and she promised that if there were any developments she would immediately telephone him.

In the taxi that took him home Mark withdrew so deeply into himself that he remembered nothing of the journey. Familiar landmarks didn't register, well recognised milestones passed by totally unseen, and it was only the driver asking "Are you alright Mate?" and then requesting his fare that made him realise the journey was over and he was back at his empty house. He paid the man with a note, he had no idea of what denomination, and didn't wait for change; the cabbie pocketed the cash and wished fervently that all his customers could be as generous.

Mark entered the empty house, shut the door behind him and sank into a chair alone with his thoughts. He had never felt so lonely or so completely useless. Wherever he looked he could see Helena, her presence was everywhere and her absence was shocking and unthinkable, and it was his fault that she was in the situation that she was in. Whoever the malign, vindictive, vengeful, person was who had sent the charming gift to his wife it was not her he really meant to hurt: it was him, and he was trying to do that by threatening to destroy the most precious and irreplaceable thing in his life. If he ever found out who had caused him so much agony, Mark promised himself that the perpetrator would pay in time and in blood. What he had attempted to do to a gentle, loving, beautiful creature was cruel beyond belief, and he had to be made to suffer in return for the suffering he was causing now. If Mark lost his wife or his child there could be no civilised or measured response, and if that put him at odds with his oath as a policeman to uphold the law, if it risked de-railing everything that his life had stood for up until then, then so be it: he would have no choice and there could be no compromise.

The telephone rang, and Mark jumped out of his skin. What if it was the hospital? What if Helena had taken a turn for the worse? What if it was already too late? His hand was shaking so much he could barely pick up the phone; in utter panic he waited to hear the words "I'm afraid I have some bad news for you Mr Hobson." The caller was Helena's mother; in his confused and emotional state Mark had forgotten that he'd telephoned Helena's parents to tell them that she'd been taken into hospital and had promised that he would let them know what the doctors had said. He tried to be self-controlled, he tried not to spread alarm and, in order to protect her father, he tried to put a positive slant on the situation, but he failed miserably. Such was his distress that his mother-in-law offered to come over to be with him. He lied to her. He told her he was alright and that that was not necessary, he said that he was coping, but he added that he was sure that both he and Helena would benefit from seeing them both the following day. She knew he was not telling the truth but, if he didn't want her there, then so it had to be and she said that she and her husband would be at the hospital the following morning. Mark ended the call by promising faithfully that he would let them know if there were any further developments overnight, and that this time he would not forget.

The hours passed at a snail's pace, each minute dragging a hundred fears behind it as it made a weary circuit of the clock face. Sleep was impossible, the thought of lying in the marriage bed without Helena was unbearable, so Mark sat in silence, in the semi-darkness, playing and replaying his memories, and becoming more and more unsettled and distressed. At one stage he went to the cupboard and took out a bottle of whisky. That had been a prop once, that had helped him deal with the recriminations that had followed the death of his first wife; but whisky had proved a false friend and had nearly wrecked his career. Disgusted with himself for even thinking about drinking and also conscious of the fact that he might need to drive at any time, he replaced the bottle unopened in the cupboard and sank back into his seat to await the dawn.

It was well after three o'clock in the morning when the telephone in Detective Superintendent Gratton's bedroom rang, and it was a most unwelcome sound. Tim had enjoyed a good night. He had dined with Amanda in an exclusive little bistro in Dore and, although the meal had cost him an arm and a leg, it had been superbly cooked and presented. Cheered by the food, and a bottle of truly excellent French wine, they had relaxed in each other's company. He had wanted her to stay the night, but Amanda was in rehearsal for a new play and needed an early start, so she had continued in the taxi to her hotel and Tim had returned home alone shortly after midnight. For the next hour or so he had listened to some of his favourite jazz C.D's and consumed two glasses of fine Napoleon Brandy before retiring to bed. Content and mellow, he had slipped easily into warm, embracing sleep; then the strident bell had wrenched him from his slumbers: he was therefore very far from content when he picked up the receiver.

"Tim it's me Mark. I'm sorry to phone you so late at night, but there's nobody else I can turn to."

The torment in Mark's voice was obvious and Tim's annoyance at being woken from his dreams was replaced immediately by concern.

"What's the matter Mark? I can tell from your voice that something is wrong. Is it Helena? Tell me for God's sake what's happened!"

Once Mark started to unburden himself, he couldn't stop. He told Tim about Helena, and about how worried the doctors were about her, he told him of the magpie and the promise of sorrow, he told him about his fears and his anger and his frustration. "If she hadn't met me she wouldn't be where she is now!" he cried and he blamed himself for putting her life in danger.

"I can't talk to anybody else like this," he stammered. "Her dad's about to go into hospital for major surgery, I can't inflict my worries on him or on her mum can I? And since my mum had her stroke I daren't put her under pressure either. There isn't anybody at work who I can unburden myself to, and if I didn't speak to someone then it felt like my head was going to explode."

Tim felt the agony; Mark's pain overflowed into his room.

"Mark, Is there is anything that I can do? Do you want me to come down? I can re-arrange a couple of non-urgent meetings and be with you soon after lunchtime, would that help? You know how much I think of Helena and of you. If you think me being there would do any good then I'm practically on my way."

"Not yet," replied Mark. "I pray there isn't going to be a need, but if she gets any worse then maybe, yes please, I don't know what I'll do if I if I lose her." And, try as he might, he could do nothing to hide his sobbing.

"It won't come to that Mark, it really won't. Believe me. You and Helena were made for each other, and you're meant to be happy, I really know that to be true. She's a brave girl, she's already proved that, and she's a fighter. She'll pull through; I passionately believe that to be the case."

"But why is it all happening now?" blurted out Mark. "At any other time we could manage. If Helena wasn't pregnant, if I was able to spend more time with her, if I wasn't working nearly every hour God sends on a double murder inquiry that doesn't seem to be getting anywhere, then we could deal with the situation, but not now, not when we're at our most defenceless."

"Use your head Man, use your head." said Tim. "What's the one most obvious thing about you? I'll tell you. It's as plain as the nose on your face to anyone who sees you together with Helena, even for just a few moments, you adore your wife; that fact is simply self-evident, you couldn't hide it even if you wanted to.

I've got no doubt that in a small town like Burrdale, where you've got some very scary festivals, and occasionally you re-enact an ancient ritual and the jungle drums tell people of your plans even before you have finished making them that everybody knows that. It's your strength and it's also your Achilles heel. I'm absolutely certain that if your inquiry was bogged down in the way you think it is, if you were heading in entirely the wrong direction with no prospect of finding out anything at all, you'd have been left alone to carry on making a pig's ear of matters and Helena wouldn't have received the terrible package that she did."

"Do you genuinely believe that?"

"I certainly do." said Tim. "Somebody in that little town of yours thinks that you're beginning to get too close, somebody wants to divert you away from the path that you're following, and if you're worried sick about your wife and child he reckons that you can't concentrate on anything else. That's what he's banking on and, if enough time passes, the whole process will collapse. If you back off the crimes remain unsolved and he gets away with murder!"

"Are you sure of that?" asked Mark.

"I'm bloody certain you idiot." laughed Tim, "and I'll tell you this as well in all seriousness. It may not seem like it now, but the best thing you can do for both yourself and Helena is to get these murders solved. Once you've done that the stress disappears, and everything gets back to normal. Try to get some sleep now, and let me know tomorrow how Helena is progressing

Chapter Thirty

Mark did try to follow Tim's advice, but for the rest of the night all he managed to achieve were odd moments of slumber which did nothing to alleviate his tiredness. He couldn't stop thinking about Helena and the baby boy inside her womb. At any second there might be a phone call bringing news that he dreaded to hear, but slowly the night wore on and thankfully no such call came. Every minute, every hour without bad news brought with it a tiny strand of hope that things would improve, but these were very fragile threads to hang the weight of all his wishes upon.

Occasionally, and almost contrary to his desire, for brief periods he found himself thinking like a policeman again. As yet the effort couldn't be sustained, and was always overwhelmed by the personal drama that was being played out, but his innate compulsion to solve the crime was now beginning the battle to re-assert itself, and it was at those times that the words of his friend came flooding back to him.

It had to be right that the most likely motive for this grotesque hoax was to disrupt the murder inquiry. As Tim had said, nobody goes to such lengths without good cause. Some of his reasoning had to be hitting the target, and somebody was obviously getting worried. When he felt up to it, it had to be more of the same, but with increased vigour and even more commitment. Every inch of ground had to be re-visited, the movements of every suspect had to be re-examined, old data and new had to be cross checked and re-appraised and somewhere amidst the mass of information already to hand, Mark felt sure a key would be found to unlock a current mystery and a past secret.

Before 8am he had telephoned the hospital. Helena had rested fairly well, but, that said, there was little overall change in her condition and there had been no significant reduction in her blood pressure, which remained worryingly high. With so much uncertainty there was no possibility of going into work, so Mark telephoned John Lomas to explain what had happened and why he had to be at his wife's bedside. He did however make arrangements for the package and its gruesome contents to be handed over to a Scientific Support Officer for fingerprint and forensic examination. He was not hopeful of a result. Bank notes and documents can be NIM tested, fingerprints can be recovered from paper and saliva is an excellent source of D.N.A; but if the stamp was self adhesive, if the offender had worn gloves, if subsequent handling of the packet by counter clerks, sorting officers, postmen and even by Helena herself had overlaid the original prints of the culprit, no positive result would be achieved. All the indications were that the criminal the police were looking for was a clever, resourceful and ultra-careful individual.

It was already patently obvious that Helena wouldn't be coming home in the immediate future. Last night had been a rush, and only the very basic needs had been catered for. Today soap and toiletries, night clothes, dressing gown and all the personal objects that a woman needs had to be taken onto the ward. Books and photographs might help to relieve the boredom and flowers might help to brighten up the room. Mark remembered the first time he had taken flowers to Helena, and how awkward he had felt buying them from the posh florist shop. He hadn't known then, but he knew now, how she liked simplicity and scent, and natural colours, and flowers in tune with their season. She loved old English white roses and sweet smelling cottage garden flowers, but on a cold October morning he knew that he would struggle to find the blooms that would most please her. In the end, just as it had been on that first occasion, he couldn't make up his mind so, when he visited the florist's shop in Lower Burrdale, he left the final decision to the girl behind the counter. He did tell her the sort of flowers Helena especially liked and, although she couldn't exactly match his preferred choices, she did put together a very pretty bouquet which Mark felt sure Helena would be glad to receive.

He arrived at the hospital well before official visiting hours commenced, but these were not rigorously enforced and he was allowed to go straight in to see his wife. Helena still looked pale and tense, but there wasn't the same sense of dread that there had been the night before. Mark kissed her gently and sat on a chair by her bed, holding her hand, gaining solace from the physical contact.

"I'm sorry Mark, I'm such a nuisance. You should be at work, you don't need all this." she said.

Mark squeezed her hand. "Oh, don't be silly Love. How could I possibly be anywhere else when my whole life is in here with you? You're everything to me, I'm nothing without you, you're the most precious thing in my world, and I have to be here. I've phoned John Lomas and he completely understands, and Tim Gratton sends his love and his very best regards."

"You haven't been bothering Tim, have you? He's got so much on his plate; it isn't fair to burden him with me."

"I had no one else who I could talk to, and I thought I'd go mad if I didn't speak to somebody. The one person I really wanted to speak to was you, but that was impossible; everywhere I looked I could see you, but you weren't there, and I was so unhappy, and so, so afraid."

"Oh Mark," said Helena, and her eyes filled with tears, "I love you so much." and she squeezed his hand tightly as she spoke.

At times during that morning they talked, at other times physical exhaustion caused long periods of silence, but the mere fact that they were together was enough, and neither Mark nor Helena wanted more. When Mark spoke, he tried to ensure that Helena was never upset or disturbed by the conversation. He talked positively of the future, he told her that Tim was sure that everything would be alright, and somehow that promise sounded convincing when it came from him. They talked about ordinary things because they needed ordinary thoughts and ideas. Mark told Helena that both her parents would be coming to visit her and that his mother was also thinking of her, and some slight sense of the re-assuringly mundane began to be felt by them both, although neither Helena nor Mark could forget for a moment that, at any second, they could still find themselves being dragged centre stage in a highly charged medical drama.

The doctor, when he visited, was giving nothing away. "So far, so good," he said. "Anything could still happen," and Helena's condition was still critical, but maybe, just maybe, it was "a little better than it had been last night."

Around midday Helena's Mum and Dad arrived, bringing with them a large bunch of flowers, and soon after that a huge bouquet was brought in by a nurse. The card simply read "To my all time favourite Enchantress, Get better soon." It was signed Tim.

"That's nice" murmured Helena, "He's so very kind."

"He's full of shit." laughed Mark, "He probably uses the same line of patter on all the girls he chats up." but he was still very glad that his friend had acted in the way that he had.

Helena's parents stayed for nearly two hours. Both looked

strained, and Mark thought her dad appeared frail, but waiting to undergo major heart surgery in a matter of weeks, it was understandable that he didn't look relaxed or robust.

After they had gone, it became very apparent that Helena was tired. She said that there was no point in watching her sleep. She said that he should get a break from the hospital for a couple of hours, and then maybe come back in the early evening when she had rested. Mark didn't want to leave her, but for the moment his presence served no useful purpose and, on the strict understanding that he would be contacted immediately should he suddenly be needed, he left the warm, stale atmosphere of the hospital and found himself walking alone in a nearby park. The autumn colours gave it a late season facelift as the feeble sun briefly split the grey sky to illuminate the beech and sycamore trees with a soft hazy light.

Mark thought about the photograph of Shane Chadwick: if he had been able to lead a normal life, if his health, complexion and mind hadn't been poisoned by toxic drugs, what would he look like now? A face came into his mind. That couldn't possibly be right! Stress and tension were playing tricks upon him, but he had to try to find out: although he had not planned to go anywhere near the police station at Burrdale that day, he was now inexorably driven towards his office and the double murder file.

When he arrived he found the place to be unusually subdued and half empty. Everyone was surprised to see him and there was a great deal of concern expressed for Helena's health; Alan Nadin explained that the news of her ordeal had upset a lot of people. The depressed mood of the office had then been further darkened by the fact that Paul Burgess and Dick Norton had had a major slanging match at lunchtime. Becky had been dragged into it, and that this time she had sided with her father, so Paul had left her feeling unhappy, angry and very, very short tempered.

"There's another bit of interesting news too, Gov." he said. "Yesterday somebody poured paint stripper on to the roof and bonnet of John Winston's new car and scrawled words like "Pervert" and "Pedo" all over it in red lipstick. He hasn't reported it to us, but he was in a right state last night by all accounts. He turned up late for his class, he kept losing his place, and I'm told, all in all, things were pretty shambolic. He didn't hang about afterwards like he normally does, and he didn't hold court in the Royal Albert as he pretty well does every Wednesday night."

"That's interesting." said Mark. "Somebody is scraping away the veneer and he doesn't like it; even though he doesn't want to involve us, I think we need to pay Mr Winston another visit as soon as we possibly can. If Helena's condition remains stable, I'll be in work tomorrow. I can't be with her all the time, much as I'd like to be, and if I keep busy it will stop me obsessing about all the things that could still go horribly wrong. Will you come with me and together we'll try to peel off a couple more layers of skin to see what sores we can uncover? I want Paul to speak to Joe Broadbent again, and I want to trace all the movements of Shane Chadwick since he left Burrdale. He's the central figure in this investigation. I'm still absolutely clear about that."

After having spoken to Alan, Mark briefly entered his office; he opened the Brocklehurst file and stared intently at the photographs contained within it. It was so difficult to tell. There was a likeness, but people age in very different ways and whilst some faces don't appear to alter at all, others change so much as to be completely unrecognisable. This was just idle speculation in any event; if any of the faces he saw on the file or in town looked like Shane Chadwick might have looked had he lived, did it really matter? He was long since dead and, although he seemed pivotal to all the events that had taken place, he couldn't have had a hand in any of them. Mark closed the file with a sense of frustration and returned to the hospital to be close to his beloved wife.

Chapter Thirty One

The ferocity with which John Winston's fist had struck the wooden table would have alarmed and distressed the *nice* ladies who made up the backbone of his night school class, but it was as nothing to the blow he would like to have smashed into the face of the person who had vandalised his car if he had the opportunity to do so.

His reaction was born out of, hatred, frustration and fear. His first response when saw the Audi 2.0 litre Sportback with its blistered paintwork and its jeering graffiti had been that this crime had been conceived in envy and that some brain dead, moron resented his tangible success; but, after he vented his initial rage in a mouthful of obscenities, another altogether more potent feeling had overwhelmed him. Somebody knew, or somebody at least suspected, things about him that were better kept well hidden.

In his own mind he was capable of justifying his actions, and he could have had no more passionate advocate in his own defence; and if some people didn't understand, if they couldn't comprehend that he had no choice, and that there was no harm in it, then that was their inadequacy for which he couldn't be blamed. He was entitled to his own life. His *interests* were his own affair. His talent shone like a beacon in a fog of mediocrity and surely gave him the right to be different. Why should he be judged by his intellectual inferiors, some of whom were not fit even to receive the smallest scraps of wisdom from his table of Knowledge? But, regrettably, in the flawed world around him, all too often the ignorant held the power and *the System* protected worthless under achievers.

Tabloid newspapers often trumpeted the supposed "wisdom" of the great British public; what wisdom was that? Was it found in the millions who watched inane quiz shows on television or who drooled over so called celebrities making fools of themselves in front of the camera? He thought not. Could it be discovered hidden amongst the army of football supporters who brought shame to the cross of St George, or in the words of the raucous and tuneless hoards who sang of "Jerusalem" or "Flower of Scotland" when international rugby union matches were being played? No, that was impossible! Yet, men of genius had frequently been brought down by the mob. Oscar Wilde had been destroyed by the prejudices of inferior minds and many modern day icons had been battered into defeat by a self-righteous puerile press: the same could happen to him, and John Winston knew that he would go to any lengths to prevent that from happening.

What a difference a week or two make! When Virginia had burnt in effigy, the world had been on his side and, even when she had been killed, there were many people who would have applauded her dispatch; then the police had come and the mood had changed. They had invaded his privacy and they had failed to respect his special status. The vile rumours that were beginning to circulate about him might even be the direct result of their intervention. He didn't like them. He didn't trust them. He could not report the damage to his car to them because they wouldn't limit themselves to the narrow task of discovering the identity of the offender. They would search for motive, they would ask awkward questions and, in a pressure situation, he was not certain that he could cope. Whether he capitulated or whether he went on the attack, in the end the cards would be stacked in their favour and there could only ever be one winner.

His dilemma had been greatly increased when he received the anonymous letter. It had called him a "sick fantasist" a "child molester" a "self-deluded piece of shit," and much, much more besides. The writer had claimed that he knew everything about him and there was arrogance and a confidence in the text that had made him fear this claim could be true. The sender threatened that he would destroy him by posting revelations about him on the Internet and taunted him that if he wanted to save his rotten, morally corrupt skin, he should slink away, deserting his coterie of sycophants and abandoning everything that he most prized. That was too high a price to pay. It would rob him of the gushing adulation of his students which was a powerful aphrodisiac, it would wipe out the celebrity status that he had nurtured over so many years, it would take away his livelihood and, perhaps most destructive of all, it would blow away his self esteem. He could not do that, he just couldn't. A life without praise was no life at all, and the writer of the hateful letter knew how true that was. He was offering him a slow, lingering death. Loneliness, rejection and despair were the bitter pills that the anonymous scribe was seeking to prescribe for him.

But what else could he do? If he showed the letter to the police it would cause him even more trouble than a report of the damage to the car would do. It would become an exhibit in any trial if a suspect was ever identified and charged. Winston shuddered at the very thought of a jury of the mediocre sniggering at the contents of that vile missive. Any decent defence barrister would have a field day cross-examining him. It would be like pulling the wings off a butterfly, a beautiful Peacock butterfly, exposing a crippled insect underneath; and it would all happen under the intense spotlight of media interest.

He took the letter and tore the single sheet into shreds and then tried to flush the pieces down the toilet. They wouldn't sink, but floated to the top like dirty confetti on a puddle. He plunged his hand into the bowl and pulled out the sodden scraps of paper. He compressed them into a ball, which he wrapped in toilet tissue, and then tried again to flush them away, this time to better effect, although some fragments still managed to escape and the process had to be repeated for a second time before it was finally successful. As he washed and re-washed his hands in strongly scented soap, his whole body shook and, although the perfumed lather made the bathroom smell sweet, somehow Winston still felt defiled, unclean, victimised and abused.

Those intensely uncomfortable feelings lasted for several hours, and it was not until it started to get dark that his mood changed. What proof could there be? He'd always been careful in his dealings with people. Nobody could possibly have any evidence that was capable of establishing any link between himself and Mike Skinner, and nobody could claim to have seen him with Virginia at any time after their ill-fated encounter at the Royal Albert. Assertions could still be made, of course, but, so far as he was concerned, they were groundless. If a man of his eloquence and education couldn't see off the uncorroborated wild claims of some spineless tittle tattler it was a pathetic state of affairs.

The computer presented a bigger problem. He had never used credit cards to acquire explicit images of children so none could be found if it was expertly examined, but the number of times he had searched the websites, late at night, to view bizarre, unusual sexual practices was very great. He could explain that this was a kind of therapy, that it stimulated his imagination, that it gave him an insight into the behaviour of human beings which assisted him when he prepared his lectures and that it was research for a possible book, but he knew he wouldn't be believed: but if the computer could be cleared of its search history then maybe he would be safe after all.

The problem was that he wasn't really computer literate. In the past he had often wanted to ask how to cover up his excursions deep into weird and strange sub-cultures, but it was an impossible question to ask without revealing that you had unsavoury secrets to hide. He had deleted images, of course, any fool could do that, but sometimes he would accidentally press a wrong key and something unwholesome would then leap out onto the screen. He knew that there had to better ways to cover his tracks, but he had nobody to teach him what they were, and certainly no time at all to learn. The computer had to go, and to go quickly. Winston cursed the sender of the contemptible correspondence; this person was costing him a great deal of money. He couldn't claim on his car insurance without first reporting to the police that a crime had been committed. He dared not fake the loss or destruction of the computer to claim on his contents insurance for the same reason, so he had to stand all the loss and damage himself. He had told the police inspector the last time that he saw him that he was not a violent man, and that he was one of "Nature's cowards", which was true, but it wasn't the whole truth. People living a lie, terrified of being exposed can kill; even a physically timid individual can lash out in extreme panic if pushed too far.

Winston knew that was true of him, and he knew that was also true of virtually every man and woman alive on the planet. He also knew that if he could meet the person who was seeking to destroy his life then, in the right circumstances, in the right place, if there were no witnesses and with the right weapon to hand, he would kill; he certainly wouldn't hesitate to do so.

He wondered where to get rid of the processor; the deep waters of the Upper Derwent Valley sprang to mind. In mid-October, after dark there would be very few people around and, if he drove beyond the Howden Dam, there was very little chance that he would be seen, but first he had to get there.

The state of his £20,000 motor car suddenly leapt into his brain. It was his only vehicle. He couldn't try to borrow a car without advertising the fact that he wanted to make a journey, but if he drove his car like it was, the smart paintwork wrecked by caustic liquid and covered in lurid accusations scrawled on windows and doors, it would be noticed by every person who happened to see it. Frantically he searched the kitchen cupboard to find something which would remove the vengeful writing. He found a bottle of cream cleaner which claimed it would cut through grease, but which carried a warning not to use on plastic, aluminium or glass; but he had nothing else, and his car was as good as written off in any event. In cold drizzle, like a man possessed, he attempted to clean his vehicle. He squeezed the thick liquid onto an abrasive pad and scrubbed furiously. The crimson lipstick was for the most part removed, but not without inflicting further damage on the car which up until its transformation had been his pride and joy.

He waited until it was nearly 10pm before he set off. It had become very foggy, which made driving conditions difficult, and had this trip not been essential he would never have undertaken it. He loaded the processor into the boot of his car, it was surprisingly heavy, and began his journey. He didn't realise until he had descended into the Hope Valley that he had left the torch that he had intended to take with him on the kitchen table; but it was too late now to turn back. Whenever headlights shone in his rear view mirror, which mercifully was not often, he was on tenterhooks. Suppose it was a police car, suppose they stopped him because the condition of his vehicle made it look suspicious, suppose they searched the boot, suppose they asked him what he was doing and where he was going: he could hardly say "I'm just popping over to the reservoirs to drown my extremely expensive computer because it is full of images that you might call pornographic." He wished with all his heart that this journey was over, but he still had a long way to go.

When he crossed the Ashopton viaduct and turned onto the Snake Pass road, his mind created pictures of the drowned villages, which had been abandoned when the reservoirs were built, and the thought of the unhappiness their construction had caused almost overwhelmed him. He was unhappy too. His life was being disrupted by a ruthless outside force. Why did people have to meddle? Why couldn't he be left alone? He turned right and, with the reservoirs on his right hand side, he made his way as far as the King's Oak which marked the extremity of the distance you could travel by car. He had driven the whole length of the road to see if there were any other vehicles about, but there had been none.

He travelled back towards the Howden Dam and stopped by the roadside about half a mile before he came to it. He opened the boot and picked up the processor; it was very dark and he could hardly see what he was doing. Twice he slipped on the embankment which was wet and greasy, staining his clothing with brown mud and, on the second occasion he landed awkwardly and severely jolted his right wrist. A shooting pain ran up his arm and he yelled out in agony, and for several moments he was convinced that he had broken a bone; but then the pain subsided a little and he forced himself onwards towards the water's edge and, finally, with a splash so loud that he thought could have been heard in Sheffield, the evidence of his obsessions was hurled into the still waters. Wet, tired, wretched and in extreme discomfort, he began the slow and difficult journey back to Burrdale.

Chapter Thirty Two

As John Winston was inching his way home through the now even thicker fog, his wrist throbbing and his eyes straining to peer through the dense gloom, Mark Hobson was sitting alone in his silent house. Earlier in the evening the doctors had examined Helena again and the news had been a little more encouraging; her blood pressure had dropped, not by much, but it had dropped, and the intense pain that had so terrified them both as they had believed it heralded the onset of a miscarriage, had further eased. The doctors had discussed amongst themselves if they needed to insert a stitch in her womb and had decided that it was not necessary to do so at the moment, although it remained a very possible future option, and that a regime of complete rest, rigorous monitoring and avoidance of stress might be sufficient, at least for the time being. There was not the equipment or the manpower to deliver the required level of care at home, so for the next few days, if not weeks, Helena was to remain in hospital.

The panic that had gripped Mark when Helena had collapsed, and for many hours thereafter, had now largely subsided: but the anger that somebody could engineer a situation to put in jeopardy the lives of his wife and his unborn son hadn't lessened: and Mark knew it would never be expunged until the person responsible for causing it had been caught and dealt with. He needed sleep, he was well aware of that, but he was too wound up to even think about it. Sometime soon he would have to force himself to lie alone on a cold and empty bed, but not yet, so to postpone the evil day he had spent more than two hours re-reading yet again the scrapbooks and diaries from the hidden box. From within the pages of their history something evil had sprung, and for the first time, Mark realised that before Helena returned home, they had to be banished from the house. The sad story they contained was taking over both their lives; it wouldn't be possible to move on whilst the crate and its contents remained with them. He and his wife were on the verge of what could be a bright new future; the last thing that they needed was to be constantly reminded of a stranger's sombre past

When Mark finally compelled himself to look for sleep he found it was hard to discover. More than once he awoke from fitful slumber convinced that he could hear Helena's gentle breathing beside him only to realise that it was his mind playing tricks. Occasionally he dreamt, but his dreams were not sweet, and always they jolted him back into a state of consciousness that he didn't desire. So it was that although he had done everything he could do to try to rest, he had only managed to sink into a deep sleep just minutes before the alarm clock had dragged him back into the start of another day.

A telephone call to the hospital confirmed continued slight improvement, so Mark headed to the police station to carry on with his search for a killer. It was personal now; he wanted this man so badly. He had felt pity when he saw the legacy that the killer's deeds had left to Jackie Skinner, now he felt outrage at the legacy that had been bequeathed to him and to his wife. The murderer would be caught, Mark made that solemn vow, and he would rot in prison: nobody else would be permitted to fall victim to his insane cruelty.

Before meeting Burgess and Nadin and then briefing all the investigating officers on the tasks he wanted them to carry out, Mark spoke to John Lomas; he left the Detective Superintendent convinced that his D.I. was fully focussed on the job in hand, but a little worried that he was now too committed to be proportionate. Mr Lomas had advised him to keep a cool head and not to pursue a private vendetta but he wasn't sure that much of that advice had actually been listened to.

Back in his office Mark talked with Paul and Alan.

"I think the man we're looking for is becoming more and more dangerous. Unless he's stopped now, I believe it's likely that he may kill again. I think John Winston could be a possible target, although I accept that it's perfectly possible that he staged the attack on his car himself in order to divert suspicion away from him, and he still remains a principal suspect in this murder inquiry.”

In that case, Gov, why didn’t he report the matter to us?” said Alan. “To be honest, I can’t see him wrecking a brand new motor. It’s not the type of thing the self-opinionated windbag would do; besides, he likes money far too much to throw so much of it away.”

“You’ve got a fair point there, but whether he did or whether he didn’t, we do need to speak to him again in any event. We also need to speak to Joe Broadbent and to all our other suspects, to see between the three of us, just how much crap we can stir up for them. As I asked last night Alan, will you come with me to pay Winston another visit? We made a pretty good team last time; there’s no reason to suppose that we won’t do so again. Paul, will you have further words with Joe Broadbent and with that self-opinionated git Henry Osbourne? And somebody needs to talk to Mr “Foghorn on Legs” Patterson. He’s a waste of space, but he’s shit scared about something, so he needs to be put under a bit of pressure. Get one of the other lads to go and see him if you haven’t got time to do it yourself.”

“I’ll go myself if I’ve got time,” said Paul. “He’s likely to behave like a total tosser, and if he does I’m just in the mood to put him in his place.”

“Well, if you’re sure,” said Mark. “But if you find time running out on you, get one of the lads to help out. You could send

Ollerenshaw if you wanted to, it might even be an advantage to use an experienced uniformed office to put the fear of God into the miserable little bull shitter."

The main briefing then followed and the rest of the detectives on the team were then set a simple collective task, which was to find out every scrap of information they could about Shane Chadwick and the Chadwick family between them leaving Burrdale until the time of Shane's death and beyond, and to have all the details available for consideration by the end of the working day. Whilst they went about that task, Mark and Alan left the police station to commence their mission to disconcert John Winston.

When examined at close quarters, the full extent of the damage to the paintwork was breath taking; the car looked as if it had been pelted with acid bombs, and the intensity of the attack upon it had to be seen to be believed. Alan Nadin turned to his boss "Popular guy, ain't he?" he commented. Mark nodded. "As you rightly say Alan, a popular guy, a very popular guy," he remarked.

The knock on the door initially failed to bring a response so D.S. Nadin thumped the woodwork with the side of his clenched fist, making the door rattle in its frame, and causing dogs to bark at houses half the length of the street away: it did the trick and eventually the door was opened by a distinctly under par John Winston. His left wrist was heavily bandaged, black rings were clearly visible around both of his eyes, he hadn't shaved and he looked like a man who was operating under considerable strain.

"What in God's name do you want?" he asked angrily. "I've not sent for you. I don't want you here. Just clear off the pair of you and leave me alone." Hobson ignored the request.

"That's a nice motor car you've got there," he said sarcastically, "but I'm not certain about the choice of paintwork. In my opinion a nice shade of dark blue would have been a far better colour scheme."

"You think yourself so very clever! You know some moron has trashed it."

"We do," said Alan Nadin. "And we also know that you haven't reported the crime to us, and we'd like to know the reason why not. What exactly are you trying to conceal Mr Winston? You must have a bloomin' big secret that you want to keep well hidden if you're willing to ignore that degree of vandalism to your motor."

"I don't know what you are talking about," snapped Winston. "And I think what you're implying is outrageous and quite improper!"

"Have you checked your computer recently?" asked Mark. "Only it is plastered all over the Internet that you have got some very exotic tastes in sex; someone out there doesn't like you one little bit and he wants you out of town. Have you any idea who that person might be?" Winston didn't speak.

"I'm investigating a double murder," said Mark. "There's a very real chance that if you don't co-operate with us you could become victim number three. Don't you think that it would be better for you if you told us everything that you know?" Winston shook his head, but his complexion turned a paler shade of grey.

"If you won't talk to us, then maybe your computer will," said Mark. "I've got reasonable cause to believe that it may contain criminal material and I propose to seize it for proper examination, and to preserve the evidence."

"You'll have a job," retorted Winston, "it's gone." and he was unwise enough to allow himself a smug grin as he did so, which was not a clever thing for him to do. The next second the big detective had grabbed him by the collar with both hands and the lecturer found himself being forced back against the door jamb and almost lifted off his feet, such was the strength of this officer.

"I could break every bone in your body, and I could say I acted in self-defence. You saw him attempting to strike me didn't you Alan?"

"As plain as I can see the clock on the church tower. Be careful Gov, I think he he's about to have another go at you!"

There was something pathetic about the way in which Winston crumbled; maybe he believed he could kill, but he knew he couldn't fight. "Don't hit me." he begged. "For the love of God, please, please don't hit me."

Mark let go the man's collar. "You disgust me," he said. "One day I will show the world what a deviant little slug you are, but right now I'm not concerned with your sordid secrets. I have good reason to believe that you may be the third intended victim of a killer and, much as it pains me, I have a duty to try to save your miserable skin; so tell me, Mr Winston, why a person who we know has already murdered two people might be looking at you as his next victim?"

The entire colour had now drained away from the man's face.

"I don't know," he cried. "I really don't know, except Mike Skinner once told me that he'd found out that somebody who hated my uncle Crawford had also got a grudge against me. He offered to name names, but the price was too high, and in any event, I thought he was lying and just trying to rip me off, but then he was killed and now all this is happening. I'm scared Mr Hobson, I'm very, very scared; what do I do Mr Hobson? What do I do?"

"Keep indoors Mr Winston. Don't go to your classes, don't go anywhere for the time being, and if you receive any threats or experience any disturbance, telephone the police. And, whatever you do, don't mess about with any more evidence, otherwise it could be your funeral, maybe in a very literal sense indeed, and I tell you now, if it is, I won't be sending any flowers," replied

Mark brusquely.

Like a rabbit hypnotised by a stoat Winston stood as in a trance, his lips quivering barely able to keep in the scream of terror that echoed around his brain. Confident that this wretched man would do nothing to imperil his own safety the two officers left. Instantly the door was slammed shut behind them, the sounds of keys being turned and bolts being rammed home were clearly heard by both officers.

"He hasn't got much bottle has he, Gov?" said Nadin. "When you grabbed him, he near enough shat himself. I suppose he might be capable of stabbing somebody in the back, or hitting 'em from behind with a pick axe handle if he were desperate enough, but he could never look anyone in the face and do the deed. I think if he'd seen Mike Skinner's stomach explode like it did he'd probably have fainted on the spot. We had a violent robber do that once, you know. He struck his victim in the face with an iron bar. Her blood spurted everywhere; some even went into his eye; that totally freaked him out. Although the victim was badly injured, she came round before he did and she managed to telephone the police while he was unconscious; he were still out cold when we arrived to nick him."

"I'm afraid you're right, Alan. I'm very much afraid you're right; but never-the-less this meeting with Winston has been an extremely useful exercise.

"How's that Gov?"

"Well, we now know for sure that Winston thinks he is being targeted because of his connection to his uncle, and that links him to Virginia and indirectly to Lucas Norton and to Mike Skinner." said Mark. "He was old enough to have spoken out, but he didn't do so. Had he told somebody at the time Virginia might have been helped and Lucas Norton might have been saved, but he did nothing, so, in a way he precipitated the whole catalogue of events by acting like a Peeping Tom. It's easy to see how the killer could blame him."

"I see where you're coming from Gov, but if everything that has happened is linked in some way to the death of Lucas Norton and to Shane Chadwick, shouldn't we be talking to Dick Norton again? It's as clear as anything that he were a victim, and that his lad's death near drove him barmy, but when he went berserk at the Chadwick household he scarred a little lad for life. If anybody can be blamed for the way in which Shane Chadwick turned out, then in my book Dick Norton's got to be that person."

"I think you're right again Alan," agreed Mark. "How much he'll tell us though I couldn't begin to guess. I suspect it will probably be bugger all, but we have to see him and, if he has received threats, then there's logic to everything that's gone off so far."

Back at the police station the emerging pattern became clearer when Paul Burgess reported back the results of his dealings with Joe Broadbent, Henry Osbourne and Tony Patterson.

"A bit of a dead loss Boss," he said, "Joe Broadbent has a severe chest infection, he doesn't look after himself. He's currently being treated by Dr McAllister; he's been pretty much housebound for the last fortnight. He can't add anything to what he told me before."

"Did he say if anybody had threatened him?" asked Mark.

"No, he didn't," said Paul, "and I'm pretty sure he hasn't been; and that goes for Osbourne and Patterson as well so far as I can tell. Osbourne was his usual stuck up self, and Patterson's just an arsehole. I'd stake my life that neither of them is more worried now than when we last spoke to them."

"It all fits," said Mark. "Those three all have links to Virginia, but certainly Broadbent and Osbourne don't have links to Shane Chadwick or Lucas Norton. They weren't involved at all in the events of twenty years ago. That's why he's left them alone; he's got no score to settle with them. With Patterson I don't know, but for the time being it looks like he is ignored as well."

"Who's he?" asked Paul.

"In a very real way its Shane Chadwick," said Mark. "But clearly it isn't him, and I can't give you another name at present." Paul said nothing, but the look on his face was one of total incredulity, and Mark completely understood how outlandish it was to focus the entire breadth of a murder inquiry on a dead man, about whom he personally knew so very little. The time had come to remedy that lack of understanding.

A careful reading of the dossier on Chadwick which his officers had compiled that day filled in many gaps. It confirmed that he died in 1994 from a heroin overdose aged just twenty four years. He had amassed a criminal record entirely consistent with the archetypal drug addict. He had progressed from shoplifting, through domestic burglaries, to knife point robberies. A wide range of penalties had been imposed; Probation, Community Service Orders, Prison, all of which had been totally ineffective. As was already known, he had died alone in a stinking inner city squat.

The history of the wider family was hardly more inspiring. Shane's mother and father separated less than two years after the Lucas Norton tragedy. One day his father just walked out, never to be heard of again, leaving his wife to cope with the burden of looking after a deeply traumatised child and his younger brother and sister. She had struggled on for three years, but the task had become impossible and she had committed suicide by throwing herself under a train at Cardiff Central Station: thereafter the three children had been looked after by relatives. Shane had either detached himself from the family, or been expelled from it, at about the age of 15 and after that he had lived at dozens of short term addresses, and sometimes on the streets. The relative who looked after the younger children was believed to have been married, and it was thought that she had already lived away from the rest of her family for a number of years before she took the children in. It was reported that that marriage had subsequently failed, but that she had then met, and maybe married, another man. Her current details were not known, nor were the present whereabouts of the two younger children.

Chapter Thirty Three

When Mark visited Helena in hospital that night he was dismayed to discover that there had been a setback. Her blood pressure had risen again after two days of coming down, it wasn't by much, but the trend was sufficient to worry the doctors.

When Mark looked at Helena she appeared to be fine, Mark thought she looked beautiful, but it was soon clear that she was tense and that was a real concern. The reason for her anxiety was not hard to discover; her father had just been told that his heart bypass operation might have to be postponed and, if that didn't go ahead as planned, Helena dreaded to think how he would cope with the delay. He was mentally prepared; he had steeled himself for an imminent ordeal. If the surgery didn't happen now it would knock him for six, and there was a distinct possibility that he would never be able to repeat his current state of readiness; there was also the ever present risk of a catastrophic heart attack whilst his condition remained untreated. Helena's mum was worried sick both about her husband and about her daughter; and although she had tried to make light of a potential re-scheduling of her husband's operation, her underlying agitation had been obvious, and this had clearly affected Helena's state of mind. As yet there was no cause for excessive alarm, but it did mean that any slight hope that Mark had harboured of an early home coming for her had now sunk without trace.

At home Mark sat in the armchair to the right of the fireplace, near to the window. When they had first moved in, he and Helena had talked about an open fire, cold winter nights, and feeling cosy and secure despite falling snow or hard frost. It was cold tonight, but Mark had no incentive to light the fire, and for reasons he couldn't really explain, he had chosen not to turn up the thermostat on the central heating system; something inside his head told him that he did not want to be comfortable when Helena was not by his side.

The first nuisance fireworks were beginning to disturb family pets and unsettle some of the older people of the town, but Mark was so pre-occupied with his own thoughts that he did not hear them. In order to pass the time he picked up the local newspaper; he wasn't really in the mood for reading, but then again he wasn't in a mood for doing anything else either. There was quite a long article about a lady celebrating her hundred and first birthday. She had been born two years before the start of the second Boer War and, as the article pointed out, she had lived through two World Wars, five Monarchs (if you included the uncrowned Edward VIII), and twenty different Prime Ministers, and she was still an active member of the Burrdale Methodist Church and very interested in all current affairs. The photograph showed a small intelligent looking woman surrounded by four generations of her family; her name was Mrs Caroline Hambleton, and she lived in sheltered accommodation in the centre of Burrdale. Mark wondered why her name was familiar and, because he was tired, he didn't immediately make the connection. Then he realised that she could be the writer of the letters that had so impressed him when he had checked the archive material relating to Lucas and Dick Norton and to Crawford Winston. He decided that, provided she was agreeable and that there was no medical or other reason why he shouldn't do so, he would very much like to meet and talk with Mrs Hambleton; somehow he felt sure that the experience would be a rewarding one.

It was nearly midnight; another night of shallow sleep lay ahead. Up until now Mark had resisted the temptation to have a drink. Tonight he felt weary, tonight he reasoned that one glass of whisky couldn't hurt; he poured himself a small tumbler of supermarket own brand cooking whisky, this was not an occasion for a good quality Single Malt and he settled back into his chair, intending to sit for a few moments until the spirit made him feel drowsy and then, when no longer fully awake, to climb the stairs and collapse onto his bed: within seconds of consuming the drink however, he was sound asleep.

Mark didn't see the dark figure approach his front door, he didn't hear the letter box rattle, nor did he hear running feet pounding the concrete path, but, seconds later, he heard the volcanic explosion right outside his front door that reverberated down the whole length of the street, setting off car and burglar alarms as it did so. Bleary eyed, he looked at his wristwatch; it was twenty three minutes past two.

When he went outside the cause of the blast was easy to discover; the remnants of a massive display firework were scattered all over the pavement and on to the road itself. All down the street front doors were opening and confused and angry people were flooding out into the night air, wrapping their dressing gowns tight around them to keep out the October chill. This had been no crass joke of the sort that could be expected on Mischief Night, this was deliberate, wilful harassment; and Mark had not the shadow of a doubt that he was the intended target.

After returning inside to put on a pair of gloves Mark set about the task of retrieving the fragments of the firework. He was not hopeful that there would be fingerprint evidence, but they would still have to be checked, and attempts to trace the shop from which the firework had been bought would also have to be made. He attempted to calm down his neighbours, telling them that it was all over now and that they should get back to their beds, and dispirited, disgruntled and tired he then returned to his own house.

Seething with rage he poured himself another whisky, and this time resolved to drink it upstairs and not to risk further uncomfortable slumber in the armchair. It was as he crossed the hallway to the stairs that he saw the envelope; it had not been there a few hours ago, of that he was sure. It was a large, bulky, brown envelope, and it looked to be very full. He opened it, not knowing what to expect, but anticipating something bad; his instincts didn't let him down. The envelope contained a great many articles which had clearly been downloaded from a variety of web sites. All of them discussed death in childbirth, and made the risk of that occurrence seem to be far greater than Mark had ever believed it to be. His hand was shaking with fury; he hurled the whisky glass across the room, it struck the solid stone wall of the cottage and shattered into hundreds of tiny pieces. Somebody was trying to destroy his mind. He felt near breaking point. There was every possibility that this person would succeed.

Whatever chance there might have been to rest had now gone. If Helena had been there, and not herself in a situation of real danger, she would have comforted him and he would never have thrown the glass. The carpet was damp where the straw coloured liquid had landed and the paintwork had been chipped where the tumbler had hit the wall. In his rage he had damaged their house, Helena's house, and Mark thought how disappointed she would be if she could see him then. He bent down and started to pick up the razor sharp shards of glass, cupping his left hand to receive the broken fragments; when it was he cut his finger, he did not know, but the bloodstains on the hearth rug added to the task of cleaning up and further increased the feeling he had of being overwhelmed by events.

It was a little after six o'clock when he telephoned Tim Gratton and for the second time in three days unburdened himself to his friend and former colleague.

"The bastard's got to me, Tim," he said. "He's finally got to me. I'm almost scared to think what he'll do next. I can't read this man at all, I can't figure out how he thinks, but I know he is putting me through hell and I've no idea how to fight him. Yesterday I grabbed a suspect by the throat because he wound me up. It doesn't matter this time because he is scared shitless and he's got too many secrets to hide to cause any trouble. I've also got a witness who would support me to the hilt, whatever I said, but, after the night I've just had, I can't trust myself to show any restraint today. I've got no self control left. If I'm provoked today, who knows what I might do. I think I could do absolutely anything."

"Don't you see that's just what he wants? Listen to me, Mark. You've got to talk to your Detective Superintendent today. Tell him exactly what's happened and show him the firework and the envelope and its contents. If I was you I'd ask for a couple of days off. Take some time to think about things, I think your boss will give you that. In my view, it would be no bad thing for the person who is doing all this to you to believe that he's beginning to make you crack up; mistakes happen when people get over confident; they get careless, that's what your man will do if he thinks he's winning.

"I've never lived in a small town so I don't really know how things work, but I think it's possible your killer is getting information from inside the police station. I wouldn't presume to tell you how to do your job, but if I was you I would check very carefully any links the civilian staff may have with the known suspects, and I'd even do that with police officers as well. If you unearth anything watch that person like a hawk. Don't tell Helena too much about tonight's events, she's got enough to worry about at the moment, but make sure everything is done to keep her safe."

"You're right as usual Tim, you're so right, but I can't just sit back and do nothing, even if John Lomas allows me to do so; unless I'm actively trying to catch this bastard, I'll feel like I'm letting myself and Helena and everybody down."

"Well, at the very least, for God's sake, don't put yourself into a situation where you can be made to snap." said Tim. "That's just playing into his hands, and if you end up suspended you're no good to anyone, particularly Helena. If you can't take a step back, at least make sure you only operate in areas where your anxieties can't be exploited. Go and see this Mrs Hambleton, you've told me about, but first tell your Superintendent what you're intending to do, but tell nobody else and, whatever you do, don't let yourself react to any provocation from anyone. You're a bloody good copper, Mark; I know it's hard, but don't blow it now. I think you're within a hair's breadth of feeling your man's collar, that's why he's reacting like he is, I really feel quite convinced about that."

Chapter Thirty Four

The first words John Lomas spoke to Mark were not exactly encouraging.

"You look absolute shit," he said. Even though Mark felt totally shattered, he managed a wry smile.

"Thanks for the compliment, Sir," he said, "You might be heartened to know that I don't feel much better than I look either," and he explained to the Detective Superintendent the reasons for his appearance and described the events of the preceding night.

Lomas already knew of the disturbance on Bear Pole Lane. There had been several phone calls to the police complaining about the incident, but he hadn't known until Mark spoke to him that one of his senior officers had been the target of the malicious prank. As Mark outlined the full facts, he became aware for the first time just how nasty the intent had been behind what he had up until then believed to be a random act of drunken stupidity. When Mark told him of his suspicions that information on the progress of the police investigation was being passed from the police station directly to the killer, Mr Lomas became very concerned.

"Have you got any evidence to back this up?" he asked. Mark shook his head.

"Nothing concrete, Sir, It's just a gut feeling, but I'm convinced that somehow the killer seems to know our next move almost before we've decided upon it ourselves. It could be paranoia, I feel so knackered at the moment that I may not be thinking straight, but that's just the way it feels to me."

"It could simply be careless talk," said Lomas, "or the worst case scenario is that you're right, and somebody in here, for whatever motive, is deliberately leaking our plans to a murderer. If there is a mole in this nick then we've got to find out who it is, and if turns out it's merely some lippy buffoon shooting his mouth off, then I promise you his arse will be out of here before you can whistle God save the Queen! Meanwhile, I agree with what your mate in Sheffield has said, you need a couple of days to get some sleep and to spend a bit of time with your wife. Shall I let it be known that you've gone off sick? If anybody in here is talking out of turn, then the news that you've cried off ill will get back to our killer faster than a dose of salts and, as your pal in South Yorkshire says, people get cocky when they think they're winning, and that's when basic errors are made."

Mark shook his head "Thank you Sir, but no thanks." he said. "There's too much to be done. Somebody needs to speak to Dick Norton again, and that really should be me. And I want to be the one to speak to Mrs Hambleton; at least that way if I do it, I can be certain that what I'm told will remain secret. In any event, I'm not up for doing nothing, it'll just make me depressed and I'll end up feeling even more flipping useless that I do at present."

"Look Mark, I do understand how you feel and I know that you don't want to be seen to lose face, but you're practically dead on your feet. At least take a few hours to snatch a bit of rest then, if you want to, go and see Mrs Hambleton, but don't tell anybody else what your plans are; and whatever you do keep way from the nick for a couple of days; much as I know it goes against the grain, I think it could be useful if people on the outside think you are on the verge of some sort of meltdown. From now on make sure that anything you find out is reported directly to me, that way we can keep a lid on what gets out. Don't worry about Dick Norton. I'll arrange for Alan to go and see him. I'll get the rest of the lads looking at Crawford Winston again; if we can find one person above anyone else who really hated him then we may be tapping into a very rich seam indeed."

The chance for a little much needed rest was ultimately too tempting to turn down. Mark could sense how run down he had become. "I'll go and see Helena," he said. "Then, if you're sure Sir, I will try to get my head down for a bit, but it can't be for more than an hour or two. If I let things slide now then events may spiral out of control, and if that happens, God knows how long it will take to get them back on track again."

It was not the unusually early visit of Mark that surprised Helena, it was the pallor of his skin and the charcoal shadows under his eyes that alarmed her. He looked washed out; there was no sparkle in his gaze or energy in his movements. She couldn't help herself; the sight of the man who was her rock, her champion looking so tired and so vanquished touched every raw nerve, and tears flooded her eyes as she held onto his strangely leaden hand.

"Oh Mark." she cried. "Look at you, look at you. You look so worn down and it's all my fault. If I was stronger you wouldn't be this way and it hurts so much to see you looking like this. What's happening to us? What's happening? Why can't things be as they were before?"

Helena's grief somehow cut through the exhaustion which had almost paralysed him. For a second or two there was real fire in his soul and warm blood seemed to flow back into his veins; he held Helena and he kissed her. "You make me better my darling. You give my life purpose in a way that no other person ever could, I had a disturbed night last night because some lunatic decided to let off the biggest firework in the world has ever seen outside our front door in the wee small hours, and that woke up the whole flipping street. I was asleep on the chair because the whisky had knocked me out. I couldn't get back to sleep after that and I've been feeling sorry for myself ever since; but I can see clearly now, providing you're fine and that bump inside your tummy keeps on kicking, everything will come right of that I'm absolutely bloody certain," and his words were uttered with such conviction that Helena could not help but believe that they would be true.

When he eventually returned home, having spent much more time with Helena than he had originally planned to do, for several hours Mark slept. He slept far longer than he had intended to, which that meant that any visit to Mrs Hambleton would have to be postponed until the following day. He had unplugged the bedroom phone and switched off his works mobile, leaving only his personal mobile still functioning. He had thought that when he checked the various phones later he would discover that the World and his wife had been trying to contact him, but amazingly it turned out nobody had. When at last he woke up, although he felt disorientated like any mid-day sleeper awaking in the early evening always does, he could tell that his senses were becoming more acute, and he had real hope that if these sound foundations could be followed up with a good night's sleep, then tomorrow offered genuine prospects of being a better, brighter, keener day. The key word, of course, was "if." "If pigs might fly" he had thought as he had laid his head on the pillow that night, but they had taken to the skies, and within seconds he was dead to the world.

Against all his expectations, he did sleep again. He slept deeply and without dreams to discomfort him and, for the first time in many days, when he awoke the next morning he felt optimism: these murders had to be solved, and he would be the one to solve them and, in doing so, at the same time he would ease the pressure on Helena and on himself. It had been three days since he had shaved and the stubble on his face, which although predominantly black was mottled with grey to a far greater degree than he would have wished, had grown rampant. The thought of becoming a father for the first time at his time of life was a thrilling and daunting prospect. As the sharp blade cleared some of the most tangible signs of age from his cheeks, he wondered just how he would cope. He smiled a genuinely contented smile; as long as he had Helena, he knew they would cope very well indeed.

The telephone call to Mrs Hambleton was as positive and friendly as he could have wished it to be, and by eleven o'clock he was sitting in her front room talking to a remarkable lady.

She wasn't tall, compared to Mark she looked tiny; old age had caused her to stoop and old bones limited her mobility. She was practically blind in one eye, although she retained reasonable vision in the other, but whatever physical restrictions she had were compensated for by an amazingly sharp mind and, an interest in life, far greater than that possessed by many people who were not yet a quarter of her age. She lived alone with local authority support, but there was no feeling of loneliness; the room was full of photographs of children, grandchildren and great-grandchildren, and of a broad handsome man who had obviously been her husband. Mark accepted the cup of tea which she insisted on making for him and he then explained to Mrs Hambleton the reason for his visit.

"I read your letters," he said, "and they stood out from all the others. You seemed to me to embody a sense of reason, and you spoke from a position of knowledge. I don't know why it should be, but I know these recent terrible murders have their roots in the death of Lucas Norton and the perversions of Crawford Winston; if I'm to solve them, I need to really understand who these people were and what made them tick, and the impact that they had on other people's lives.

Mrs Hambleton smiled. "I fear I will be a huge disappointment to you," she said, "but ask anything you want and I'll do my best to try to help you."

"Tell me about the Chadwick family please. I think that's where we should start."

"I suppose that they were what you would call today rather a dysfunctional family," said Mrs Hambleton. "I watched Sidney Chadwick grow up, he was the same age as my youngest daughter Anne. He was a strange youth, a bit slow, he was often picked on at school; sometimes he used to lose his temper and lash out if he was upset, but he wasn't big and he frightened nobody. He found it difficult to stick at things, but when he worked he worked very hard. To the best of my recollection he never had a girlfriend in town; it was quite a surprise to everyone when he went away for a few months and came back engaged to Lizzie."

"What was she like?" asked Mark.

"She was a simple good hearted girl," said Mrs Hambleton, "Extremely disorganised. People in town called her a hippie because of the way she dressed; she was something of a figure of fun, but she was very kind and well meaning, I liked Lizzie a lot."

"Tell me about the rest of the family. I know a little about Shane, but what about the other members of it?"

"The person I knew best was Lizzie's sister, Norah. She was quite a lot older than Lizzie and she was wheelchair bound; she was one of the victims of the Polio epidemic of the 1950's, I can't remember the exact year. She was a teenager when it happened, which was quite unusual, because most of the children who suffered were quite a lot younger than that, or so I believe was the case. She came to Burrdale to be near her sister, she was much brighter than Lizzie and she was a devout Christian. I met her through the church. We became good friends. She continued to correspond with me even after the family were forced out of town; she died in 1985 or 1986 of a brain tumour.

"There was also a younger half sister who I didn't know at all. Norah hardly ever spoke of her; her name was Lillian. Norah resented the fact that her father had left home for a while to be with Lillian's mum, and later she disapproved of the fact that Lillian had set up home with a married man. She was teaching somewhere in Lancashire by then and at the time Lucas's tragedy happened she had been virtually cut off from the rest of the family. She was using the name Widdowson, or Williamson or Willoughby, or something like that, but she was the one who eventually gave the children a home when their mother committed suicide in 1984. Sidney had walked out two or three years before, nobody knows where he went. Poor Lizzie couldn't cope. It was very, very distressing." And there was genuine sadness in Mrs Hambleton's voice as she spoke.

"What about Shane and the other children?" asked Mark, "Did you know them? What were they like?"

"Shane was a lovely boy," said Mrs Hambleton. "He tried so hard; I think he was probably mildly autistic, but nobody recognised the condition in those days. He just wanted to please. He tended to take things too literally, he was very impressionable and I think easily manipulated, but very gentle, and very, very trusting. What Dick Norton did to him was absolutely criminal. His sister Sharon was only six years old when the tragedy occurred. She was a sweet little thing, but I never saw her growing up, and the other boy, Derek, had only just had his fifth birthday when the family fled Burrdale; how he turned out I really don't know."

"Talking about Dick Norton, what sort of man was he? And what was Lucas like? Tell me about them both."

"Dick Norton was six months older than my middle son Robert," said Mrs Hambleton. "He was a bright kid who was extremely good at sport, particularly rugby, but he was a bully at school and a bit mardy if he didn't get his own way. When he got married, he mellowed a good deal and he was certainly devoted to Lucas. Lucas was an incredibly good looking little boy and very, very clever like his dad, but he was spoilt, and he did have some of his father's temperament. He thought he was better than the other kids, which meant that he didn't seem to have too many friends. I think that was one reason why he tolerated Shane, he looked up to Lucas and Lucas loved being looked up to. After Lucas died Dick was devastated. What he did to the Chadwick family was awful, but he was in so much pain that I can understand why he did it. I don't think he's ever fully recovered from the shock; it destroyed his marriage and it blighted poor Rebecca's life, and she's the one I feel most sorry for."

"That leaves Crawford Winston," said Mark. "What did you think of him?"

A sudden coldness came over Mrs Hambleton. "He was an evil man, Mr Hobson," she said. "He seemed so generous and so cultured, and was outwardly very charming, but it was all a charade; inside he was morally corrupt. One of my grandchildren was one of his victims. God forgive me, but I prayed that he would rot in Hell, and even after so many years I still feel the same way.

"Yet you wrote those letters asking for tolerance and forgiveness for his relatives" said Mark.

"They were innocent," said Mrs Hambleton, "and they were victims too. Why should anybody seek to punish them?"

Chapter Thirty Five

The meeting with Mrs Hambleton behind him and, with a further good night's sleep under his belt, Mark Hobson felt like a new man. There had been no new setbacks for Helena, her blood pressure had stabilised, and with that worry for the time being lifted, he was raring to get back to some proper police work. Mark's only problem was that Detective Superintendent Lomas didn't want him at the police station, he preferred to continue with the deception that Mark was absent on sick leave. Mark understood the reasons behind his senior officer's desires and, he agreed with them, but never-the-less he found the thought of imposed idleness hard to bear. He came from a background in which being straight with people mattered. You didn't cheat the system: you didn't claim your pay without earning it. Even on the worst of the bad old days, on those occasions when the pounding inside his head had seemed sufficient to shatter the entire outer casing of his skull and his stomach had churned like a turbulent sea, he had still turned in for work. It felt wrong when he was in better physical and mental shape than he had been for weeks that he should be instructed not to be at his desk, but, worse than that, it felt like he was back pedalling in his fight against a killer who had also quite deliberately put the life and health of Helena at serious risk. Mr Lomas had understood this, and had promised that his enforced absence from Burrdale police station would be short lived, and he had suggested that he could do worse than spend the next few hours logged on the computer to see what, if any, relevant information might be found hovering in the outer reaches of cyberspace.

Mark was not a computer illiterate, no modern policeman could afford to be, but his literacy barely exceeded the level of a "Jane and Peter" book and it therefore seemed odd to him that he was having to search the Internet as a first, and not a last, resort to see if he could find any reference to Shane Chadwick's youngest auntie. There were so many websites it was almost impossible to know where to start and he had such very limited information to go on. "Widdowson", "Williamson", "Willoughby", or maybe any other multi-syllable surname beginning with the letter "W", it was an extremely vague description; and although Mark had worked out the year this lady was born, Mrs Hambleton had been unable to give him a day or date or month to assist his search. She hadn't even known if she shared a maiden name with her two elder half-sisters. "Friends Re-united" might hold the key and amongst countless thousands of personal diaries, which were now available for worldwide scrutiny, something could possibly be discovered; but more likely there would be absolutely nothing.

The records of teacher training colleges were available to be sifted, and it was almost certain that within the membership registers of one of the main teaching unions relevant details would be recorded, but access to those records would be zealously guarded and little or nothing was likely to be divulged voluntarily to the police. If nothing was forthcoming, then in time, with the help of a court order, details might be prised out, but time was a luxury that Mark could ill afford. He couldn't say why, but he was fearful that the end game was about to be played. The stakes had been raised, and he worried that another death formed part of the killer's overall intent.

The rage inside the murderer had intensified; of that fact Mark was sure. Almost certainly there must have been critical points along his journey when he had agonised whether to carry on, but not any longer. After the first death all his boats had been burned and Mark suspected that the feeling had been good. He wondered how often in his mind the killer had tightened the garrotte around Virginia's neck until it could tighten no more, and how many times had he recalled with satisfaction, the force with which he had plunged the knife into her defenceless chest. Did he strike his pillow at night re-living every day the moment of his absolute triumph? Would he have inflicted further vengeful damage on the corpse if he had had more time? Mark was sure that he would have done; and if before her violent death he could have heaped ritual humiliation upon a once proud woman, he would not have held back, and his victory would then have been complete and total.

Somewhere along the way, maybe not until he had killed for a second time to silence Mike Skinner, he had come to the realisation that one ruthless execution wasn't enough. That killing had not been part of the original strategy. It had been a reaction to events, but, thereafter, had he decided to embark upon a war of extermination to ensure that everyone he perceived to have been an enemy paid a heavy price? John Winston had been threatened with the destruction of everything he valued most. Mark shuddered as the thought suddenly struck home that in the eyes of a psychopath he was an enemy because he opposed him, and because of that so too was Helena. Did he see her as Mark's Achilles heel, as Tim Gratton had suggested might be the case? Did he think by attacking her it would fatally wound him? And did the killer have future plans to neutralise the threat Mark posed to him by harming Helena yet again?

In the early afternoon, after three hours of tedious browsing, to little worthwhile effect, Mark telephoned John Lomas. He asked him to use the considerable resources the police had available to try to trace Shane's mother's surviving younger half-sister, and through her, or by any other means, to try to locate Shane's sister and younger brother if they were both still alive. Lomas promised to do his best, but like Mark, he felt it wouldn't be easy, and in the short term it might even prove impossible. He did, however, consent to Mark returning to work the next day, but only if the impression was created that this was the D.I. being stubborn, and ignoring all sensible advice to the contrary

In the evening Mark visited Helena. He didn't leave the hospital until long after the final visitors' bell had rung and, even after he left the ward, he didn't leave the building until he had spoken to Hospital Security to urge them to be on the alert for any suspicious strangers.

The time that he had spent with Helena had been good, it was never anything else so far as he was concerned, and she had been a lot more composed than she had been the day before. The reason for the improvement was mainly due to the fact that her father had now learnt that his operation was to go ahead as planned after all, and his relief had lifted some of the pressure from her shoulders; Mark's own improved physical state had also helped to do this. As a consequence of being more relaxed, Helena's blood pressure had started to drop significantly and the satisfaction the doctors had expressed had been a further boost to her self-confidence.

That night at home, because he had nothing better to do, Mark returned to the computer. He sat glued to the monitor until well after midnight, by which time his strained, abused eyes could take no more. Here and there he found odd references to Lillian

"Widdowsons", "Williamsons", "Willoughbys", "Warringtons", "Waddingtons", "Watkinsons", "Wellingtons" and "Winchesters", but nothing that could clearly and unequivocally be said to relate to the lady he so desperately wanted to find. Eventually he could take no more; frustrated and tired he waved the white flag and retreated to the cold comfort of his sterile, empty bed.

The next day, although awake in good time, he didn't shave, nor did he take particular care over his appearance. The image he presented was far from a flattering one, but it was a necessary one. He looked like a man struggling to hold himself together, which was exactly the impression Mr Lomas wanted him to make, and that was certainly the perception that people who met him gained when they looked closely at him.

His meeting with Mr Lomas turned out to be very interesting. The Detective Superintendent had instructed Alan Nadin to go and talk to Dick Norton but, before he left the police station, a telephone call had been received from Jackie Skinner. She had sounded frightened and upset and, because Alan knew her, and could be trusted to be compassionate and re-assuring when the situation demanded, Lomas had agreed that he should go and see her first before visiting Dick Norton.

It turned out the cause of Jackie's distress had actually been Dick

Norton himself. He had repeatedly telephoned her, alleging that Mike had confided to her details which related directly to the death of Lucas and the murder of Virginia. When she had told him that he was wrong and that she didn't know what he was talking about he hadn't believed her. He had offered her money, a very substantial amount of money, to tell him the information Mike had passed on to her and, when she had protested that she knew nothing, he had called her a liar, and threatened to go round to the house personally to ransack it if necessary, and not to leave until she'd given him the answers that he knew she had.

Alan had been outraged at her treatment: at a time when she most needed sympathy and understanding, she had been threatened and vilified. When he subsequently met Norton he had not held anything back and had torn into the butcher with barely concealed fury. At one point he had actually arrested Norton using powers contained in the Protection from Harassment Act and, although he had subsequently de-arrested him because he was sure Jackie would not support a police prosecution, when Norton refused to tell him what it was he believed Jackie knew he gave him the bollocking of a life time. The butcher was left under no illusions at all as to what he might expect if he were unwise enough ever to try to intimidate Mrs Skinner or anyone else again.

An unfortunate postscript to whole incident was that when Paul Burgess had called to see Rebecca later that night to try and patch things up between them, Norton had barred his entry into the flat. Unwisely, Paul had tried to force his way in, Norton had blocked his path and, in the struggle that had followed, Paul had received a black eye. There was nothing he could do. Legally Norton was within his rights. He had used reasonable force to prevent a trespasser from entering into his home. The whole affair had degenerated into an unpleasant slanging match: torn between her father and her boyfriend, a distraught Becky had once again come down on the side of her father, and her relationship with Paul was now at an end. He had returned to the police station in a state of fury and had paced around the nick like a wounded panther, which had made life very uncomfortable indeed for everyone else in the C.I.D. office.

The results of John Lomas's covert inquiries into possible "moles" within the nick had been unproductive. There had, of course, been a connection between Paul Burgess and Dick Norton, which had now so dramatically come to an end, but nobody in their right mind could ever have considered that relationship to be close. It was inconceivable that, given the degree of underlying distrust there had always been between the two men which was manifestly obvious, Burgess would have risked his job to help a person who so plainly disliked him. Two civilian staff, one a typist, the other a front desk counter clerk, turned out to be distantly related to Joe Broadbent, but neither of them had access to classified information. P.C.Ollerenshaw's wife was John Winston's second cousin, but there wasn't a shred of evidence to suggest that that relationship had caused Ollerenshaw to jeopardise his long police career by leaking information to a remote relative with whom he could only ever have had the most tenuous of links.

Mr Lomas's inquiries into teachers had born better fruit. Despite having to overcome a number of obstacles, and only after promises had been given that this was off the record and would not form part of any prosecution case, he had found out that a Lillian Wrenbury had been at a teacher training college in Bolton in the late 1970's and that she had lived with a man called Martin Willoughby for more than eight years before they separated. She had later formed a new relationship with a person called Lloyd Bannister and sometime in the late 1980's she had apparently married him. Lomas had discovered that Mrs Bannister was still teaching at a school in North Yorkshire. All the information he had so painstakingly teased out from his contact ticked the boxes Mark needed to see ticked, and so it was agreed between the two men that he would secretly arrange to meet Mrs Bannister to see what, if any, light she could throw on those dark corners of this murder investigation which were still badly in need of further illumination.

Chapter Thirty Six

An unusually sharp frost for late October had turned the earth hard and painted the trees and the parked vehicles Arctic white. Mark scraped at the windscreen of his car with a credit card. He hadn't yet bought de-icer believing it to be unnecessary so early in the year, but that assumption had proved to be entirely wrong. Did this cold snap herald the onset of another savage Peak District winter such as the one that happened twenty years before? He didn't know, but the ice that clung stubbornly to the glass seemed to foretell as much, and the cold which numbed his fingers and frustrated his efforts to make an early start seemed to promise that there would be much worse still to come. Not too far away the sirens of emergency vehicles wailed and Mark wondered if the icy roads had claimed their first victims of the approaching season; perhaps even at that precise moment cutting equipment was being used to free trapped and injured people from tangled and jagged metal. The depressing thought struck Mark that if the weather remained bad no doubt there would be many more occasions when this equipment would need to do its work.

Eventually he managed to clear the last vestiges of Siberia from the outside of his car but he was still not able to set off. He had to sacrifice precious minutes of his journey time waiting for the heater to evaporate some of the condensation from the inside of the windscreen before he could be on his way and, because to begin with, only part of the screen was clear, and because the sun was low down in the sky, he had to drive slowly for the first couple of miles of the journey to avoid colliding with parked vehicles.

Telephone calls to Mrs Bannister had confirmed that she was indeed Shane Chadwick's auntie and, although initially she hadn't wished to speak to him, she had ultimately agreed to do so. The omens weren't good; she had told Mark over the phone that she remained in regular contact with Sharon, to whom she said she was very close, but that she had not seen Derek for at least ten years and had no idea at all as to his current whereabouts. She had assumed that Mark would abandon as futile his plans to visit her when he realised she had no up to date information to give, but Mark had explained that historic recollections that she might possess could be absolutely vital and so, without any enthusiasm, she had agreed to see him; but personally she still doubted the usefulness of the entire exercise.

The drive to the small North Yorkshire town where Mrs Bannister still taught turned out to be far less straightforward than Auto Route had predicted it would be. Low lying mist in the Hope Valley severely restricted visibility for the first part of the journey and road works on the M.18 then caused long tail backs. A broken down articulated lorry in the contra-flow system had also added substantially to the congestion, and what on paper should have been a two and a half hour drive, in fact took over four and a quarter hours to complete.

Perhaps it was the frustration of queuing in seemingly permanent traffic jams that caused Mark to once more to wonder if any end to his murder investigation would ever be arrived at. He had expended so much of his energy and almost all his personal credibility on pursuing the Shane Chadwick connection that he just had to succeed; but what if he was wrong? Suppose Mrs Bannister pointed him along a trail that led to a discovery that Derek Chadwick was dead, or in prison, or living abroad, or fighting for his country overseas, or in some other way provided conclusive proof that he couldn't possibly have committed the murders. If that occurred then he had nothing left. Paul Burgess would have been right all along. The identity of a double murderer would still be completely unknown, and the risk to any potential victim would have greatly increased because there would now not even be a recognisable motive to help investigators divine what a killer's next actions might be. He and Helena were previous objects of the man's hatred. If there was no discernible reason why this man was acting in the way that he was then how could their safety be ensured? Mark didn't know and that lack of knowledge frightened him; he had no other cards up his sleeve, no plan B to revert to and, like a goat tethered to bait a tiger, he had every reason to fear and no reason whatsoever to feel confident.

Finally, and not in the best frame of mind, Mark arrived at his destination. The school in which Mrs Bannister taught was a 1960s concrete structure, and a drab monument to bad architecture. It was not quite a failing school, but it didn't rank highly in any school league table. Government money appeared largely to have passed it by. An air of fatalistic under-achievement hung over the whole edifice which seemed to challenge the political boasts of the Secretary of State for Education.

Mark parked his car in one of the empty visitor spaces on the car park. An east wind had picked up, an idle wind that blew straight through you, and there was dampness in the atmosphere that chilled the bone to the marrow. Mark made his way to the reception desk in the main entrance hall. He could have been a mad gunman or a predatory rapist but he was not stopped or questioned by anybody at any time. Graffiti defaced the walls of the Assembly Hall; paint was peeling from ill fitting metal framed windows and chewing gum pock marked the fading wood block floor.

After introducing himself and explaining his business he was taken to a small, sparsely furnished office, and there he met Mrs Bannister. She was a tall, thin woman in her early fifties. Made up and dressed to go out she could probably still cut a very striking figure, but the shapeless grey sweater that she wore didn't flatter, and the thick tweed skirt did nothing to recapture her lost youth.

"Mrs Bannister, I'm Detective Inspector Hobson," said Mark. "We spoke on the phone. I think you know why I'm here; I'm investigating the deaths of two people and I'm hoping that you might be able to help me with my enquiries."

Mrs Bannister shook her head. "I very much doubt that, Inspector Hobson," she replied, "but ask what you will, if I can assist you at all then I will do so."

"I think you cared for Shane, Sharon and Derek Chadwick after their mother died," stated Mark, "will you tell me the circumstances as to just how that state of affairs came about?"

"I often ask myself that same question," pondered Mrs Bannister. "I suppose it was a pity really, I don't honestly know. For a long while Norah and Lizzie would have nothing whatsoever to do with me. Norah was the worst! She blamed my mum for breaking up her family. She was supposed to be a Christian, but that didn't stop her calling me a bastard, and when I moved in with Martin and we lived together, that was the end so far as she was concerned. If she referred to me at all it was always as "Jezebel" or "that slut": I really, really didn't like Norah."

"What about Lizzie?" asked Mark? "What were your feelings for her?"

"Lizzie was completely dominated by Norah, but she wasn't nasty like her. She always wanted to do the right thing, but she made so many mistakes. The man she married was a complete washout; he had no brains, and very little courage. When he left her alone with the three kids because he couldn't cope with the problems, it came as no surprise to me. Lizzie had no one else to turn to and so she wrote to me. I tried to help her as best I could, but things had gone too far; but I did get to know the children a little during that period and that really infuriated Norah! After Lizzie died who was left? Norah didn't want them, and in any event she couldn't have coped. Either I had the kids or they went into care. Martin had been in care himself for a short while; he knew how awful that could be. He was brilliant. He said "We can't let it happen to them and that's why they came to live with us." explained Mrs Bannister.

"Tell me about the children" said Mark, "What were they like?"

"In a sense I never knew the real Shane." said Mrs Bannister. "Everybody who had known him as a child said that he had been a really lovely, gentle little boy, and I think that was true; but when he came to me he was very disturbed and insecure. He was depressed, angry, frightened, introverted and inadequate. He did appallingly badly at school, partly because he truanted most of the time. He had no friends: the only person he was close to was his little brother. Maybe that was because Derek looked so much like he had looked when he was a small boy. Shane more or less ignored Sharon completely, but he would do anything for Derek, and he'd stand up for him through thick and thin. Derek adored him. Shane started using hard drugs when he was just fifteen years old. I know that seems common place now, but it was a truly shocking thing in those days. Time and again he stole money from us, and we never knew from one day to the next whether he would come home or whether he wouldn't. He didn't only steal from us. He started shoplifting to fund his habit, and there was a time when the police seemed to live at our house, he was in trouble so often. Sometimes he'd even take his sister's pocket money he was that desperate, but he never took anything from Derek. If I tried to stop him he would scream and yell and once he hit me in the face with his fist, making my nose bleed and splitting my top lip. That was the final straw. I threw him out. I wouldn't take him back even when he begged and pleaded to be allowed to come home. I don't think Derek ever forgave me for not letting him return."

"What about Sharon?" asked Mark, "Did you have any of the same problems with her?"

Mrs Bannister shook her head vigorously. "Sharon was and is an absolute delight." she said. "I sometimes ask myself, if I had the chance to live my life again would I do the same things? And if Sharon had to be part of a package, then my answer would have to be "yes". She may not be very academic, but she's grown up into such a sweet natured, loving, honest person. She still rings me two or three times a week, even though she's now married, and she still calls me "mum;" I'm grandmother to her two little girls, and my happiest times are all spent with her and with them."

 "The youngest child Derek," said Mark, "do you mind telling me everything you can about him?"

Mrs Bannister was silent for a long while.

"I know I failed him," she said. "He could have done so much, but after I refused to take Shane back, he hated me and from then on I could do nothing to help him. He had truly awesome potential. He was only just over eight when his mother died, and somehow that didn't seem to affect him because he had Shane, and whilst Shane was in his life he had an anchor. I've never seen such a bright little child. By the time he was ten he had the reading ability of the average sixteen year old; he was good at every type of sport and he had the most beautiful singing voice. Martin used to say he was special, and I truly believe he was, but after Shane had gone things changed. He started to have terrible tantrums and he wouldn't listen to a word I said. He would deliberately damage my things and throw food around the house for me to clear up. He was always worst if he saw Shane on the street, there was no controlling him when that happened; and time and time again he demanded to hear the story of that little boy's death and of his family's flight from Burrdale. I didn't know names, and I never met any of the people concerned, but Derek always accused me of hiding their details from him. Little boys often make threats and it's just so much hot air, but Derek was different; he said he would find out who they were and he would kill them and you really felt he meant every word he said."

By the time he was fourteen the situation was impossible. He wouldn't speak to me or let me touch him and sometimes he would even spit at me if I went near. He had to go into care because there was a total breakdown of our family life. I believe he stayed with a number of foster parents up and down the country; in the end, I think one placement really did work and he stayed with that couple until he was at least sixteen. When he was old enough I am told that he changed his name by deed poll, and effectively he became their son. He air-brushed his sister and he airbrushed me completely out of his life. We never hear from him, we don't know where he is, or even what he's called; as far as he's concerned we don't exist, and I think that's how it will stay." Mark noticed the sadness in Mrs Bannister's eyes as she remembered those turbulent and traumatic years.

"We were all scarred," she added. "The legacy of bitterness and recrimination even got to Martin and me. I nearly had a nervous breakdown, and I took my feeling of anger and guilt out on him because he had encouraged me to take the kids in the first place; we drifted apart, it was my fault, I'd become such a miserable person to live with."

"I'm sorry," said Mark. "I can see all this is distressing for you; we've nearly finished, I promise you, but, before I go, will you have a look at this please?" and he pulled a copy of the photograph that had been recovered from Virginia's purse from out of his wallet.

"This picture was being carried by my first murder victim," he explained, "We really have no idea why. We think its Shane, but to be honest, we're not entirely sure. Can you confirm that for us?"

Mrs Bannister shook her head: "No," she answered, "its Derek, it must have been taken when he was about twelve years old. How did your murder victim get hold of it?"

"I truly have no idea," said Mark, "until thirty seconds ago I thought it was Shane. It's possible it could have been given to her by a man called Mike Skinner; he was a childhood pal of Shane once upon a time. Is it possible that Shane could have sent it to him?"

"I don't know. Shane wasn't very good at writing, but maybe

there were times when he was feeling wretched and lonely he could have scribbled a note to a one time friend, and he perhaps felt easier talking about Derek than he did about admitting what a sorry mess his own life had become."

It was as Mark was about to take his leave from Mrs Bannister that the thunderbolt happened. The door of the office was flung open, and in walked a small bearded man who was obviously a teacher. He seemed surprised to find the room occupied.

"I'm so sorry, Jenny," he said. "I didn't know anybody was in here, will you be long? I just need a quiet place to make a telephone call."

"Nearly done Frank," replied Mrs Bannister. "Just give us five more minutes and then the room's all yours."

"I'll pop back in ten. Will that be O.K?" and on being told by Mrs Bannister that that was "fine," he left the room, carefully closing the door behind him as he went.

"He called you, Jenny," said Mark. "I thought your name was Lillian."

"It is, Inspector," answered Mrs Bannister, "but my mother's maiden name was Wrenbury. My dad never married her and his name doesn't appear on my birth certificate. My friends at school all called me Jenny because of the songbird and the name sort of stuck; I prefer it to Lillian in any event. Somehow it just makes me feel younger."

Suddenly the neon light in Mark's brain burned bright. He hadn't listened carefully enough. He had misheard! The name was "Lill," not "Jill". All the missing pieces of the jigsaw were tumbling headlong into place.

Chapter Thirty Seven

"You can fuck off! She doesn't want to talk to you." Richard Norton sat in the small office at the back of the shop behind a battered desk and relived his triumph of two nights before.

The lad had called at just the wrong time while he was still seething. What Alan Nadin had said to him was completely out of order. To be threatened and abused by a police officer in your own home was totally unacceptable. He hadn't threatened Jackie Skinner, he just asked for information that she had. Mike Skinner had always been a devious bastard, with his grubby fingers in a great many pies. There wasn't much that went off that he hadn't known about, and from previous conversations they had had it was obvious that he had found concrete evidence to connect specific individuals to Lucas's death. Jackie had no money. She needed cash. He had been generous in his offer. Why had the silly bitch not just given him what he was after? If it had been anybody else he would have thought she was trying to get a better deal but not her. Maybe she didn't know the value of what she had? Why couldn't she just have sat down and talked to him rather than getting upset? He'd been trying to help her, and in the same process help himself; there had been no need for her to go off the rails in the manner that she had.

Alan Nadin had been way over the top. He needn't have reacted in the way that he did. The police had no sense of proportion, and the young lad who had been dating Becky was no different. She'd told him quite clearly earlier in the day that she wanted to end their relationship; he should have got the message. Any sensible youth would have accepted it was over. It hadn't been working for some time, he should have acknowledged that but stupid young idiot wouldn't do that.

He couldn't have timed his second visit to the house worse. The fury that he felt at being verbally beaten up by that bastard Nadin had increased tenfold his contempt for the Derbyshire Police force so when the wet behind the ears ex-boyfriend had pounded on his front door and demanded to speak to Rebecca, he was ready for him.

They had argued in the street. The daft sod had tried to force his way inside; the smack he got for his pains was well deserved. For a moment a smile flirted with the corners of Norton's mouth. He'd put the good looking copper in his place. A pretty boy with a humdinger of a black eye; Norton laughed as he recalled the results of his handiwork.

Becky had heard the commotion and rushed downstairs. She was screaming at them both to stop. The lad was saying "I just want to talk, I just want to talk." She had dithered, and for a second he had thought she would crumple then, praise be, she had told him she couldn't cope anymore, she just wanted him to go, and eventually he had stormed off in a rage.

"Don't ever come back here you fucking loser," he had yelled after him, and that moment his victory had been complete. For the first time in twenty years he felt like a winner, and momentarily his inner grief had gone away: it didn't stay away long.

Immediately after the fracas he had worried about how Becky would react. She had told him in the past that she couldn't stand living at home anymore, and when the exhilaration of the moment melted away, he had been terrified that she would turn on him and announce that she was leaving. That hadn't happened. True, she had said very little to him since the incident, but nothing bad. She was a good girl; he would reward her for her common sense. He would buy her something nice, maybe some expensive jewellery, or even a new car, and throw a holiday into the bargain. That would please her that would make her happy.

He opened the bottom drawer in the desk and pulled out a bottle of whiskey, he didn't look at what brand it was, unscrewed the cap and poured himself a drink. He pulled his chair away from the desk, it didn't move far, the room was really no bigger than a cupboard, and mainly used by him to write up his order book and lock up his petty cash, and sometimes as a bolt hole when he found himself being savaged by Churchill's black dog of depression.

He heard the front door of the shop open. Becky was home. She was going to a party tonight, she'd enjoy that; to let her hair down a little would do her good, and tomorrow, when she was still bubbly after a nice night out, he would tell her of the treats he had planned for her.

She came into the back room to seek him out. She looked pale, and far from well.

"You're late home Love," he said. "You've not got much time to get ready to go out."

"I'm not going out," she replied. "I feel like death warmed up. I'm going to go to bed, but I've something to tell you first. I've found a flat of my own in Manchester, and I'll be moving out at the weekend. I can't live in this atmosphere anymore."

He started to protest, but she cut him short. "Not another word Dad," she said, "or I'll go tonight. My mind's made up. There's nothing you can do to make me change it so please don't try. I feel cold, I feel achy, I feel sick. If you care for me at all, just let me get some sleep. If you don't I'll find somewhere else to rest my head, even if it is a park bench. I mean it Dad, not one more word."

The finality of the decision, and the conviction that it was set in stone hit him like a sledgehammer. He was numb, he was speechless, and he was utterly broken. He leant forward to try to grab her hand, to beg her to stay, to plead for his life, but she was gone. Tears welled up in his eyes, only the death of Lucas had been as bad as this. He had nothing left. He threw a tumbler of whisky down his throat; the unkind liquid burned as it travelled to his stomach; he poured another large drink and repeated the process.

If he was to be left truly alone, then it meant that the monster who was Shane Chadwick had won, but he hadn't achieved victory all by himself. The actions of others had helped him on his way. Jackie Skinner knew who they were, or at least where Mike had stored away vital information. And the nephew of the pervert Crawford Winston, he must bear some of the blame, and probably there were others. Tomorrow he would hunt them down; tomorrow he would make them talk; he wasn't going to be cowed by the threats of any police officer. Detective Sergeant Alan Nadin hadn't seen anything yet.

His mood got incrementally blacker as the amber spirit disappeared. By midnight he was well into his second bottle. The thought then struck him that later that morning he would have terrible things to do. He staggered out of his chair intent on climbing to his bed. His head span like a fairground Waltzer, and it seemed to have disproportionately increased in weight compared with the rest of his body. He lurched from one side of the room to the other, unable to control his movements. He crashed into the shop counter, and collapsed in a stupor onto the stone floor behind it. His head was bleeding from a bad cut, but he was too drunk to realise it. Tomorrow a lot of cleaning up would be needed.

How long he was unconscious for he didn't know, and for much of that time if a plutonium bomb had exploded right outside his window it would not have awakened him, but gradually he began to re-emerge into fretful consciousness. His head ached, he had been sick and his clothes stank. Unable to cope with the harsh reality of it all he closed his eyes and tried to return to sleep.

Whether it was the rattle of the letterbox, or the pungent smell of petrol, or the flickering light of the fire that finally dragged him back into reality he couldn't say. For a while he was disorientated, unable to make sense of what his eyes were witnessing, then everything began to become clear. He felt the heat. The room was in flames; everything was well alight.

The shouting of people from outside became discernible, blue lights were flashing in the night sky, a heavy implement was being smashed against the front door, any second now it would burst open and firemen would enter his home to deal with the blaze.

A terrifying thought exploded in his mind. Becky was asleep upstairs. She was in deadly danger; she had to be saved. Suddenly he realised her peril was an opportunity. He would be the one to save her, and in her gratitude for his courage she would stay. If he was injured in the process, then so much the better; she surely could not run away from the loving father who had risked his life to protect his child,

No bastard is going to beat me to it; no-one is going to rob me of this chance. As the door burst open, ignoring desperate cries to wait where he was, he rushed up the staircase to the flat above, and into a solid wall of flame.

Chapter Thirty Eight

In a strange way Mark felt that somewhere very deep inside himself, buried by layers of incredulity, had always lurked the suspicion which had now spawned a dreadful fact, but that didn't make the final realisation any the less shocking or any easier to come to terms with. Derek Chadwick had metamorphosed into Paul Burgess, that much in his own mind was now clear, and not for a moment did he doubt that this dramatic transformation would be capable of verification. Mark had always regarded Paul as bright and now, through Mrs Bannister, he had found out just how bright he really was.

Lots of things were becoming clear: Paul's total opposition to the murder inquiry focussing on Shane Chadwick could now be explained, and his subdued behaviour at the very start of the investigation could now be understood. Paul had claimed that he'd been ill at the time when Virginia was killed, but he had self-certified that sickness. Becky Norton had waited a long, long time in the café for him to arrive, and had found him poor company when he eventually did. This had been put down to him feeling unwell, but in reality there had been another, more terrifying, explanation.

Even the most inhuman of men cannot kill and feel nothing, and Paul Burgess was far from inhuman. The enormity of the act has to have an impact, and the effort of trying to suppress a wide range of conflicting emotions can mislead an observer into gaining an entirely false idea as to why a man is behaving as he is. It takes an extraordinarily focussed individual to be able to murder a woman, in a frenzy of hatred, and then drink afternoon coffee and make small talk to a girlfriend, as if nothing has happened when metaphorically speaking, the blood on his hands is still wet? To be able to carry on as normal in a highly charged situation and not to give himself away took a special kind of talent and a will of iron; but if a person has had a lifelong mission to seek retribution against people who had wronged an innocent life, then anything was perhaps possible.

There had been very few mistakes. The lack of fingerprints and D.N.A., which had so puzzled Mark, became much easier to explain when the criminal was an expert investigator and fully aware of the errors ordinary offenders often make; but not even the cleverest of persons is perfect and, despite his care there had been mistakes. Mike Skinner must have discovered something, and could only have done so if there'd been a slip up. The failure to recover the ear stud ripped from Virginia's ear was a lapse of concentration and the throw away, seemingly innocuous, comment Paul had made about his Aunt Jenny had now come back to haunt him. There were other things too, which, when looked at with the benefit of hindsight, should have pointed the finger of suspicion towards him. The depth of knowledge that he possessed about Shane's death was far greater than any ordinary detective could reasonably be expected to have had, and the ease with which he'd unravelled tangled family trees which had seemed remarkable, as had his mastery of the local geography could now be viewed in a very different light.

Mike Skinner had to have been the anonymous caller who had wanted to speak to Paul Burgess at Burrdale police station. How Paul had maintained self-control when he received that call almost beggared belief. Most people would have panicked at that stage, and their anxiety would have been obvious, but although Paul had been furious about Becky's treatment, he'd been almost casual when he talked about the supposed informant. In a time of war he would probably have made an extraordinarily successful spy. He must have known when he left the police station that Mike had to die, realistically there could be no other outcome, but nobody who had seen him leave could really have guessed that murder was his intent.

The change of attitude that Mark had seen, he now understood had nothing to do with ambition and everything to do with Paul's innate personality. He was a man full of contradictions; maybe some of Shane's early gentleness formed part of an extremely complex whole. His relationship with Becky had been real, and had that been allowed to develop without the obstacle of a morose and stubborn Dick Norton, then maybe things could have turned out differently. Paul had quickly integrated into Burrdale society, he'd even gone to night school classes with Rebecca, although Mark now wondered if his real reason for doing so was to know and understand one of his enemies. At some stage early on Paul must have realised that killing Winston wouldn't make him suffer enough: to destroy his reputation, to explode his self-satisfied conceit, to expose him to contempt and derision, that was a better plan, and more terrible for Winston than anything else that he could devise.

But the Paul who was capable of tenderness and of playing the long game was also capable of inflicting savage tempestuous violence, as Virginia had found that out to her cost. Why he had waited so long to kill her Mark didn't know, and how he had lured her onto his territory to commit the fatal act only Paul could say, but somehow he had done just that. She'd been an intelligent woman, not somebody who was easily duped, but, unknowingly, she had played into his hands and had suffered terrible consequences as a result. He had slain her for Shane and that explained why her body had to be returned to the place where Shane's tragedy began, but the stab wound to the chest and the slashing of the wrists, he had done those things for himself and for himself alone.

There was no doubt Paul watched and listened intently to

everything he saw and heard and he remembered every action and every word. Mark realised that Paul had seen his closeness to Helena and had understood just how important her life was to him. Paul knew that he had been the one person above all others who had wanted to revisit ancient history, and that was an area Paul preferred to see undisturbed. The grotesque present sent to Helena had been calculated to cause her maximum distress, and the stunt with the firework had been intended further to turn the screw. How he would keep his hands off him Mark didn't know, but on his journey from Yorkshire to Derbyshire he would have to find a way; he would also have to speak to John Lomas before he did anything to precipitate a crisis.

As he was driving back home other thoughts filled Mark's mind. He knew a dreadful truth, and he was confident that he would be able to convince John Lomas of that truth, but could he convince a sceptical C.P.S. that there was enough hard evidence to charge Burgess with murder? Even with proof that Paul was Derek Chadwick, what did that really establish? It gave him a motive and there was a good deal of circumstantial evidence but was that sufficient? Without a confession or some new physical evidence Mark feared it wouldn't be.

"Where's the forensic evidence, Inspector Hobson? Where are the eye-witnesses? Have you got any fingerprints?" He could hear the lawyer's scornful voice and, given that he had already experienced many occasions when the Crown Prosecution Service had refused to run cases, which he'd believed to be evidently strong, because there were a few slight loose ends, he doubted if they would be brave enough to bite the bullet on this occasion.

And if Paul wasn't charged, what then? He would be suspended whilst the investigations into his actions continued but he would probably retain his liberty, and whatever reasons he had had before to injure himself and Helena would have increased tenfold. And, God willing, there would also be a new born child whose life could be put in danger. Mark broke out into a cold sweat: there is only so much protection the police can give and a clever, resourceful, experienced officer would know that fact, and would know precisely what the limitations were.

He had intended to go directly to the police station to speak to John Lomas, but fears about Helena drove him to the hospital instead. Tonight he had to be with her, tonight she was not under threat because Paul didn't know what he had discovered; tomorrow it would be different. Before then he had to understand everything about the layout of the ward so he could think about the security measures that would have to be put in place. He was on edge all the time he was with her, and she could sense his unease. He told her everything was fine, that he was just a little bit tired, and that he'd had one of those days at work you just simply want to forget. He said he didn't want to think about it, and she respected his wishes and didn't ask questions.

After he left Helena for the night he spent many hours considering the best way of dealing with the explosive information he now possessed. He paced the kitchen floor trying to organise his thoughts, at times talking to himself, urging his brain to think, and it was very late before he went to bed. He locked and bolted the door before he did so, and it shocked him to realise how jumpy he himself had actually become.

The next morning he arrived at the police station early. He'd expected to find the place half empty but he found the car park to be full and it was obvious that a large number of additional officers had been drafted in from Divisional Police Headquarters and beyond. The first person he bumped into was Alan Nadin.

"You don't know do you?" he said.

"Know what?" asked Mark.

"There's been another death; and Dick Norton is lying in hospital with serious burns."

"What's happened?" asked Mark, "What the Hell's been going on?"

"Dick Norton's shop was attacked by an arsonist early yesterday morning. Somebody stuffed a couple of petrol soaked rags through his letter box and then set them alight. Dick had got very drunk the night before. He couldn't make the stairs, so he slept where he fell behind the counter; that probably saved his life. The flames went straight up the stairwell. Becky was asleep in an upstairs bedroom; she shouldn't have been there at all, she should have gone to a friend's birthday party, but she wasn't feeling very well so she didn't go. She may have taken some sleeping tablets; we'll know that for sure when the doc's examined her, but for whatever reason she failed to hear the smoke alarm. Although the firemen got her out of the room before it was engulfed in flames, and there wasn't a mark on her, she had suffocated; she was pronounced dead at the scene by the *Grim Reaper*. Just before the fire crews arrived Dick Norton came to. He realised Becky was still upstairs. He tried to force his way through the flames He suffered 70% burns, and has less than a50% chance of survival. Paul Burgess was distraught when he heard the news, he ran out of the police station, tears streaming down his face screaming "She should have been at Janine's; she should have been at Janine's." He hasn't been seen since, he doesn't answer his phone, and at the moment nobody at all knows where he is."

"Good God." gasped Mark. "Is John Lomas in yet? I've got to see him immediately; this is so bloody awful!"

Mr Lomas listened with more and more amazement as Mark told him everything that he had discovered.

"So Paul Burgess is Shane Chadwick's younger brother!" he said.

"I can't believe it! It's incredible! None of us had the slightest idea; and now it looks like he's killed two people to conclude a twenty year old vendetta. God! It's going to get very, very messy."

"Three people," corrected Mark, "three people. Paul's got to be the prime suspect for starting the fire that killed Becky Norton. He didn't intend to do that, the way he rushed out of here shouting "I thought she was at Janine's" is a clear indication of that, but he did intend to kill Richard Norton. Dick more than anyone else had ruined Shane's life with his wild rage; the kid was immature and vulnerable. He believed himself cursed; Norton deliberately set him on a path to disaster. Paul saw every sad step he took; he had plenty of reasons to hate him even before Becky dumped him. I'm certain he blamed Dick for turning her against him. When he gave him a black eye it meant more to Paul than just a minor injury. It was loss of face; the story was all over town; the Saturday night drunks would have taunted him about being beaten up by somebody old enough to be his grandfather; he couldn't have taken that. He needed to get the better of Dick, and he chose to do so in a deliberately final way. Triumph turned to disaster when Becky died. Paul's not a mindless thug; he's capable of deep thoughts and real emotions. Right now I don't think he's knows what's hit him. He's dreamt about a day when the slate would be wiped clean for most of his life, and now it's all gone horribly wrong. He's risked everything and done terrible things, and it's all been for nothing. What he'll do next is anybody's guess."

"We've got to locate him without delay, and get him under lock and key somewhere where he can't hurt himself or anyone else. This is so bloody awful. I can see the headlines *"killer cop's trail of slaughte*r", *"Derbyshire detective murders three people",* and those will probably be the least sensational ones we get The Chief Constable will go mental when he learns of this; before we do anything else I need to put him in the picture.

"Mental" wasn't far off the mark. Extracted from a meeting when he had given strict instructions that he should not be disturbed unless there was an earthquake, within minutes it seemed to him that the Peak District of Derbyshire had been hit by a major tremor measuring at least 9 on the Richter scale. Many difficult questions were going to be asked.

He informed Detective Chief Superintendent Lomas that he would travel to Burrdale to arrive within the hour. He ordered that until an appropriate Press Liaison Officer had been appointed no statements should be issued by the police. If the press started to ask for information only "no comment" replies should be given at this time. If a lid could be kept on the matter, at least until the suspect had been apprehended, it might just divert some criticism away from his force if he could point to the fact that as soon as the identity of the man thought to have been responsible for 3 brutal murders had become known, Derbyshire Constabulary had moved Heaven and Earth to apprehend him, and they had been successful. He hoped that this would blunt some of the choreographed anger the less responsible tabloids would level against his officers.

"And it won't be at all fair," he later complained to John Lomas. "When we accept recruits we don't ask them if they've lost a brother or a sister in a car accident or a street fight, or in any other way at all. It's their character, their level of education and their potential we're interested in. The fact that somewhere on our records it will be recorded that Burgess changed his name by deed poll would be seen as a minor detail, it wouldn't be highlighted in his personal file. The appropriate checks were all done. The lad was of good character when he joined the force, his record until now has been exemplary. How the hell could we be expected to put two and two together?"

The briefing to the men and women given by Mr Lomas and Detective Inspector Hobson immediately after the former's telephone conversation with the Chief was a sombre affair. In the strongest possible terms, it was stressed to everyone that there was a complete embargo about talking to anyone outside this room about the case; (except of course those conversations that it was necessary to hold with potential witnesses to obtain evidence and/or to locate the missing suspect). Detective Inspector Hobson then briefly put forward four possible ways in which the case might develop.

One obvious way in which Paul Burgess might react was to flee. His flat would have to be searched of course. If some or all of his clothes were missing, and his passport had disappeared that would give a clear indication of his intent. Ports and airports would need to be contacted urgently, and his landlady and the other residents in the house would all need to be spoken to to see if they could shed any light on his possible whereabouts.

Another possible response to the situation he found himself in was to fight, not only against capture, but also against anyone he blamed for his personal tragedy. This was the most dangerous of all the possible outcomes. It was suspected that Detective Sergeant Burgess had used extreme physical violence on two occasions, throttling and then stabbing one victim with a large knife, and shooting the second victim with his own shotgun, He wasn't afraid to use weapons, the only slight crumb of comfort was that he didn't seem to own or to have ready access to an easily available firearm. Nothing could be taken for granted however so a police armed response team had been called in. The instruction given to the men and women present was that their erstwhile colleague could be armed and dangerous and that if seen he should not be approached but that back-up should immediately be called for.

The names of potential targets for any revenge attack were then read out. John Winston's name came top of the list, closely followed by Tony Patterson (on the basis that there was great uncertainty as to exactly where he fitted into the wider picture). Henry Osbourne featured on the list of people at risk of harm because for a short time he had been a close confidante of Virginia Brocklehurst, Joe Broadbent's name was absent, his loathing for the widow of Jack Brocklehurst was well known and made him immune from attack by one of her enemies. Detective Inspector Mark Hobson and his wife Helena were the final two names disclosed.

"I don't need protection Sir," he had said to John Lomas, "I can look after myself, but if Paul does now see me as an enemy and wants to do something to hurt me then he knows that the best way to do that would be to attack my wife. I want total protection for her until this is over. Until Paul Burgess is apprehended I can't be sure she will be safe from attack."

The third way Paul could react to the desperate situation he was in would to throw in the towel, to take his own life, to commit suicide. The cloak of secrecy had been stripped from his life, he was naked and totally exposed. The beautiful girl he had loved had died as a direct result of his desperate actions. He was now a wanted man with nothing to look forward to except a life in custody, which in his case would be unbearable. He would be a good looking, young, former police officer, the sort of things that would probably happen to such a man were almost unthinkable. What had he got to live for? In some ways suicide could seem to be the least worst option. For all Mark Hobson knew he could already have swallowed a bottle of pills in the privacy of his own bedroom, and his body might be lying on his bed awaiting discovery.

"And if that's happened, it may not be pretty," the D.I. warned the assembled officers. "Some people think an overdose is a way to die with dignity. It isn't necessarily the case. Sometimes people choke on their own vomit, sometimes they cough up blood, and it can be an agonising and disgusting way to die."

But in Mark's mind there was another place where Paul might choose to end his life; the place where it all started, the place where Shane Chadwick killed Lucas Norton, the place to which he carried Virginia's body to hurl it into the dark water as a final act of settlement, to bring to a close twenty years of hurt. To end everything where it all began, there was something about that conclusion that would resonate with Paul's innate sense of order.

The fourth and last way Paul could try to come to terms with the overwhelming problems he now faced was surrender. He could simply walk into any police station and meekly hand himself in. This would be by far and away the best solution from the police point of view, but it was also completely at odds with the personality of the man they all knew. Very few bets indeed would be placed on this particular outcome.

A phone call just as the briefing was about to finish put an end to all speculation. It was made by David Wright. One of his men had returned to his farm in a state of shock having found the body of a man hanging in the barn where Virginia's ear stud had been discovered and where it was now believed she had been slain. He wasn't sure, but he thought that the dead man could be one of the police officers involved in the murder investigation. His suspicion proved to be well founded. The dead man was Paul Burgess. The *Grim Reaper,* when he examined the body at the scene estimated that he had been dead for around 18 hours. Mark realised that his speculation that Paul might seek to end his tragic tale at the place where the story started had been incorrect, but to a lesser degree the fact that he had chosen to kill himself at the same place where he killed Virginia demonstrated something of the same mindset. Mark could feel no satisfaction in being proved partially right.

 Paul's death surely signalled an end to the killing, but it was such a waste of a remarkable talent. When Mark told Helena she wept openly, and there were many people that night who couldn't understand why this terrible tragedy couldn't have been averted.

Chapter Thirty Nine

The suicide note arrived the following morning. Mark recognised the handwriting immediately, but why Paul had written to him he didn't initially understand; perhaps the catastrophe of Becky's death had reminded him that Mark had once offered to try to help him if ever he needed to unburden his soul to anyone.

"By the time you get this" it read, "it will all be over. It shouldn't have ended this way. I didn't want any regrets; I've had a life time of those already. Mostly I'm not sorry about what happened. You with your happy life will find that shocking; but I am sorry there was ever a need for those things to happen. Shane never deserved to be used in the way that he was used, or abused in the way that he was abused. If he hadn't been picked on we could have been happy here. He had good memories for the first nine years of his life, and then he had nothing but pain. I watched him fall apart as a human being; there was so much hopelessness and so much unbearable sadness. The world is a cruel place, but it doesn't have to be deliberately cruel; what happened to Shane was as deliberate as it was unmerited. I've known about this place all my life and, even though Jenny couldn't tell me, I learnt from Shane the names of the people who had caused his suffering; and afterwards that the story never left me. It wouldn't go away. I had no choice, I had to come here; I didn't know what would happen when I did, but I knew for sure that coming here would change my life forever.

I met Becky by chance. I knew she was the daughter of Dick Norton, and when I first saw her I thought she was both beautiful and arrogant and, to begin with I think I intended to use her to hurt Dick in some way.

I couldn't help myself, I fell in love with her and just for a little while I hoped that things could change. I saw how Dick's lifelong anguish had destroyed him, and maybe I recognised that in him I saw myself unless I allowed myself to become a different person.

His utter loathing of the girl who caused the tragedy was deep seated and eternal, as was his hatred for Shane, it was also destructive and infectious. I discovered that that girl was Virginia completely by chance. I heard two locals at the Royal Albert talking about Virginia Brocklehurst, and what they said wasn't complimentary. One of them mentioned Crawford Winston in the same breath, and suggested that he might have been responsible for the way she had turned out. That intrigued me. I started to dig and eventually I found out everything. I think I thought to begin with that, if I could force her out of town in the way my family had been chased out of town that might be sufficient. If before she went, I could in some way be responsible for making her keep her husband's promises, then, although no-one would know but me, the new Amenity Centre would really be down to me and be my secret peace offering to the people here. It almost worked. After I told her everything I knew and what I was demanding she became a very worried woman. I saw impotent fury and fear in her face and I liked what I saw. I gave her time to ponder and to think. She had caused Shane a lifetime of suffering so I couldn't possibly give her a quick solution. That was a mistake; it gave her an opportunity to fight back. Somehow she discovered who I was, maybe it was through Mike Skinner and, if it was, then it would have cost her a packet; and after that the tables were turned. I knew then what I had to do. She thought she was so clever; she thought it was her choice to meet in that stone barn, but I knew that Freddie Skinner had frequently taken young girls there to have sex. I guessed that he had taken Virginia there and it turned out to be a good guess and I was well prepared when I met her .The rest you know, but you'll never know how good it felt to lay a ghost to rest; but the ghost wouldn't die. Mike Skinner saw me dumping her body into the pool; he tried to blackmail me which was a very stupid thing for him to do. I shot him with his own gun and it gave me pleasure to watch him die in agony; Virginia should have experienced more agony than she did, but when I killed her I didn't know then what I was truly capable of. I had to punish Dick Norton in a very final and terrible way, but then it all went wrong and I killed Becky by mistake.

I can't bring her back to life, and with her death, I killed my own future. The past makes prisoners of us all and the sentence is a life sentence. I can't live with what I've done to her, so like my pathetic mother I take the coward's way out and choose a quick death rather than a slow agonising one. If I live I know my mind will disintegrate, and that would be the final degradation.

Before I end this letter and my life I will do one good deed and give you the hideous head of Tony Patterson on a plate. Mike Skinner tried to blackmail me, as he tried to blackmail Virginia, and when threatening to expose me he bragged that he could fill a courtroom with defendants if he chose to reveal the information he possessed to the police. "They might put you and Tony Patterson in the same remand cell," he sneered, which confirmed in my mind suspicions I have had about Patterson for a long time."

The statement made by Jackie Skinner that she thought Mike had been getting money from "more than one source" flashed into Mark's mind. He knew he should have done more at the time. He should have explored the possibility that Patterson's unease could have been linked to blackmail, but he had been pre-occupied with thoughts of Helena, and Patterson had seemed such a peripheral figure in the unfolding drama. He had dismissed him as a bombastic buffoon with a backbone of jelly and a quivering heart. That had been the wrong thing to do. Angry with himself, he continued to read the letter.

"I remembered people talking about an incident in a pub some years ago when Mike Skinner prevented a woman from stabbing the fat councillor. Somebody joked that even with his record that was the worst crime Skinner ever committed. I found out who the woman was, but she is now dead. Intriguingly I discovered she divorced her husband soon after this episode; he later went on to do time for child sex offences. I have written all my findings down in a file, if you haven't already found it you will find it in a chest of drawers when you search my flat. I learnt that Patterson the merchant seaman seemed to have visited every brothel in the Far East as well as many on the near continent. In Thailand, as you will see, he saw just how many sick British men would pay large amounts of money to have sex with young children. He found places where there could be add on bonuses; kids being fucked by dogs, even necrophilia if the price was right, and he photographed these activities. He put together an album of his disgusting photographs, rather like a sales brochure, I'm sure you will find it hidden somewhere in his house if you look hard enough. He became a "facilitator." People paid handsomely for his knowledge.

With him as their "tour guide" perverted businessmen and bankers could find exactly what they wanted in order to be able to indulge their sick fantasies. I had hoped to destroy him, but I cannot do that now. You can. Maybe through this one act I may gain a measure of redemption in your eyes.

I'm sorry for the hurt I caused your wife. She was blameless in all of this, and I have already expressed my sorrow at Becky's death. The others ruined my life. Why shouldn't I destroy theirs? "They have reaped as they have sown," as my Aunt Norah might have said. I have done likewise and I have been punished accordingly."

Chapter Forty

The wood smoke hung in the damp November air, scenting the night sky with the smell of burning pine. Soon there would be a new smell, the smell of gunpowder, and the mist that blanketed the old market square would be ripped asunder by explosions and red, gold, blue and green balls of light would cascade down onto the ancient rooftops as the townspeople celebrated Bonfire Night. For as long as anyone could remember it had always been this way, and the ancient tradition would live on so long as it was observed annually, but should the chain ever be broken, then the right to build a fire would be lost. And so despite frost, fog, rain, sleet and hail there had always been a bonfire on Burrdale Market Place on the night of November 5th. The only exception to the rule had been in the dark days of the Second World War; and even then the local scout leader had paid homage to the spirit of Guy Fawkes Night by lighting a tiny fire under the cover of a large cardboard box in the place where the big bonfire always stood in happier times. If the box itself caught fire, a bucket of water was on hand to extinguish the flames, and the A.R.P. wardens were never troubled by the light.

As usual, a large crowd had gathered in the square, some to drink mulled wine from the stall outside the Wellington Inn, or winter ale in the doorway of the Royal Albert, but mostly young and old alike were there to watch the fireworks as their parents and grandparents had done before them.

The fire burned brightly now, and the shadows of the watchers could be seen on the white walls of the Wellington Inn. At the top of his funeral pyre Guy Fawkes awaited his inevitable fate, a sinister figure dressed all in black created from old newspapers and cast off clothing. As the flames caught hold there was a cheer, but perhaps not as full throated as it had been in other years. Maybe the mood was subdued because so many people remembered how loudly they had cheered, only a few weeks before, when the well-dressed facsimile of a rich and powerful woman had been sacrificed to feed their anger and their recollection of the terrible events that had followed on from that primitive display of rage.

At precisely the same time the guy caught fire, in the delivery room of a hospital not more than fifteen miles away from these celebrations, three weeks prematurely, Christopher Samuel Hobson (weight 5lb 3oz) was born without medical intervention.

The End